Taash
and the Jesters

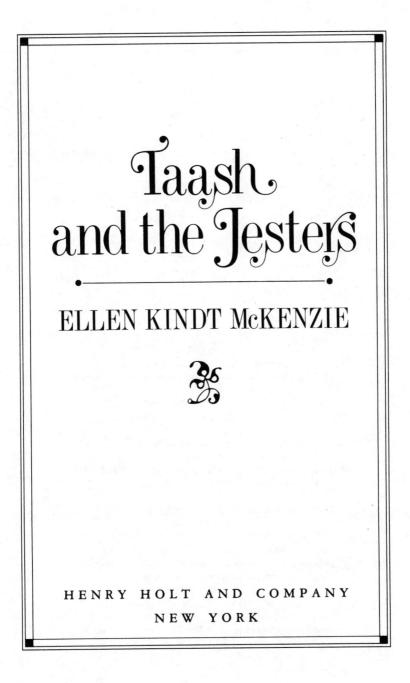

Taash and the Jesters

ELLEN KINDT McKENZIE

HENRY HOLT AND COMPANY

NEW YORK

Published by Henry Holt and Company, Inc.,
115 West 18th Street, New York, New York 10011.
Published simultaneously in Canada by Fitzhenry & Whiteside Ltd.,
91 Granton Drive, Richmond Hill, Ontario L4B 2N5.

Library of Congress Cataloging-in-Publication Data
McKenzie, Ellen Kindt.
Taash and the jesters / by Ellen Kindt McKenzie.
Summary: An orphan boy, who lives with a witch, becomes
involved in a dangerous adventure, from which he eventually
emerges as the brother of a king.
ISBN 0-8050-2381-X
[1. Fantasy.] I. Title. PZ7.M478676Taas 1992
[Fic]—dc20   92-12378
Printed in the United States of America on acid-free paper.∞
1   3   5   7   9   10   8   6   4   2

To Alison, Bobby, and Jamie

Taash and the Jesters

1

"Sit!" ordered the old man. "Sit and eat!"

Taash's lip trembled. How he hated that old toad crouching there over his porridge with his elbows on the table!

Unfortunately that "old toad" had a strong arm and a heavy hand for he had been a woodcutter all his life. And there had been little sign of either the age or the rheumatism that had begun to cripple him when he had seized Taash the night before, held his head firmly between his knees, and laid into the exposed area of the boy with a stick.

"I said sit!"

The old man paused in his eating and glared at the boy. Taash lowered himself gently on the hard bench and leaned on one hand while he picked up his spoon with the other.

The old man finished his porridge and reached for the dish of strawberries. He poured all of the milk from the cracked pitcher over them and spooned the ripe fruit into his mouth.

Taash pushed the wooden spoon around and around in his bowl. Yesterday's porridge was cold, and he was as cold as the porridge. The chilly morning air crept around his bare feet and found the holes in his tattered breeches. Shivering in his thin shirt he pressed his elbows against his ribs for warmth.

"If you won't eat your food the pig will have it."

The voice rasped in Taash's ear and the woodcutter swept his dish from the table and emptied it into the trough beside the door. Then the old man went to the cupboard where he cut bread and cheese and wrapped them in a square of cloth. He tucked the food into his pocket and swung his axe over his shoulder. Turning to the boy he stared at him for a minute. Then he grunted.

"You're old enough now to do more for your keep. Today when you have finished your chores you will go to the Witch Bargah for herbs."

Taash was unable to believe his ears.

"Do as I say or there'll be another whipping for you to-night," the woodcutter threatened. "And one of these days there'll be a dungeon and the end of a rope for you if you don't stop your misbehaving and your lying. You'll go to the witch today. Do you hear?"

Then out the door he went.

Taash sat stunned, his heart in his lap. And it was not because of the cold that his teeth suddenly chattered. The name of Bargah the Witch filled him with terror. He saw her now and then, an ancient withered creature wrapped in a black shawl, who hobbled through the village clutching her basket. Everyone feared and shunned her. They said she could dry up a cow's milk, strike a man dumb, or change a boy into a toad.

Now Taash was not a boy to cry, but the thought of going to the solitary hut at the edge of the great marsh was more than he could bear. He put his head down and wept.

He sobbed until he was quite dried out.

Then he stared hopelessly at the smoke-blackened stones of the cold fireplace. In a little while he began to frown and a minute later he jumped angrily to his feet. He would *not* go to the witch and he would *not* take one more beating from the woodcutter.

He cut bread and cheese for himself. He took up his jacket, shook the straw from it and tied the sleeves around his waist. Then he went out the door.

He would never come back.

Taash went down the path that led to the village. On either hand the plowed fields of the hillside lay steaming under the morning sun. Below him the night fog still clung to the surface of the river, and where the stream branched and meandered to form the great marsh, the broad valley was completely hidden by a blanket of mist. On the other side of the valley the mountains rose like islands from a white sea.

The village was astir. Smoke drifted from the chimneys. A cart rattled through the deep ruts in the road and several farmers passed Taash on their way to the fields.

Taash kept his eyes open. He had no friends here. Why hadn't he thought to go around through the fields? He hoped no one would notice him. Then he heard a whoop and a shout.

"Look who's here! It's the woodcutter's boy!"

It was the fat red-haired boy and two or three of his friends. Taash's heart sank.

> "Taash, Taash,
> He ought to be ashamed!
> He can't read,
> He can't write,
> He don't know his name!"

The red-haired boy started the chant and the others took it up. Taash ground his teeth and clenched his fists. Of all days they would have to catch him today! Perhaps if he paid no attention they would leave him alone. But he had no such luck. A shower of stones fell around him.

Taash stooped quickly, picked up a stone, and sent it flying. Red-hair shrieked and bent to find another while Taash snatched a second stone from the road and weighed it in his hand. But Red-hair did not aim at Taash again.

Instead he looked carefully around, hurled the rock, and took to his heels at once, his friends following him.

The shattering of the glass in the baker's window so startled Taash that for an instant he did not move. When he did turn to flee it was too late. He was caught by the arm.

"Throwing rocks, eh?" a voice said in his ear. "Drop that now!"

A twist of the wrist made the boy cry out. His fingers opened and the stone fell to the ground.

"Did you catch him?" The baker rushed up and seizing Taash shook him until the boy felt his head would come loose from his shoulders.

The baker was so furious he could not say another word. His ill-humored face above his flour-dusty apron waxed purple.

A crowd began to gather.

"It's the woodcutter's boy," someone said.

"Broke the window." Another pointed.

"Outrageous!"

"Throwing rocks at it, he was!"

The mutter grew.

"He's a good-for-nothing scamp."

"Needs a good thrashing!"

"Look! There's the mayor! Call him over and let him teach the boy a lesson!"

The talking stopped, the circle parted, and Taash found himself looking into the face of the mayor.

It is not quite true to say that Taash looked into the *face* of the mayor. For at first he found himself staring at the gold watch chain that stretched across a wide expanse of waistcoat. As the boy's eyes moved upward, they discovered a cataract of gravy-spotted lace and ruffles. Higher still was a collection of chins—three at least before the original came into view. Above this mountainous whole appeared a pro-truding lower lip and the end of a nose.

The mayor stepped back, creased himself slightly, and ex-amined the boy.

"What's this? What's it all about?" he demanded.

"It's a boy, sir," said the man who had caught hold of Taash.

"He smashed my window!" shouted the fuming baker. He shook his fist under Taash's nose. "And I'll smash him, I will! Let me get my hands on the young rascal!"

Taash shrank back.

"I didn't break the window," he protested. He was ready to believe that he should come to an end like a stepped-on blackberry.

"Oh, didn't you!" The baker was beside himself with rage. "What broke it then? The wind? An earthquake, perhaps! Or did it die of old age?"

"It was a stone, but it wasn't mine," Taash insisted.

"Ah, so it wasn't your stone! Then whose was it?" And the baker brought his red face within an inch of Taash's nose.

"I—it was the red-haired boy who threw it," Taash stut-tered.

A silence fell on the crowd. The mayor cleared his throat.

"Hmp!" the baker snorted after a minute. "A likely story! I don't believe it. I didn't see a red-haired boy here. Did anyone see a red-haired boy?"

He looked around the circle of faces and a murmur rose. No, indeed, no one had seen a red-haired boy!

"Everyone knows this boy is a liar," someone said.

"He should be punished."

"It was the only glass in the village!"

"Teach him a lesson. Throw him in prison."

"Ay, throw him in prison and send for the woodcutter."

The last piece of advice was taken. Taash was led off and locked in a small dismal room. The walls were of stone and the floor of dirt. High up, a single narrow window let in a small amount of gray light. It was cold and damp. There was no chair, not even a pile of straw to sit on.

Taash untied his jacket and pulled it on. He felt in the pocket but his bread and cheese had vanished. He sat down on the floor in a corner.

"Here, you, wake up!"

Someone was shaking Taash by the arm. He opened his eyes, sat up, and looked around. How could he *waken* into a bad dream?

"Come on now. They're going to have a trial and make the woodcutter pay for the glass." The boy who had roused Taash shook his head. "You shouldn't have broke that window!"

Taash followed the boy. He hadn't the least idea what a trial was, but he hoped he might be given something to eat or drink. His mouth was dry and his head was aching.

The boy led him down a hall and through a door into a large room full of people.

It looked as if the whole village was there. The woodcutter was there and the baker and the man who had caught Taash. There was the red-haired boy too with his fat jeering face. All of them and many others were sitting on the rows of benches that filled the room.

At the front of the room was a table behind which the mayor and two other men sat. Taash was told to sit on a chair between the table and the rows of benches. Everyone looked at him. The man on the mayor's right, the one with the long wrinkled face that resembled nothing so much as a prune, gave Taash such a look that the boy hastily straightened his back and put his legs down from under him. They dangled uncomfortably over the edge of the hard chair.

The mayor stood and struck the table with a mallet. The room grew quiet and he began to speak.

Taash grew more and more miserable. The mayor's words were too long to understand, but they had a terrifying ring to them. Besides the boy was growing numb from sitting still, for every time he moved the thin prune-faced man glared at him until he scarcely dared breathe.

At last the mayor finished what he had to say and the baker stood and talked. He trembled as he spoke of his window. His brow grew black and his voice rose until he shouted so loud that the men on either side of him pulled him down on the bench and the mayor pounded the table and called for order.

After that many spoke concerning the boy, the stone, and the broken window. It seemed that everyone in the village had witnessed the catastrophe. Taash was bewildered. He didn't remember seeing any of them on the street.

Finally the mayor called upon the woodcutter.

The old man refused to come to the front of the room. He stood beside his bench and his face was dark with anger.

"You've no right to make me pay for the glass," he said. "I've had all the expense of this boy for seven years. You were quick to forget your promises when the fear left you. But I've not forgotten. And I've not forgotten the cowards you were! Witchcraft! That's what you cried! And you ran and hid. Ay, you feared the old woman even after she died, and you feared the baby too. But you were more fearful to let him die for what might happen to you then. So you came with him to me!"

The old man snorted and glared at the faces around him.

"*I* never feared your witches nor your spells nor any of your cock-a-doodle and you knew it. You promised me money, but I've never seen the color of your gold. As for the boy, he's never been but trouble to me. Lazy he is and defiant. He has no respect and such a liar I've never known. He might profit by a lashing in the morning as well as the evening, but whatever, *I'll* have no more to do with him. *You'll* take him now, for I'll have him no more in my house. I'll have no more of his doings. And I'll not pay a penny for the glass!"

He sat down.

The courtroom was buzzing like a bee in a bottle. The baker glared at the woodcutter and the woodcutter glowered at the baker. The mayor pounded on the table.

When at last a reasonable calm was restored the thin sour man on the mayor's right rose to his feet and began to talk through his nose. His face was more puckered than before and Taash wondered if it were possible for a prune to eat a pickle.

"As I am the judge," he was saying, "it is my duty to see that justice is done, that this boy is punished, and that the glass is paid for. If there is no further evidence . . ."

"Your Honor!" a voice came from the back of the room. "Are we not to hear what the boy has to say for himself?"

A pained look crossed the judge's face.

"The boy?" he asked. "We know that he is lying!"

"Indeed! Then I have something to say!" the voice replied.

"Say it quickly," said the judge, frowning.

The mayor frowned too and his collection of chins quivered. He was hungry. They were wasting time. The boy should be flogged at once, the woodcutter should pay for the window, and everyone should go home to dinner.

"Your Honor!"

A fair, slender young man—three and twenty perhaps—stood before the table and bowed low to the judge.

"And my Lord Mayor!" His second bow was lower still.

"It's the beggar!" A surprised murmur ran through the crowd.

The mayor leaned back and drummed his fingers on his paunch.

"Permit me to apologize for my speech," the beggar began. "I know how much better you are versed in the law than I. Your devotion to justice is famous through the country. And surely with such a pair to lead them these honest folk are as eager for the truth as yourselves."

The mayor cleared his throat and the judge folded his face into an even more stern and righteous expression.

How eloquently the young man spoke of the capable mayor and the irreproachable judge! How sincerely he praised the upright parents and the well behaved children of the village! He was remarkably honest—a rare fellow, for beggars are generally such liars!

Perhaps he is something more than a beggar? The villagers nodded knowingly to one another over the elegance of his speech and the grace of his manner. They soon fell captive to the subtle expressions of his face and words. In another moment they were enslaved by the near dancing madness of his keen blue eyes. No one could turn his look from the man before them.

He was worth their attention. In no time the courtroom was in a roar with laughter, for the fellow had a wonderful stock of tales concerning boys and the mischief they did. He told them with a marvelous droll humor and the listeners hung on every word.

Story upon story he built until he was telling one that had a familiar sound to it. Yet so comical it was that tears of laughter rolled down faces. Ah, that red-haired son of the mayor was a clever one the way he brought the entire village down upon the luckless Taash! They would have the story from the boy himself!

Red-hair, with a smirk, was flattered to tell them. The mayor swelled with pride, and the room was filled with good-natured chuckles and guffaws.

But now the beggar held up a hand for silence.

"The matter of the boy Taash must be settled," he said. "If the woodcutter doesn't want him who will take him?"

The mayor called for order.

"Let us settle this quickly," he said. "Who will take the boy?"

No one spoke.

"Come now!" The mayor's dinner was calling loudly to him. "Surely there is someone who can use a . . . a . . ."

He glanced at Taash to see what commendable quality the boy might possess. But considering the woodcutter's words and seeing him there, a hunched-up rag of a child—pale and small even for a possible ten years of age—there was little to say. The mayor frowned. Why *must* the boy look so ill?

"Well . . . well, it is a *boy*!" he remarked heartily.

Several in the room laughed with the mayor. Still no one offered to take Taash.

The mayor's annoyance was visible. *He* didn't want the boy on his hands. The silence grew long.

At last from the back of the room an old and crackly voice spoke.

"I'll take the lad!"

Heads turned and a breath of fear swept across the room. There, sitting alone for no one cared to be near her, was Bargah the Witch.

"I'll take the lad," the old woman repeated.

Benches creaked. Someone cleared his throat.

"Excellent!" cried the beggar cheerfully. "If anyone can get some work out of a ne'er-do-well of a boy our good Witch Bargah can!"

The mayor smiled. If you looked at it *that* way—of course!

"She shall have him!" He banged the table three times. "Henceforth the boy Taash shall belong to the Witch Bargah! Court dismissed!"

"For shame!" a voice cried.

But any further remark was lost in the noise of the scraping of chairs and the scuffling of feet. Suddenly everyone was in a hurry to leave.

As for Taash, he did not know whether he was waking or sleeping, whether this nightmare would ever end. The judge told him to stand and go with the witch. He got to his feet but the room began to turn and reel around him. Darkness came over his eyes and he knew no more.

As the beggar carried Taash out the door, the baker's voice was heard rising above the noise of the crowd.

"But when will I be paid for my window?"

At that moment Red-hair received such an unexpected squeeze on the arm from his affectionate father that he howled aloud.

The next Taash heard was the sound of rushing water and a voice speaking.

"He's coming around now, poor lad."

He opened his eyes and recognized the beggar who was bending over him and bathing his face with water from a stream. The young man smiled.

"Are you all right?" he asked.

Taash nodded.

"Have a drink of water."

The young man scooped some water from the stream and Taash drank from his hand. The boy tried to sit up but he felt so faint he put his head down again. The young man sat beside him and looked at Taash with his sharp eyes. Taash raised his head and stared back. The beggar's eyes seemed to see more in one glance than most eyes see in a week of looking.

"Are you hungry?" he asked Taash suddenly.

"Yes," the boy said.

The young man handed him a piece of bread from a sack he carried. Taash munched on it.

"Didn't they give you anything to eat?" the beggar asked.

"No." The boy sat up. "And I hadn't any breakfast or any supper the night before. I was hungry!"

"And that gross mound of fat sat there the whole time thinking of nothing but his dinner!" the young man snorted. "He would have thrown you to the wolves if he thought it would get him to the table any quicker. Ah, Bargah, it made me ill flattering that bag of jellied pudding. And Horse-face sitting beside him whinnying the law through his nose! Aagh, what a pair! The pig and the donkey sitting in the court of justice!"

"Watch your tongue, Kashka. You will get us into trouble."

Taash turned around and saw the old witch sitting on a rock nearby. The young man caught the expression of dismay on his face and burst out laughing.

"So you think you have jumped from the kettle to the hot stove! Don't be afraid. The talk about the Witch Bargah is as true as that pot of a mayor is thin. Look at me! They call me a beggar, and they would swear by the mayor's belly that I am a beggar. Yet not one of them would be able to recall once that I ever begged anything from anyone—even his pardon!"

The young man leaped to his feet and snapped his fingers in a way that dismissed all the villagers as idiots.

"But let me introduce myself. I am Kashka." The young man bowed with a flourish. "And this is the good Witch Bargah."

Taash glanced fearfully at the old woman. Kashka smiled.

"Don't you worry. She won't harm you. She'll never beat you or let you go hungry. If you feel the need of a whipping, praise the mayor to my face and I shall give you a beating you will never forget!"

Kashka then pulled a flute from beneath his ragged tunic and began to play a lively tune. He twirled around, dancing and bounding high in the air. So light his step was, his feet seemed scarcely to touch the ground. Taash was amazed. The music made his spine prickle and he wanted to leap and pipe himself.

When he had finished his dance Kashka made a deep bow to the boy and the witch.

"Hey!" he shouted. "I am out of breath! This will never do, Bargah. Either I am out of practice or I am growing old. Or is it your cooking, you old witch, that has made me fat?"

He tucked his chin down, thrust his thumbs into his belt, and puffed and strutted in a perfect imitation of the mayor.

Taash was no little scandalized but delighted all the same. He covered his mouth with his hand. Bargah shook her head.

"You are naughty, Kashka," she chided.

Unable to hold the pose any longer from the mirth that bubbled in him, Kashka threw back his head with a laugh and turned a somersault in mid-air. The witch cackled. Taash, gaping, was overcome by the antics and was conscious of nothing but the leaping, whirling figure before him.

"You've finished eating your bread," said Kashka stopping suddenly. "And I have used up my bag of tricks. Shall we go on?"

The three of them set off together. They crossed the stream at the ford and followed the path which Taash knew led to the Witch Bargah's hut.

The day was at the end and the evening mists were rising over the marsh and drifting out across the meadows. The forest had grown dark and still. The last golden touch of sun faded quickly from the mountains. The jagged masses of rock, alive in the day with changing patterns of light and shadow, now thrust their barren peaks bleak and menacing against the darkening sky.

Upon all the land fell a hush so compelling that the three travelers stopped and waited, breathless, with the rest of the world in that moment of eternity between day and night.

"Garrumpf!"

The great bullfrog of the swamp broke the stillness.

"Trrrr trrrr trrrr!"

He was joined at once by a small cousin.

Soon the marsh was alive with the songs of frogs. A night heron rose and flapped away across the reedy swamp. A tawny owl hooted and glided out of the forest. The world that wakes to the moon came alive as darkness softly gathered up the corners of the earth and folded them into the shapes of night.

"Hurry now," Bargah said impatiently. "Let's get into the house."

"Dear old woman," Kashka teased. "Anyone who didn't know that you were a witch might think you were afraid of the dark!"

He crouched in front of her and waggling his fingers as if they were horns on his head, he sang.

> "There's dreadful things that come in the night,
> Things that shriek and things that bite,
> Goblins that revel,
> Ghosts sent by the devil
> Whose moans and screams
> Will haunt you in dreams.
> But the fright that will bring your life to an end
> Is the unmasked face of an untrue friend!"

At the end of the song he pulled at the corners of his mouth with his fingers, stuck out his tongue, and rolled his eyes upward.

"Get on with you and your nonsense!" snorted the old woman. She gave Kashka a push that nearly sent him sprawling. "Your face is bad enough as it is. Don't be frightening us out of our wits trying to improve it!"

Kashka laughed and they hurried on.

Taash was glad to hurry. The white vapors rising from the fen went through him to the marrow of his bones. And Kashka's banter made him even more uneasy. How dared he mock the witch? Any minute she might turn and change him into a toad or a frog or—or a mosquito!

They were at the house at last and Bargah pushed open the door. Kashka hustled the boy inside.

Taash blinked at the sudden light. He had expected a cold room, dark and musty and filled with ancient books of spells and the weird tools of witchery. But he found himself in no such place. The room was bright with the light of a fine blaze in a wide fireplace. A bubbling pot did hang from a metal arm over the fire. But from it rose so delectable an odor of stewed meat and vegetables that Taash grew faint again. A large cat leaped from a chair. But it was a comfortably fat orange and white tabby that wound herself in and out between Bargah's feet, rubbed against her legs, and purred loudly.

In the center of the cheerful room was a table set with three earthenware plates and mugs together with a pitcher of milk, a round loaf, and a bowl of flowers.

Taash did not see everything. The polished copper pots, the bright curtains, the painted dishes standing on the scrubbed wooden shelves—all these he did not notice. But the cheer and comfort of the room reached out and surrounded the lonely boy with a warm friendliness he had never known.

Not quite so friendly was the face of the little girl who stood in the middle of the room and stared at Taash.

"Hi-ho, Nanalia!" Kashka greeted her. "We have a guest for dinner. This is Taash."

"The woodcutter's boy?" asked the little girl.

"Not any more," the young man told her. "He is ours now and he will stay with us."

"Always?"

"Always!"

Nanalia stared at Taash and Taash stared at her. She was not as old as he, two years younger perhaps. She had black eyes and long black braids. As she stood gazing at him she caught her underlip between her teeth in a pout.

"Well," she said at last, "if he is going to stay with us, I suppose I must put another plate on the table."

She climbed upon a chair, took down a plate and mug from the shelf, and set a fourth place.

"I didn't think you would ever get home," she complained to Bargah. "I've been waiting ever so long."

"It took longer than we expected," was Bargah's reply.

"We were unavoidably detained by some long-winded oratory, Your Highness," Kashka said with a bow. "We humbly hope you will forgive us."

Nanalia giggled. "You're silly, Cousin Kashka. When I grow up I shall make you behave."

"Heaven protect me!" Kashka rolled his eyes upward. "But we're hungry. May we dine with you, Princess?"

Nanalia giggled again and nodded.

Taash had never tasted anything so good. It was hard to believe that he could have all he wanted besides.

After supper Kashka took him outside and they sat on a bench beside the door. The moon was full and the night air soft. The frogs and crickets croaked and chirruped and trilled. Altogether the evening was so pleasant that the boy's uneasy fear grew somewhat less.

"I know you're tired," Kashka began. "And I won't keep you long. But what I have to say is very important."

He paused a moment to admire the moon. Then he continued.

"I am going away tomorrow and I shall not be back for some time. While I am gone you must look after Bargah and Nanalia. Bargah is old and she is growing blind. She needs your help. She will be good to you. If she does know a bit of witchcraft don't be frightened by it. She never uses it for any evil."

He paused again. Taash was disappointed. He had hoped that Kashka was going to tell him something really important, not just that he must be helpful!

"You must learn your letters. Bargah will teach you to read and write, and when I come back I shall see what you have done. If you have done well I may bring you something." He turned to Taash. "Is there anything that you would like to have?"

No one had ever before asked him if he wanted anything. Indeed, all he had ever possessed were the things he needed to stay alive—his ragged clothes and the amulet to ward off evil that he wore around his neck.

Taash thought for quite a while. At last he spoke rather shyly.

"I should like to have a pipe like yours, and I should like to learn to play on it and sing and jump the way you do."

Kashka stared at him in astonishment. Then he flung his arms to the sky and cried aloud.

"Do you hear, Moon? If Taash behaves himself he shall have a pipe and I myself shall teach him to play!"

Openly delighted with the idea, Kashka leaped to his feet, twirled around three times, and did a row of handsprings down the path and back again.

"Ugh!" he gasped when he again stood in front of the startled boy. "Don't ever do that on a belly full of stew! Now, sir, off to bed with you!"

It was in the small loft above the kitchen that Bargah had prepared a thick pile of straw covered with a heavy quilt for him. There was a warm fleece for a cover if the night grew cold. It looked so comfortable the boy could not wait to lie down and sleep.

But in the dark his fear of the witch came back to him and grew like a monstrous shadow. What would she do to him when Kashka was gone? All the eerie tales of witchcraft came to his mind and he could not bring himself to close his eyes. The creaking of a board or the sudden cry of a night bird set his heart knocking against his ribs. He stared into the blackness of the room and strained his ears with listening. The witch would not catch him sleeping!

Below him the door of the kitchen creaked open and was gently shut again.

"Well, old grandmother," Kashka spoke. "We could hardly have planned it this nicely."

"No, indeed," Bargah's wavery voice answered him. "He has fallen at our feet like a fledgling from the nest."

"It was a stroke of luck," Kashka's voice came clearly through the boards under Taash's head. "We couldn't wait any longer. I was afraid that we would have to steal him away."

He laughed softly.

"But he is ours at last and we must take good care of him."

After that his voice dropped so low that Taash could not hear what Kashka said, nor could he understand Bargah's muttered replies. The murmur of their voices lulled him to sleep. It was not until the next day that he wondered at what he had heard. But it made no sense to him. What could they want with him?

3

Kashka was gone when Taash rose in the morning. How he wished the young man had stayed for breakfast! He scarcely dared speak to Bargah. The witch was such a very old woman. Her face was wrinkled and yellow like crumpled parchment. Her hands were bony and wrinkled too, and because she could not see well she would peer at Taash with her old amber eyes in a way that frightened him. Sometimes she muttered to herself and then he grew more fearful. Was she putting a spell upon him? What could he do?

After breakfast Bargah set the boy to work milking the cow and splitting wood for the fire. When he had finished a stack of kindling, Nanalia took him to see the garden. As she showed him about she kept up a constant chattering.

"Sometimes the grasshoppers come and eat the garden, and sometimes the rabbits get in and eat it. Once the mule got loose and ate rows and rows of things so that we had to plant the whole garden over again, and by that time it was so late in the season that everything froze before it was ready to pick and all we had to eat all winter long were rutabagas and parsnips, and we were so tired of them we wanted to eat the mule.

"I don't think the frogs eat the garden. They eat bugs so they are good to have nearby. The cat doesn't like to eat frogs but she does catch mice and sometimes she catches a rabbit.

"When Kashka is here he catches rabbits for stew and he goes hunting for other things too. Kashka is clever but he is terribly silly and I can't ever make him mind his manners. Don't you think he's silly? Grown-up people shouldn't behave that way! But he does help Great-aunt.

"Bargah is my great-aunt. I came to live with her when I was born because everyone else died of the fever and there wasn't anyone to take care of me. Everyone says she's a witch. If she is a witch, she's a good one and I don't mind. When I grow up I am going to be a witch too. Then I shall put a spell on Kashka so that he stops making funny faces and teasing me.

"I don't like being teased. You never know when Kashka is teasing.

"I don't suppose you want to be a witch when you grow up. I don't even know if boys can be witches, but I suppose they can. I don't like boys very well. The boys in the village used to throw stones at me so Great-aunt won't take me there any more.

"Do you throw stones at girls?"

She paused to catch her breath and, perhaps, to find out if Taash did throw stones at girls.

"No," Taash told her. "I only throw stones at other boys because the ones in the village throw them at me too."

"Well, then." Nanalia took a deep breath and was off again. "I might like you. Of course, that's hard to tell. Kashka is the only one I like, but I don't know anyone else so I can't tell.

"I suppose we'll have lessons together. Bargah teaches me to read and write and add numbers and it's all horrid. I get so bored adding numbers that I want to scream and sometimes I do scream. I stamp my feet and I scream. Once I screamed and screamed and Great-aunt took a pitcher of water and poured it all over my head and I was so angry with her that I stopped screaming and I wouldn't speak to her all day.

"Then wouldn't you guess? Kashka came that night

and when he found out what happened he wouldn't talk to me. He was horrid! He was as horrid as the numbers. I told him I hated him and he picked me up and I thought he was going to hug me and beg my pardon. But he took me outside instead and held me over the well. He said he would drop me in if I didn't behave, and I was frightened.

"I really didn't believe that he would drop me in, but it's frightening to be held over a well even when you *are* holding tight around his neck. So I had to say I was sorry and promise not to scream or stamp any more. And I haven't. It's not really that I'm keeping my promise, it's just that it was a very childish thing to do and I'm getting older now.

"I don't like Kashka to be angry with me. He frightens me then. His temper is worse than mine. Great-aunt tells him so and she says he's old enough to know better and it will get him into trouble some day. But he just laughs and says he saves all his tantrums to have here because she won't tell on him. He says he behaves as long as he can stand to, and when he has to have a tantrum he comes for a visit. I don't know where he goes when he goes away. It's time for lessons now. We'd better go in."

The days and weeks went by. There were times when the boy was filled with fear. When the thick fog crept around the house and the only sound was the pat, pat, pat, as the heavy mist gathered into drops on the roof and fell from the eaves, Taash would wait for it to happen. What he waited for he didn't know, but with all the world hidden by the white veil that hung before his eyes he was sure the witch would do something.

Other times he would wake in the night and hear sounds he had never heard before. Mysterious sounds rose from the swamp, the hollow booming of the bittern or the terrifying squeal of some creature caught in the sharp talons of a winged night hunter.

On windy nights the branches of the apple tree creaked and scraped against the house. If the moon was out wild shadows leaped and danced on the sloping walls of the loft. Taash would crawl under his fleece and shut his eyes and stop his ears.

One night, shortly after he had come, he wakened and looked out through the small window. By the white light of the moon he saw the Witch Bargah wrapped in her black cape and hood and carrying a basket. She walked through the meadow and vanished into the forest. Taash crept back into his bed and pulled the fleece over his head. Over and over he repeated Kashka's words.

"She will be good to you. She never uses it for any evil."

But the growing plants in the garden, the reading and writing and talking and playing with Nanalia all brought so many new ideas to his mind that Taash had less and less time to be fearful. He was never beaten and scarcely ever scolded. It was not so hard after all to speak to the witch. The air seemed sweeter to him, the sky bluer, the sunsets more brilliant, and all the colors of the earth more beautiful. He wondered if the air at the woodcutter's house had not some strange heaviness in it that blotted out light and color.

One day he was working in the garden and Bargah came out to help him.

"Look at that!" he exclaimed. "Just look at how things have grown since I came. The beans are taller than I am and at first they were only as high as my finger! Here, give me that!"

He took the bucket from the old woman.

"You mustn't carry water. It's too heavy for you. I'm much stronger than I used to be. Feel my arm there!"

"You have a fine muscle," Bargah smiled. "More things

are growing than the beans!" And in more ways than one, she added to herself.

"They certainly are," Taash agreed. "Look at the carrots and the onions!"

Nanalia talked constantly of Kashka. Taash wished the young man would return.

"Do you think he will ever come back?" he asked Nanalia one day. They were sitting outside studying their lessons.

"Don't be silly! Of course he will. Kashka always comes back, only you never know when to expect him."

Taash looked at the piece of wood on which he had written with charcoal, "The red hared boy has the fase of a gote, acts like a donky and has the brane of a chickin."

"Do you know—" he said thoughtfully, "maybe it is worthwhile to learn to write."

"Who says it isn't?" came a voice from behind him and a hand took the board from Taash.

Taash caught his breath as he looked up. He turned scarlet while Kashka studied the words before him.

"You must be sure that you can prove what you say!" The young man shook his head gravely. "That he looks like a goat and behaves like a donkey is obvious. But that he has the brain of a chicken can be debated even though it appears to be true. How did he get such a brain, through witchery or surgery? The court physician is a very clever man, but I have yet to hear that he successfully transplanted the brain of a chicken into the head of a boy."

He returned the board to Taash.

"You had better rub that out and do the lesson Bargah has given you."

"Yes, sir." Taash scowled to feel his face burning. He ducked his head as he rubbed hard at the writing. He wished he knew whether or not Kashka were laughing!

"And what have you been doing to improve yourself?" Kashka asked Nanalia.

"I've been drawing a picture of you and your long nose," she told him. "Why did you stay away so long?"

"To tell you the truth, I was on my way here a long while back when some mad fellow tied a handkerchief over my eyes one night as I slept," Kashka began. "So that when I woke in the morning I thought I was blind. I had to ask everyone I met to direct me on the road for I couldn't see the way. But I encountered a parade of such ignorant people that I had nothing but misfortune. Not a one could read the signposts and I was sent halfway across the country in the wrong direction.

"The only reason I'm here now is that I was told to cross a certain bridge over a river. But the bridge happened to be washed out and I fell into the water and caught a very bad cold. I sneezed so much that I had to take the handkerchief from my eyes in order to blow my nose. Then I discovered that I could see after all, and I was able to find my way by myself.

"You see what happens when people are too stupid to learn to read? I might have been here a month ago!"

Nanalia looked at him with a slight frown on her face.

"I don't believe you," she said at last. "Besides, *you* weren't very clever either if you didn't know you had your eyes covered!"

Kashka sighed.

"I expect you're right. But where is Bargah?"

"She went into the village to get some flour from the miller," Taash told him.

"So that's why you're playing instead of working at your lessons, is it?" Kashka shook his head. "What am I to tell her when she comes back?"

"You could tell her that the cow got loose in the garden,"

Taash began. "Or that a wolf . . . or that . . . or you could tell her the truth," he finished lamely.

"And what would you have told her?" Kashka's keen eyes studied the boy's face.

"He would have told her the truth," Nanalia answered when Taash remained silent. "He always does now. It's no fun at all. You never heard such stories as he could tell when we were late for supper. And Great-aunt never punished him for it. I don't know why he stopped!"

"Ah, run along and play, you two," Kashka laughed. "I'll go to meet Bargah."

"May we come along?" Taash asked shyly. "We often go to meet her, though she won't let us go all the way to the village."

"Indeed you may." Kashka smiled. "And on the way I can give you your first lesson on this."

He rummaged in the bundle he had dropped at his feet and found something that was wrapped in a piece of cloth. He unwound it carefully until before Taash's delighted eyes he held a beautifully polished wooden flute. Kashka handled it lovingly.

"It was made by a fine craftsman," he said. "You must take very good care of it. It has a sweet true tone, but if you leave it out in the sun or the rain, the wood will not sing for you. Here, if you hold it this way . . ."

"Didn't you bring anything for me?"

"Oh ho, Nanalia! Of course I brought something for you. Did you think I would forget you?"

"I didn't know," said Nanalia. And the look she gave Taash was far from fond.

"Here." Kashka drew from his sack a piece of cloth. "This is from the same piece that the Queen herself had a dress made. Look! How beautiful it is! Bargah will make a dress for you from it."

Nanalia stroked the cloth.

"It's very pretty. But you never told me you knew the Queen! You're teasing me again!" And she suddenly burst into tears.

"Perhaps I didn't say I knew the Queen," said the astonished Kashka. "But I know the weaver. He made a mistake somehow and wove an extra length of this. And do you know, he saved it especially for me to give to you! No one in the kingdom will have a dress of this except you and the Queen!"

Nanalia stopped crying and looked at Kashka with round eyes.

"Is that really true?" she whispered.

"Cross my heart!"

She hugged the folded material close to her, laying her cheek against it.

"It is very pretty!" she murmured. "But I suppose you will spend all your time teaching Taash to play that old flute!"

4

"What! Just up? Why, so lazy a lad will scarce be in time for the noonday sun!"

The basin in which Taash gingerly dabbled his fingers was suddenly emptied over his head.

"Aaaaiii!" Taash gasped and sputtered as the cold water ran down his neck and back.

A towel was thrust into his hands and he mopped his face and eyes. There beside him stood Kashka grinning like a red fox.

"Good morning!" he said cheerfully. "By heaven! It's Taash! I thought it was some good-for-nothing lout afraid he might get his face clean or I'd never have done such a thing! How are you this bright morning?"

"I was fine a minute ago," said Taash shivering. "But it's not a bright morning. The sun isn't up yet."

"Ah, but it will be! You can count upon *that*! And you and I shall watch it rise. Where is your shirt? I was hoping that Bargah would have put a bit more fat on your ribs by now. Come along, let me see you stand on your head, dance in the air, knock down dragons!"

"I would if I could!" Taash laughed. "But I don't know how."

"What? What have you been doing with your time? What has Bargah been teaching you? Stuffing your head with nonsense and letting your feet take root! Watch this!"

Kashka leaped into the air tapping his heels together three times, jumped and twirled, did a somersault and a handspring all in the blink of an eye. Then he drew out his pipe and blew upon it, the notes running and leaping and twirling just as he had done.

"I can't!" Taash cried when he had finished. "But I want to!"

"Bargah," Kashka said sternly to the old woman who had come to the door and was standing sleepily in her nightgown. "What has the lad been doing while I was away that you haven't taught him the proper way to walk upon this earth? Is he such a wastrel of his time that he cannot so much as stand on his head?"

With these words, Kashka upended himself and calmly surveyed the world with his feet in the air.

"Go on with you," old Bargah chuckled. "If all the world had brains of jelly such as you have, there would be no harm in their standing on their heads. But luckily they haven't! Come in and light the fire. After breakfast you can see what the boy has learned."

"We'll come in as soon as we have seen the sun rise," Kashka answered. "There, from the roof!"

He leaped upon the bench, caught hold of the eaves, and pulled himself up. Then he gave Taash his hand and with some scrambling the boy found himself seated astride the ridge. He watched with Kashka as the sun came up over the mountains.

"That's the way a day should be started," Kashka said. "Pleasure first, work later. Some people think differently, poor creatures! They have no idea of what is really important.

"What are you cooking, Bargah, that's making my mouth water? Filet of wolf? Bear steak with sauce? Or is it just bare bear?"

"Oh, Kashka, it's porridge and muffins, of course. Where would we ever find a bear or a wolf?" asked Nanalia as she set the table.

"Why, the forest is full of them, Nanalia. Who ever heard

of a forest without bears and wolves? But come to think of it, I really do not think I could bear to eat a wolf or wolf a bear so early in the morning."

"What makes Kashka so silly, Great-aunt? Was he always that way?"

"Indeed he was," Bargah said. "He was silly before he was born, so I am afraid there is not much we can do about him."

"Slander," sniffed Kashka, looking hurt. "I am the most serious man in the kingdom. Why the King himself will not make a move without consulting me. Only last week I was strolling with him through the palace gardens when a bee lit upon the back of his hand. 'Don't move, Your Highness,' I said to him. 'Let me converse with this insect before you take action.'

"I tried to reason with the beast but it refused to respond to either reason or the most eloquent of arguments. So I armed myself with a spear, a battle-axe, and a good broad sword. Then borrowing the King's own dagger which I held between my teeth, I rushed at the creature. It bowed before my fierce and terrible attack, flew off at once, and went about its proper business of making honey. The King was spared, the country saved, and I was the most important man of the hour! And *you* say I am silly!

"Now to me there is nothing more foolish than two children dabbling soggy muffins in cold porridge when they ought to be walking in the woods. Who'll come with me?"

"I will!" Nanalia cried. "But Taash has work to do so he can't go."

"Poor Taash," sighed Kashka. "Perhaps though, he'll be clever enough to finish the milking by the time you have finished washing the dishes. Then he can go with us."

Nanalia's face grew red and she pinched her lips together.

"You think Taash is so clever! Well he's not!" she snapped. "He didn't know anything when he came here. He didn't know a weed from a vegetable. He didn't know his letters or his numbers. We had to tell him everything. And if you really want to know how stupid he is, I'll tell you something else. *He doesn't even know who he is!* I know, because I asked him. All he knows is who he *isn't* and that's the woodcutter's son. I don't know why he had to come and live with us. He spoils everything!"

Taash sat thunderstruck. Nanalia's words brought the village boys' stinging taunt to his mind. "Taash, Taash, he ought to be ashamed. . . . he don't know his name!" The old unhappy ache swept over him and the despair of knowing that no one wanted him made him shrivel and grow cold inside. The morning turned gray. He stood up.

"I'll go milk the cow."

But Kashka caught his arm and held it so tightly that Taash winced.

"No, you won't!" he said and he shook the boy. Kashka's voice was angry and his face was white.

"You will not go," he repeated and his eyes were blazing, "until a certain little girl with a very nasty temper has apologized."

"I won't!" cried Nanalia. "I hate him! I hate him! I . . . Oh, hooo!" she sobbed. "I'm sorry. But why did he have to come here?"

"Kashka!" Bargah spoke sharply. "Let go Taash's arm. Nanalia, go out and wash your face. Taash, go milk the cow. Not a word from any of you!"

Nanalia ran from the room. Kashka looked down at Taash in surprise and let him go.

"I'm sorry, Taash," he muttered. "I'm sorry, Bargah. But Nanalia makes me furious!"

"I'm not surprised," Bargah told him. "Her temper is almost as bad as yours. But you're a grown man! If you weren't I should box your ears!"

Kashka scowled and pulled at his lower lip.

Taash went out. He didn't know how the sun could shine when it had lost its brightness. He sat down on the low stool and rested his head wearily against the warm side of the cow. A cold heavy weight had settled in him. What had he done? What had he said that Nanalia hated him so? How angry Kashka had been—it seemed as much with him as with her! Taash stopped milking to rub his arm. Nanalia called him cousin, but what was he, Taash, to Kashka? Nobody. Would they send him away now, perhaps back to the woodcutter? He grew colder still. But the woodcutter didn't want him. Nobody wanted him. He closed his eyes.

"Haven't you finished milking? Cover the pail and run along. Kashka and Nanalia are waiting for you."

Taash looked up. He hadn't heard Bargah's step.

"Are you going to send me away?" he asked.

"Send you away? Where? Why should I send you away?"

"If Nanalia hates me so, I should think you wouldn't want me here."

"What! What sort of nonsense is this? Not want you?" Bargah put her arms around Taash and held him tight. "There must be something in the air today. I am surrounded by a houseful of idiots! I wouldn't give you up for the whole world!"

"Throw in the sun and the moon and the stars!" Kashka had come up behind them. "Why? Who has come asking to take him away? The woodcutter? The mayor? The baker? Bargah, you must change them all into fat piggies if they so much as look in this direction. Why, Taash, what a face you are making! Come along and show me the garden. Nanalia says you don't know a weed from a vegetable so I suppose there's nothing there for me to eat except dandelions and thistles.

"Now look at that!" said Kashka looking around in exasperation. "Just when I felt my ears growing long and furry and was hoping I would look positively elegant in my new tail, I see nothing but vegetables. I cannot become a donkey after all! The weed crop has failed. Ah, Nanalia, you have told me a lie and I shall never know when to believe you again."

He shook his head sadly. "I don't even believe that you hate Taash."

"Of course I don't hate him. Why should I? That was tantrum talk. Don't you know when it's tantrum talk?" Nanalia asked.

"Maybe I do," Kashka said, "but I don't think Taash does. He has never lived with such a spoiled bad-tempered person."

"Did you believe me?" Nanalia turned to Taash.

"Yes," he said.

"Didn't you ever say you hated anybody?"

"Yes," he said again. "But I meant it."

"Oh." She thought a little. "Well, I meant it too. Only just for a minute, because Kashka talks to you all the time and then he doesn't talk to me. It isn't fair."

"Come along," Kashka said, "or we'll be late."

"Late for what?" Nanalia asked.

But Kashka didn't answer. He had taken out his pipe and was playing upon it.

They wandered along the edge of the marsh, across the wide meadow, and into the forest. It was cool and dark there and the air was sharp with the smell of pine. Their feet made no sound on the soft forest floor. It was so pleasant they went on deeper and deeper into the woods.

Suddenly Taash stopped. Nanalia bumped into him. She gave him a push.

"Go on!"

Kashka turned. "What's the matter?"

Taash didn't answer. He was listening and the other two stopped and listened with him.

It was the sound of an axe that they heard. Chop, chop, chop.

"It's only a woodcutter," Nanalia said.

But Taash had grown pale. He spun around and began running back along the path.

Kashka was after him with a bound and Nanalia, after stamping her foot angrily, turned and ran after them.

"Stop!" Kashka called. "Taash!"

He caught the boy on the shoulder.

"Don't run so fast! Do you want to leave Nanalia here by herself? Now then, what is wrong?"

"I don't know!" Taash was bewildered. The sound of the axe had made him feel queer.

"Are you afraid of the woodcutter? Do you think that you might have to go back and live with him again?"

"I don't know," Taash repeated. "Perhaps."

"You must never think so!" Kashka shook him gently. "Do you understand that? Neither Bargah nor I would ever permit it!"

Taash nodded, but he knew that that was not what had frightened him. Kashka looked sharply at the boy.

"For goodness sake, what *is* the matter with you?" Nanalia came puffing up to them. "You are the strangest boy I ever knew!"

"Never mind," Kashka said. "It's getting late and we must go back."

They walked without speaking. Taash listened for the sound of the axe but he didn't hear it now. He tried to get hold of what he had felt. It was as if the axe had been telling him something. Telling him—what? He thought he should know, but he didn't. It made him uneasy.

"Look there!" Nanalia called out all at once. "Look at

that path there. I've never seen it before. Let's go that way, Kashka."

"No," said Kashka.

"Why not?" Nanalia persisted. "It's not *really* late. I don't know why you said it was. Please, Kashka?"

"No!" Kashka repeated.

"But we've never been down it!"

"And you are never to go down it!" Kashka stopped and turned to the two children. "Do you understand that?"

"But why not? Why is it there? It wasn't there yesterday or the day before, but it looks as if it had always been there. Who made it? Will it be there tomorrow? How can we go down it if it isn't there?"

"Be quiet, Nanalia, and listen to me." Kashka had grown very serious. "I can tell you nothing about that path except that it is dangerous. Sometimes it is here and sometimes it isn't. Don't ask me why. But if you go that way you might get hurt in such a way that you would be sorry for the rest of your life. You must *never* go. Don't even look for it."

Taash gazed down the path. It *looked* like an ordinary path. How could it be there one day and not another? It was strange. Everything today was strange!

Kashka hurried them along. Taash heard the sound of the axe again. It was farther away now, but it made him want to run. Why didn't Kashka go faster?

5

That night Taash lay thinking. Nanalia was angry with him again. All during the flute lesson she had stood behind Kashka and made faces at Taash. When Bargah called her to come and help cut out the new dress, she had said she didn't want a dress.

"Very well," Kashka had said without looking around. "I'll take the cloth back with me. I know another little girl who will be delighted to have it."

Nanalia went then to help Bargah but she was sullen the entire evening and wouldn't speak to any of them. Taash sighed. Girls were very difficult to live with. What she needed was something to play with. He sat up in bed. He could make something for her! What did girls like? He remembered seeing some little girls in the village playing with dolls. He would make her a doll!

He fell asleep with his head full of ideas.

Down in the kitchen Kashka walked back and forth and around and around.

"They should never go far into the forest by themselves again," he said to Bargah. "I didn't dream we would see it or I never would have taken them. Who knows when it might be there again? And who knows what they might not do? A child is a child, and will forget a promise, or stretch it a bit. I wish I could take him with me!"

"You know you can't—not yet. So there is no use of talking of that. I shall be more careful than before." Bargah shook her head and sighed. "There is so much time to make up!"

"He is quick to learn. Let's be thankful for that. I shall leave him with a few things to do. And I shall try to get back more often, Bargah. But it isn't easy. The King is generous but I dare not impose on his good nature. And there are those who might be suspicious. To be honest, I have never been sure but what they knew something."

"Then watch yourself, Kashka. This is no child's game."

"I know, Bargah," Kashka sighed wearily. "I have been playing the game for eight years."

Taash was up before anyone was awake in the morning. He went into the forest to look for a piece of wood. From it he would carve a doll and he knew exactly how it would look when it was finished.

The sky was growing light but the wood was a world of half-light, of gray shadows and indefinite shapes. The ferns hung dew-silvered and motionless beside the path and the trees beyond faded into the pearl-white mist. The hush of sleep still lay upon the creatures of the forest. How quiet it was! Taash walked softly, unwilling to break the enchantment of the stillness.

He found a piece of wood but it splintered too easily. Another was split, another worm-eaten. He went deeper into the forest.

Down the path he went, around the bend, and past the huge double-trunked pine. There he stopped suddenly and stared. Before him was the mysterious path. A low fog hung over it and crept out among the bushes. The trees on either side floated rootless above the ground as if rising from some obscure other world.

The boy gazed at the opening. Where did it go? How could a path be dangerous? What kind of danger could it be? No matter! Kashka had told them—and *there* was a fine-looking piece of wood! He picked it up and examined it. It was of a perfect texture, smooth, sound, and with no knots. He rubbed his hand over it. Nor would it be hard to carve!

Taash smiled happily and turned with the wood in his hands. Then he heard it. Chop, chop, chop. The mist was rising and drifting away. There was a rustling in the trees as if unseen beings moved among the leaves and the air around him was filled with soft whisperings and faint sighs. Chop, chop, chop. "I am looking for you. Come to me." The whispers grew more distinct. "Help me find you." Chop, chop, chop. "This way, down the path."

Taash stood clutching the little log. Where were the voices coming from? How pleasantly the path wandered through the trees! Now the morning sun was dappling the ground. A soft breeze caressed his face. Just one step, one little step nearer? Chop, chop, chop.

But Kashka had told him—Kashka had said . . . !

"Kashka!" he shouted. "Kashka!"

He began to run then, run as fast as he could away from the pleading, cajoling voice. Through the dark forest he ran, stumbling, tripping, terror mounting in him with every step he took. At last he was out of it and in the open fields. The sun was warm and bright and there were no hidden paths here. And there, running toward him, bounding across the meadow as if he knew Taash had called, was Kashka.

"Kashka!" Taash called again and then fairly flung himself at his friend.

"Hi! Steady! You near knocked me flat! What is it, Taash? Where have you been? I've been looking for you. How did you get so cold?"

"I went into the forest," Taash panted. He struggled to catch his breath and get hold of himself as well. "I was looking—for a piece of wood. I wanted to make a doll for Nanalia. So she wouldn't be angry about—whatever she gets angry about. Girls like dolls, don't they? The village girls have dolls."

"Yes," Kashka nodded. "Girls like dolls."

"I couldn't find a good piece. Not at first. I kept looking and then I saw the path. You know, the one we saw yesterday?"

Kashka nodded again.

"It was still there. Then I saw the wood. This piece. It was just right. But when I picked it up I heard it again. It was the woodcutter's axe. I heard it and something kept telling me to go down the path. What was it, do you know? I didn't know what to do! I ran and I called you and I ran. I didn't want to go down the path but someone tried to make me go!"

They were at the door of the house and Kashka stopped. "I shall ask Bargah about it," he said. "She will know what it was. But you must stay out of the forest until she tells you it is safe. And you must promise me that never, *ever*, will you go down that path!"

Taash had another lesson upon the flute that day. Later Kashka taught him how to do a proper somersault. The young man watched the boy with a critical eye.

"Again! Now again. Try it once more. That was better. Rest now. We'll try again in a minute. See here, like this. You're lucky you aren't all arms and legs or you would never get over three times and back on your feet so quickly. You have some ability. All right, now do it again just as I did. After this we'll do it backwards and then I'll show you how to stand on your head."

"Why can't I learn too?" Nanalia asked as she stood watching them.

"You can if you find something to wear. You don't want your skirts falling in your face. See if Bargah will fix something for you."

They were so busy that there was no time for a walk in the woods that day. Nor was there time the next or the day after that. But in the night when Taash and Nanalia were asleep, Kashka went into the forest. Bargah sat by the fire waiting, waiting until at last she heard his step. Both nights her look of inquiry was answered by a gloomy shake of the head.

The third night he went out again. The hours went by. Each time Bargah rose and went to the door the stars had made their silent way a little more to the west. But Kashka did not come.

When at last it had grown very late and still he had not returned, she went to a high cupboard. From it she took a tall flagon, a tiny phial, a small box, and a crystal goblet intricately etched and rimmed with gold. She set them on a low table before the fire. Carefully she poured a sparkling red liquid from the flagon into the goblet, and to it added three drops from the phial. She passed her hand above it uttering several syllables in a strange tongue. Gazing at the flaming logs, she held the glass, turning it around and around, warming it in her hands.

After a time she took from the box a pinch of glistening grayish powder and blew it from the palm of her hand onto the glowing embers. The flames leaped high in a blaze of blue and green and she held the goblet over them and murmured and murmured until the fire fell back. Then she set the glass in a small niche in the fireplace where it would stay warm. She added another log to the coals and sat again waiting.

A click of the latch roused her. The log had turned to a ghost of itself. The candle on the table had guttered out. But before her at last stood Kashka. He was pale and so exhausted he could scarcely draw his breath, but his eyes burned like the blue flames of the witch's fire.

"I found them, Bargah!" he whispered. "Oh, what I have seen this night!" He passed a trembling hand over his face. "But they do not know. We are still safe."

Bargah took the goblet from the niche. Now it glowed and flashed in her hand with a fire of its own. She held it out to Kashka.

Kashka took it and put it to his lips. For an instant he hesitated, gazing at her over the rim of the glass. Then he tipped it back and drank.

Bargah smiled and took the empty goblet from his hand. Kashka took three steps backward, staggered, and then collapsed on the pallet in the corner of the room where he lay quite still.

Bargah rose, took a small covered basket from the same high cupboard, and wrapping her shawl around her shoulders, went out the door and pulled it quietly shut behind her.

In the morning when Taash and Nanalia rose, Bargah was making their breakfast. She motioned to them to be quiet, for Kashka still lay as if dead in the corner.

"He is a restless one," she explained in a whisper. "Sometimes he cannot sleep at night. Then he walks and walks until he cannot take another step. Now he must sleep. Go outside when you have finished eating. There is plenty for you to do there."

Two days later, before Kashka left, he talked to Taash.

"The forest is safe now," he told him. "But I do not expect you to play there much any more. I expect you to work hard at your pipe and the tumbling."

He smiled wryly.

"Some men are kings, some are soldiers, and some wield the pen or sculptor's chisel as skillfully as others do the sword. But only a king is born to his job. The rest of us must work to succeed. Give your pipe half your heart and you will be half a piper. But *I* cannot tolerate half-done things. Do you understand?"

"I think so," Taash said.

Kashka smiled again, but his eyes looked through the boy.

"I will not bear with a sluggard. I will not trifle with one who trifles with music."

"I shall try," Taash told him.

"That will not be enough."

"I shall do my best!"

"Your best may be scarcely tolerable. You must do better!"

Taash had finished carving the doll and he showed it to Bargah.

"It needs a face now," she told him, "and some hair."

She helped him paint the eyes and the mouth. For the hair she braided yarn and glued it down tightly. Then she found a scrap of cloth and made a dress for the doll. It was done.

Taash put the doll on the table at Nanalia's place. He had grown fond of the little piece of carved wood, but now he frowned at it. It wasn't perfect. The arms didn't quite match. One leg was longer than the other. He sighed. Bargah had painted the face very well, though. The eyes looked almost real. He gazed at them and they stared back at him. "So you are Taash," the doll seemed to say.

Those eyes made Taash uncomfortable. Why did they stare as if they had something to do with him? It was only a piece of painted wood! "I am waiting for you, Taash," they said to him. "I shall wait."

"What's that?"

Taash started.

"It's a doll," he said. "It's for you. I made it."

Nanalia picked up the doll, looked at it, turned it over, turned it back, smoothed its hair, and patted its dress.

"I've never had a doll," she said at last.

"I know," Taash said.

"You made it?"

"Kashka helped me before he left. He showed me how to make the arms move up and down. See? And Bargah made the dress and the hair and painted the face."

Nanalia moved the arms and felt the braids and nodded.

"What is her name?"

"I don't know. *You* have to give her a name."

Nanalia nodded and looked seriously at the doll. She thought a long while.

"I shall call her Tiliana. That is what she looks like. Tiliana."

"That's a good name." Taash was pleased.

"You're my doll, Tiliana, and you must do everything I say!" Nanalia spoke sternly to the doll.

"First you must thank Taash. It was very kind of him to make you. There, you must bow politely even though you can't talk. And now you must—now—oh my!" Nanalia suddenly hugged the doll and ran out the door past Bargah and up the path into the meadow.

"Nanalia!" Bargah called after her. But the little girl did not stop or look around.

"Shall I go after her?" Taash asked.

"No, let her go." Bargah smiled. "She will be back when she is ready to come back."

She smiled again at Taash. "I think she likes the doll!"

In a little while Nanalia was back. She was her usual self, chattering away about everything. The doll had done this, Tiliana thought such and such about that. Tiliana must sit at the table for meals. She must learn her letters. She must have her dress washed. She was naughty and must be spanked. She must sit under a tree and see that Taash weeded the garden properly. And, of course, she must go to bed with Nanalia at night.

Taash almost felt that he had been replaced by Tiliana, but he did not mind. Nanalia no longer pouted and sulked as she had been doing ever since Kashka left.

Everything was better. Best of all, Kashka had promised not to wait so long before he came back.

6

The days passed, and the weeks, and the months. Summer turned to fall and fall to winter. Every time Kashka came he gave Taash more to do.

"I can never make such a sound come from my flute as Kashka gets from his," the boy would complain.

"Kashka has been practicing for twenty years," Bargah would tell him. "You cannot expect to master such an instrument in a week or a month or even a year. You are doing very well."

Or he would fret that he was awkward and clumsy, that his feet did not go half as high as Kashka's when he jumped in the air. He was sure that he was nothing but a stumble-footed clod! Even in the winter he would go outside and turn handsprings and somersaults in the snow to see how many he could do, or how far or how high he could leap. He would climb the apple tree in the garden and swing on the branches, chin himself and hang by his knees—anything that he might show Kashka what he had done during the long winter.

For Kashka could not come to visit during the bad weather. The days dragged and even Tiliana did not keep Nanalia from growing quarrelsome. She and Taash would argue until Bargah made them sit in separate corners of the little kitchen with their hands folded in their laps, their faces to the wall.

At last the days began to grow longer and warmer. And one day spring came.

"Will Kashka come today?" they shouted to Bargah as they raced around in circles in front of the house.

"I don't think so," she smiled from the doorway. "How could he get here so quickly? Yesterday it was still winter and it may be winter again tomorrow. He must wait until the rivers stop flooding and the roads are dry. He's not a bird!"

"Why does he go away?" Taash asked. "Where does he go?"

"He serves the King at his court," said Bargah. "When the King is sad, he jests and makes him laugh. When the King is bored, he leaps and tumbles for him. When the King is weary, he plays his pipe. He is kept very busy, do not doubt that! He is the King's favorite jester, and the King wants him near all the time."

Taash's eyes sparkled.

"I should like to be like Kashka!" he said. "Just think what it must be to keep a king happy!"

"Nay, it is not so easy," Bargah laughed. "Kings are hard to please."

"But to be so close to a king! Who could want more?"

Bargah tweaked Taash's nose. "Well, perhaps one day you will be as close to a king!"

And as he ran off leaping and bounding she murmured, "Ay, we would you were as close to a king!" Then she shook her head and sighed.

They had a week of bad weather when it rained and stormed as if the winter were beginning all over again. But when the storm finally passed and a fine day came, the grass was green, the buds on the trees were bursting open, and the violets and trilliums were blooming in the forest.

Taash arose one morning to find that Bargah had already started the morning fire, and hunched up before it, warming his fingers, sat the figure of an old man. His cloak and hood were pulled tightly around him and he shivered and rubbed his hands.

"Ay, poor fellow," he was saying to Bargah. He wheezed and coughed as he spoke. "He was caught in the storm. A terrible blizzard it was. And just before he died of the cold he gave me this and begged me to seek out the Witch Bargah's hut and give it to the boy Taash. He said he loved the boy like his own brother and he wanted him to have it."

There in the shaking hands of the old man lay Kashka's flute.

"For shame . . ." Bargah started to speak as Taash leaped forward.

No! No! It couldn't be true!

"Where is Kashka?" Taash's voice caught in a sob. Then, "Kashka!" he gasped.

For the old man stood suddenly and threw off his cloak. There was Kashka himself, hugging Taash and pounding him on the back.

"Of all the mean tricks!" Taash's laugh was close to tears.

"Ah, well, I had to find out whether you had forgotten me!"

"Shame on you, Kashka!" Bargah scolded.

"No shame at all," Kashka insisted. "Now he is twice as glad to see me that he knows I am not dead!"

Bargah threw up her hands. "You are a madman, Kashka!"

"There's no news in that!" Kashka grinned. "Now, Taash, let me see you stand on your head!"

Taash was upside down in a minute.

"And I can walk on my hands too. Look at this!"

He started across the kitchen.

"Out! Both of you!" Bargah snatched up the broom. "Now! This minute! Before you break every dish in the house!"

Kashka leaped out the door and Taash tumbled after him.
"Just like an old witch!" Kashka shouted. "Using her broom on us!"

"If you weren't so quick you would have learned what a broom felt like!" She shook it at them.

"Now then, let us have a performance fit for a king!" Kashka called to Taash.

With his whole heart in it, Taash jumped into the air, tapped his heels, twirled, did a row of handsprings, three somersaults—forward and back—another leap and a turn and then a bow.

Kashka clapped and cheered and shouted. "Bravo! Bravo! And now a tune, Sir Jester! Let us have music!"

Taash ran to fetch his pipe.

"Wait," he panted as he put it to his lips and then took it away again. "I have no breath left for playing!"

"What? Take off his head! He will never do! The King is dying of boredom and a good fool must be able to go on hour after hour. He must be able to jest when his heart is weeping, to dance when his feet are of lead, to pipe when he suffers from asthma! This fellow I see before me is useless! Bring me another . . ."

But Kashka did not finish, for Taash had leaped upon him and began pummeling him. They rolled to the ground, wrestling, struggling, and tussling, until at last Taash found himself face down in the dust with Kashka perched on the small of his back.

"Enough?" Kashka asked cheerfully.

"Ye—yes," Taash was weak from laughing.

"Now there are *two* madmen!"

Bargah stood in the door and shook her head.

"Look at you! And breakfast is ready. I will not serve such a dusty pair of rags at my table!"

Kashka let Taash get to his feet, but no sooner was the

boy up than he seized the bucket of water from beside the well and doused Kashka from head to foot.

"Bargah wants you clean!" he shouted, and collapsed again with laughter.

What happened next, Taash was not quite sure. But he suddenly found himself dangling head down in the well.

"Help!" he shouted. "Kashka, don't!"

"Shall I let go then?" Kashka cried.

"No, no! Please, Kashka! Take me out!"

"What if I can't? Ooops, there you go! No, I still have you!"

"Kashka!" Taash shrieked.

And then he was hauled back up into the daylight. He was considerably sobered.

"It never fails!" Kashka said solemnly as he poured another bucket of water into the basin and washed his hands and face.

"Hallo! Bargah!" he called. "Throw me some dry clothes. What sort of fiend have you made of this boy with your witchcraft? Last year it was 'Yes, sir,' and 'No, sir,' and now he beats me, drowns me, and probably calls me bad names when I'm not here to defend myself!"

"It's your own fault," said Bargah as she tossed him a dry shirt. "You've set him a bad example. He wants to be like you."

"Oh ho! So that's it!" He rumpled Taash's hair. "He has a fair start, but he will have to hustle to catch up. One must work hard to achieve madness! Poor lad, he's in for a miserable life!"

"No, indeed, I'm not!" said Taash. "It's I who will make everyone else miserable, just as you do!"

"Listen to him!" cried Kashka pretending to be outraged. "In another six months the boy will be insufferable. We shall be forced to send him back to the woodcutter."

Taash laughed.

"In another six months I shall be able to put *you* down the well!"

He stretched himself on his tiptoes to see if he were tall enough to measure up to Kashka's chin.

"By heaven, you're cheating!" said Kashka pushing him down until the boy's knees were bent. "There, that's about right."

"Taash is as bad as Kashka," said Nanalia who had come out with Tiliana. "I shall be glad when he *is* big enough to throw Kashka down the well. Then they can throw each other down and see who pulls which out. It will serve them right."

"Children nowadays have no respect for their elders," Kashka complained.

"You never were a respectable elder," Nanalia said. "Tiliana is much more grown up than you ever will be. I don't see how the King puts up with you!"

"Nay," Kashka laughed. "You should see what he has to put up with without me!"

Kashka's visits were too short for Nanalia and Taash. He came and went in the blink of an eye. On one of his visits that summer he cocked his head to one side.

"Nanalia, you are becoming quite a young lady. How old are you now, four years? Five?"

"Kashka, you are dreadful! You know I am ten! I shall be eleven on Roodmas."

"Ah yes, of course! And Taash is twelve. Well, then . . ."

"How do you know I am twelve?" Taash asked. "I don't know myself how old I am."

"Why, you are twelve because I have said you are twelve. If Nanalia had agreed to be four, I would have said that you were six. Now then, since you are twelve and will probably be thirteen someday—thirteen does come after twelve, doesn't it?—it would not surprise me if Bargah surprised us by saying you might come with me when I return to the court. Nay, don't get so excited! I mean later this year, or next. It's up to Bargah!"

"We'll see," Bargah said.

It was enough to drive Taash and Nanalia frantic.

"What do you think?" Kashka asked Bargah when they were alone. "Will you come back with me in the fall?"

"It is something to think about," she said. "But I'm not sure. I've taught him everything I can. He's like a sponge for learning. Yet I cannot help but feel there may still be too many dangers."

Kashka grew thoughtful.

"No, I suppose it wouldn't be right," he mused. "If he were recognized by—but by heaven! He almost caught me up today! We shall have to tell him soon!"

"Ay," Bargah agreed. "But we must not be hasty. He must be prepared to look after himself if anything should happen before all is safe. He is still young, still only a child. No, Kashka, I think we shall be safer to wait at least until next spring."

Kashka jumped to his feet and began pacing.

"I know you're right, but I can't bear to think of the long winter. What if something happens and I know nothing of it until next spring? Bargah, they're up to something again. It makes me uneasy."

"All the more reason to wait!" the old woman told him. "We're safe here. The year is almost up since they last tried, and I shall go into the forest every night now to be sure that they are not back at their old tricks. If I find any trace, I know well enough how to stop them."

"Then it's settled. I must go back tomorrow. But how I wish you were nearer! I could visit you more often. If anything . . ."

"Will you stop your fretting? To be nearer would be to

invite trouble. There are a hundred places we might be other than here, but that was settled long ago."

"Ay, ay, ay, old woman," Kashka said impatiently. "But look at him now, and think what a miserable, frightened, half-starved ragamuffin he was! I can scarcely believe my eyes! I'm fond of him—for himself, Bargah. I want to watch him become what he will be. You don't understand!"

"I understand very well," Bargah smiled. "I watch him grow day by day, nay, hour by hour! But we are both fussing like two old hens over a baby chick!"

Kashka smiled ruefully.

"I would not fuss so much if my bones were more quiet. Take care, Bargah!"

7

"Taash!" Nanalia called. "Come with me! Tiliana and I have found the most beautiful blackberries you've ever seen. Don't put your pipe away, leave it around your neck. Tiliana likes to hear you play. Bring another basket. They're the last of the season. If Kashka comes, we'll have a surprise for him."

"Bargah thinks he might come today."

"Then hurry!"

She paused to stare at him a moment. "How your good luck stone glows today! Did you polish it?"

Taash looked down at the small pendant.

"No. It must have come clean in my bath last night," he laughed.

Nanalia pouted. "Mine isn't so bright."

She rubbed her amulet with the edge of her collar. Then she dropped her doll into a basket and ran ahead of Taash. He was in no hurry to pick blackberries. Kashka might be there very soon and there was still a passage he could not play on his flute. He must have it before Kashka arrived!

"Play something different!" Nanalia called to him. But he was so intent upon the music he did not hear her.

They crossed the meadow and went into the forest.

"Do hurry!" Nanalia's impatient voice came from around the bend in the path. "They're still here."

"Why shouldn't they . . ." But Taash did not finish the sentence. He had dropped his flute and looked up to see where they were. There stood Nanalia pointing to the bushes bowed low with the weight of the fruit, pointing to the bushes that grew on either side of the mysterious forbidden path.

The boy stared in dismay. The path had not been there since that frightening morning so long ago!

"Oh don't be so silly," Nanalia said. "We don't have to go *down* the path. There are enough berries growing right here to fill both baskets and a dozen more besides. Anyway, *I'm* not afraid!"

She stepped onto the path and began picking berries.

"But we promised," Taash said, and he wondered himself what harm could come of taking one step on the path.

"*I* didn't," Nanalia tossed her head. "He told us not to go down it, but I didn't say I wouldn't."

"Well *I* did!"

Nanalia said nothing but her lips pinched together. She picked berries without saying another word.

Taash stood still watching her. The forest was so silent! There was no breath of wind, no flutter of birds. The more he listened the more silent it became. He began to feel that he would suffocate in the stillness. At last he was unable to bear it another minute.

"I—I suppose I could pick some berries," he said.

His heart pounded as he stepped onto the path. Nothing happened. Nothing changed. The world did not grow dark or burst into flames! The ground did not split open and swallow them!

Nanalia snickered.

"You *are* afraid, aren't you?"

Taash flushed.

"I promised Kashka I would stay off it. Now I've broken my promise."

"You don't need to tell. I won't tell. We'll say that we found the berries growing beside the path."

"That's a kind of lying besides breaking a promise!"
Taash frowned. He picked in silence, scowling all the while
at the heavily laden bushes.

In a little while he looked at Nanalia's basket.

"We have enough now," he said. "Let's go back."

Nanalia set her basket on the ground.

"I'm going to see what's around the bend first."

"No," Taash said. "Let's go home. You said you only
wanted the berries."

She stuck out her tongue at him.

" 'Fraidy cat!"

She ran down the path.

It was not far. When she came to the bend she looked
back at Taash who stood watching her. Then she looked
ahead beyond the trees and bushes where Taash could not
see. All of a sudden she laughed.

"Good-bye!" she called, waved to Taash and ducked
around the bend and out of sight.

Taash did not know what to do. If any harm should come
to Nanalia it would be his fault, but Kashka's warning rang
in his ears. *Never ever will you go down that path!* He was
furious with Nanalia! He picked up the baskets and set them
out on the main path. He would wait for her there.

But just as he put the berries down, he heard her scream.
She screamed and screamed again. Taash stood frozen.

"Taash!" And then there came another piercing scream
so terrifying that Taash ran blindly toward the sound. Whatever happened he must try to help her.

But when he came around the bend, he stopped. For there,
sitting in the center of the little track, covering her mouth
with the back of her hand to keep from laughing aloud, was
Nanalia. Taash stared at her.

"What's the matter?" he asked. "Why did you scream?"

She burst out laughing.

"You should see your face! You look as if you'd seen a dozen ghosts! My, aren't you brave!"

Taash grew so angry he wanted to shake her. If she had been a boy he would have thrashed her.

"There!" she said quickly, seeing what was in his mind. "What is there to be afraid of in that?"

She pointed down the path which ended abruptly in a mass of undergrowth and young trees.

"That's all there is to it. Nothing more."

As Taash continued to glare at her, Nanalia became angry. She jumped to her feet.

"And I don't expect there is anything there either!"

And she ran to the end of the path and pushed her way into the bushes.

By this time Taash had made up his mind that he would shake her and he ran after her and through the brush he scrambled too.

He came out of the tangled growth to find Nanalia standing at the edge of a still dark pool. All around the trees grew close and thick and the branches overhead had entwined in such a way as to form a dense canopy. The foliage shut out the sky. A dim light filtered through the leaves giving to the air a greenish cast.

The pool was small and black and though it was clear they could not see to the bottom. It was perfectly round and perfectly still. No breath of air ruffled its surface. No water spider skated over the glassy film. No frog croaked on its banks.

The same suffocating stillness that had distressed him earlier again enveloped Taash. It grew and grew upon him until it was a force, a living presence that weighed upon him. Yet there was no sign of life around the strange pool. Nothing moved and there was no sound but the beating of his own heart in his ears. They stood without speaking, scarcely breathing.

"It must be magic!" Nanalia whispered at last. "Look there!"

As she raised her hand to point there was a splash and a shriek.

"I've dropped Tiliana!"

The doll floated a little way out in the water. Nanalia could not quite reach it. Her fingers pushed Tiliana a little farther out.

"Be careful," Taash warned her. "You'll fall in. I can reach her."

He leaned far out over the water. There, he could just touch the dress. He leaned a bit more, stretched, snatched at the doll, caught hold of it and threw it back over his shoulder. And then—then lost his balance and fell into the black pool.

Nanalia screamed, then put her hands over her mouth and waited. Taash could swim. She knew he could swim well. He would come up soon. She waited.

She didn't know how long she waited. It was a long time. The air grew darker, then lighter. A breeze like a sigh riffled through the trees and sent a shiver across the surface of the water. It grew still again.

Nanalia waited. Then her heart began to pound and her eyes grew large and dark and her breath caught in her throat. She could wait no longer. She turned, pushed her way through the thicket and ran back down the path past the baskets of berries, back through the forest and into the meadow. Across the meadow she ran, toward the marsh. Run, run, run, she told her legs, and they fairly flew with the terror that grew in her.

At last she came to the house and pushed open the door and burst into the room. As she stood there, breathless and unable to speak, she found herself looking into the eyes of Kashka. He was sitting at the table with Bargah.

Kashka stared at the little girl and something of the fear

that showed in her pale face and dark eyes transferred itself to him.

"What's wrong?" he asked sharply. "Where is Taash?"

Nanalia began to tremble.

Kashka leaped to his feet and grasping her shoulders shook Nanalia.

"I said, where is Taash?"

The little girl began to cry.

"He fell in the water," she sobbed. "He fell in and he drowned. He fell in!"

She burst out then with such a wailing that Kashka shook her again.

"Where?" he demanded. "Where did he fall in? Was it in the marsh? Show me where!"

"No, no, no!" Nanalia cried. "It wasn't in the marsh! It was the pool. The black pool at the end of the path!"

Kashka's hands dropped from her shoulders and he turned white.

"No," he whispered. "He didn't. He couldn't!"

"Yes, yes!" she screamed. "The doll fell in. It was Tiliana's fault. She fell in and he tried to reach her and *he* fell in. He went down and down and he didn't come back. I waited and waited and he didn't come back! Oh, oh, and I've lost Tiliana too. I don't know where she is!"

Nanalia burst again into such a state of weeping and wailing that Kashka could question her no more. Indeed, he did not try to question her, for scarcely had he heard her last words than he leaped to the door, ran up the path through the meadow and into the forest as fast as the wind.

Bargah, who had said nothing, brought a cool wet cloth and wiped the little girl's face and tried to calm her.

"Now then," she said as soon as Nanalia could pay attention. "Let us go after Kashka as quickly as we can. Perhaps Taash did not drown after all. Perhaps you did not wait as long as you think you did."

Taking the child by the hand, the old woman set out with her, hurrying as fast as her old legs would go.

It was late afternoon, and when they reached the fork in the path the sun was low, its rays filling the forest with a soft golden mist. They hastened along the strange and fateful track and wondered if they might not meet Kashka and Taash coming back after all. But they saw no one until they forced aside the vines and saplings that hid the pool.

There was Kashka. He sat with his head bowed on his knees, and in his hand he held a wet and muddied Tiliana. The paint had washed from the doll's face. There was no sign of Taash.

Bargah put her hand upon Kashka's shoulder.

He did not raise his head.

"He's gone," he said. "We've lost him and we shall never get him back. Ever."

"We don't know all of it," Bargah tried to comfort him.

Kashka shook his head.

"He wasn't ready. Not yet. He didn't know anything about it. There's no telling what has happened to him."

Bargah was silent for a moment and then said, "No, we don't know. We'll go, of course. Perhaps it won't be too late."

Kashka groaned. "It will take too long. It's already too late."

He stood up sorrowfully and they turned away from the still, dark pool and went back through the shadowy forest. When they arrived home they found that the fire was out and the soup cold. The house was dark and chilly and empty.

Nanalia crept into her bed and cried herself to sleep. Bargah and Kashka, neither speaking a word, sat at the kitchen table long after the rekindled fire had burned itself out. Toward morning Bargah rose and began putting the house in order. She made up a bundle of clothes for herself and Nanalia.

When Nanalia woke, the old woman told her they were going on a long journey with Kashka. They had a little breakfast. Then they harnessed the mule to the cart in the back of which the cat curled among the household belongings. With the cow tied behind, they set off down the road.

Though the people of the village often wondered what had become of them they never knew, for no one had seen them leave. By the time a villager came seeking herbs from the witch, the weeds were already thick in the garden and a shutter, blown loose in a storm, hung at a slant and tapped gently against the wall of the house.

The visitor, peering fearfully through a window, saw that the place was dismal and deserted. He hastened back to the village with the news. It was decided that the door and windows should be nailed shut and that no one should go near the little house by the marsh. As time went on, it was said to be haunted.

8

When the black waters of the forest pool closed over Taash his first thought was that he would have plenty of time to dry his clothes before he went home. He gave an instinctive kick to bring himself to the surface, but to his surprise found that he was still under the water. He kicked again, pulled with his arms and then became aware of a strong current that was pulling him down through the darkness. He grew panicky and kicked harder, swimming strongly upward. The terrifying thought that he was being drawn deeper into a bottomless whirlpool made him fight with all his strength against the water until he felt that his lungs would burst.

Suddenly his head was above the surface of the pool and he gasped and panted. Shaking the water from his eyes, he saw that he was on the opposite side of the pond. The root of a tree grew close to his hand and he grasped it and pulled himself up.

"Nanalia!" he called.

She was standing across from him. She stared at the water, her hands over her mouth.

"Nanalia, I'm over here!"

She did not look up.

"Hey!" he shouted. "Hi! Haloo!"

That was odd. She was no more than a dozen paces from him. Why didn't she hear him?

He stooped to pick up a stone and tossed it toward her. But there was no splash of water. The stone fell short of the middle of the pool and Taash stared with amazement as it sank without leaving a ripple on the surface. He found another stone and threw it harder. Again it fell without a trace in the center of the pond.

Fear rose in him.

"Nanalia!" he shouted at the top of his voice.

A breeze sighed through the trees and ruffled the water. Then Nanalia turned suddenly and pushed her way through the brush and vanished. Only Tiliana remained lying on the bank across from him.

Taash drew a deep breath. What was the matter with her? But he must get home. He began to make his way carefully along the bank. He was afraid he might stumble or trip on one of the twisted roots and fall again into the pool.

What a long way it was around the little pond! He had been climbing over roots and clinging to vines and still the doll lay on the opposite bank! Taash paused and looked around. How odd! The forest behind him was nowhere near as dense as he had thought. He gazed through the trees upon a rocky slope. The sun shone upon it hot and dry.

He turned again to the pond and he could not believe his eyes. The pond had vanished altogether. A small stream trickled by at his feet and the country all around him now had changed. There was no forest, no pond—only the rocky slopes of a hill and a scattering of scrubby pines.

Taash gazed around himself in bewilderment. What had happened? For a moment he had the odd feeling that he had been here before. But no matter how he tried, he could remember nothing that might tell him where it was or when he had been here. It was like a dream.

Unlike a dream, the hill he stood upon stayed as it was. The sun glared upon the broken yellow rocks and the small stream continued to trickle down the hill.

Taash looked around again. There was no house or person or animal in sight.

It took Taash some time to collect his thoughts and decide what to do. Then he started down the hill following the stream. The air was very dry and he was grateful for the water. But in a short time, the little stream sank into the ground and vanished entirely. The bed of the stream continued on however, and Taash thought that at some time of the year it must be a good-sized river. He continued following its course.

He had walked for several hours, and still he saw no house or any sign of human life. Now the sun was a great orange ball balanced on the edge of the world. In a moment it would be gone and would take with it the heat and light of the day. Taash would not miss the heat, but he did not fancy wandering in the dark. He climbed out of the river bed and looked around.

He saw that the countryside had changed. The steep hills lay behind him and he was in more gently rolling country. The low mounds unfolded before him like the backs of giant sheep, and they were covered with the coarse stubble of dry, brown grass. He watched the sun sink below the horizon. Darkness rushed over the earth while the blue of the sky deepened.

Taash sighed. He was downhearted, hungry, and tired. If only there were a house! He gave one last glance around and then his eyes caught a glimmer of light. Where was it? There! There it was again! It was a flickering like that of a fire. Perhaps a shepherd was keeping watch. Perhaps he would give Taash a bite to eat and let him sleep by his fire.

With a much lighter heart, Taash set off toward the light. The stars came out and he gazed at them in wonder. He had never seen so many nor had he ever seen them gleam so brilliantly. He puzzled over them wondering if the stars here tried to make up for the barren wasteland over which he walked.

After he had gone a good distance he began puzzling over the fire too. In all that way he should have come nearer, but it was still a dancing, flickering point far away. He rested a while and then set off toward it once more. Sometimes it vanished as his way took him down into a small valley. But when he came up again over a hill, there it was.

Taash walked on and on until at last the speck of light grew larger and he could see the flames of the fire. As he drew nearer still, he saw that it was no shepherd's fire, but a great roaring blaze that leaped high into the sky. It was built within a circle of trees and as he came yet closer he could see that there were figures moving around it.

Taash paused and watched from the brow of the last hill he had come over. There were about a dozen figures circling the blaze. They held hands and moved first in one direction, then in the other in a kind of dance. He was perplexed by the sight and hesitated to rush down the slope and ask for food and shelter.

They might be gypsies, though he could see no wagons or horses. Nor were they cooking anything, just dancing, dancing. Taash watched for a long time. He could not make up his mind to ask for help. But it was tiresome standing on the hill and he was getting nowhere. Finally he decided to creep as close to them as possible without being seen. If he could understand their speech perhaps he would find out who they were and whether it would be safe for him to speak to them.

He started quietly down the hill toward the nearest tree. Taash was halfway there when the group, which up to now had swung silently around the fire, began to chant.

It started with a low moan then rose to a pulsing wail. The weird strain rose and fell again with odd catches and an eerie wavering in the voices. Strange syllables fell upon the boy's ears. And all the while the rhythmic beating of the moving feet on the soft earth accompanied the incantation. The group went around and around. Three times in one direction, then three in the other—all in all, seven times each way, they went. And as they danced the chant grew more and more wild, more terrifying, until at last they stopped, and with arms stretched upward, threw back their heads and uttered a shriek so fearful it must have made the stars tremble in the heavens.

At the first sound Taash flattened himself to the ground and lay still. The dreadful wailing made his hands grow cold and wet. A shiver went down his spine and it was all he could do to keep his teeth from chattering. There was no bush or stone to hide him and he trembled in the fear that they might see him. Covering his ears with his hands he pressed his face against the earth.

After the last terrible cry there was silence. Taash peeked cautiously through his fingers. They were dancing around the fire again, holding hands, making no sound.

What should he do? They might see him at any minute. He must hide until they, whoever they were, went away. But there was no cover except in the grove itself.

And so, though the bizarre chant was begun again, Taash inched himself closer and closer. By the time they reached the final frenzied shriek he had crept into the shadow of a tree and crouched against the rough, gnarled trunk.

For some time he scarcely dared breathe. Then he grew curious and peered around the tree. Who were these strange beings who performed such fearful rites in so desert a place?

Now they stood in one place. Back and forth, back and forth they swayed. Forward, backward, side to side, on and on they kept the same constant motion. And all the time they uttered a queer monotonous sing-song that kept the rhythm of their swaying.

Taash had fixed his eyes on the back of the long-robed

figure nearest him. He began feeling giddy and light-headed. He began to sway. He wanted to stand up and take a place among them and join them in this grotesque dance. He opened his lips feeling that he must utter the same low moan with them, when suddenly the image of Bargah rose in his mind. He saw her leaning across the kitchen table and pointing to the numbers he studied. He heard her speaking as clearly as if she stood beside him now.

"If ever an evil presents itself to you and you feel you must be a part of it, start here with your one times one, and go on through with your twelve times twelve. You will find that by the time you have finished the evil will have passed and you will be quite safe. There is this good in numbers that few know of. I shall tell you of others by and by."

At the time he had not understood what she meant, but now he thought it must be this very moment of which she spoke. Without knowing that he had begun he found himself involved with six times seven and six times eight and six times nine (which were always hard to remember). The desire to join the group around the fire had disappeared.

Taash finished repeating all the combinations of numbers that he knew. He started again and went halfway through when he noticed that these fearful beings had stopped their swaying and moaning and stood perfectly still. One of them mounted a platform on the far side of the circle and raised her arms.

"Sister Witches," she said. "Nine years have we had to watch and wait. Nine years have we had to seek and search. Nine years have we had to lay our plans. Ay, and nine years have we had to curse that meddling fool! But once again the circle's round. Once again the charm is wound. The time is ours. All portents favor us, all signs are to our advantage. All auguries foretell success. And so we meet in desert waste to shape our fate with prudent haste.

"With this in mind, dear Sisters, let us see how she who is our coven leader and the very Queen of our Black Art does now proceed!

"Behold! All fix your eyes upon these flames and let us witness her bold triumph!"

Taash, fascinated, stared into the fire from behind his tree. As he gazed into them the flames twisted and shifted, fell back and so altered themselves at the very center of the blaze that in a moment's time he found himself looking down a long and shadowy hall. Many doors, all closed, lined the walls on either side. As if he moved along the hall, he approached one door. Beside it two men-at-arms dozed, leaning on their spears.

A hoarse chuckle went around the circle of watchers.

The door swung open and a figure entered a softly lighted room. Beside the fireplace sat a woman. She slept, her head nodding on her breast. The figure hesitated but a moment then moved to the center of the room where a small bed stood. Hands brushed aside the curtains that hung from a velvet canopy. A sleeping child was lifted from the bed.

The figure turned and Taash saw the face, the gloating face of a malevolent woman. Taash gasped and clapped his hand over his mouth. That woman! That room! He knew her and he knew it! But where, where, where? How was it possible?

Transfixed, he continued to stare at the face in the fire until it faded from sight. Once more there were only the leaping crackling flames before his eyes.

The witches cheered and then a shout went up.

"Here she is!"

There was the sound of the rush of the wind. The fire blazed high and white. And there standing before them was the woman Taash had seen in the fire. In her arms was a small bundle of blankets.

Another shout rose and was lost in the desert sky.

The newly arrived one raised her arm for silence.

"My dear Sisters," she spoke. "Long have we waited for this hour and minute. Long has our patience been. But soon the honey of success shall fill our mouths and we shall hold the brimming cup of gall up to the lips of him who wears the crown! The King who rules with feeble tools of sentiment shall taste defeat, shall have his draught of bitter failure from our hands.

"Then with one clean sweep of sword and fire will we cast out love, justice, trust, forgiveness—all those meager, thin and stunted, half-starved values men so love to honor. And finally, with unrelenting power, with glove of steel enforced by our Black Art, we'll guide this land to victory o'er the world!"

A wild cry broke from the lips of the witches, but once again the speaker demanded silence.

"Hold back your noise!" she scolded. "The victory is not yet ours. We have this night to go! And oh my Sisters, must we now take care and let not one false word destroy our plans. For in the omens, good as they appear, there lies yet one dark blot that's unexplained. I've tried a thousand ways to learn its sense, to ferret out the meaning of its being. But no light has been cast upon this darkness. So I must guess. What could it be if not that hated knave, that noxious prince of mischief-making, madcap, pickle-herring, merry-andrew! Nine years ago because of him we failed. This time we'll not! The Fates have smiled on us for he is far away. That golden fox of sweet capricious fortune lies asleep, nor is there any power else within the realm that can oppose us!

"When we perform our magic rites upon this babe, he will be ours. He will be King, and ours! And if the King is ours, so is the land; and if this land, why not the world?"

For the third time she quieted the exulting witches.

"Silence still, my dear ones. Hear me out! Our rites are long and must with no mistake be done. And all must be complete and this small one must sleep again within the palace walls before the sun awakes the cock, or all our work's undone!"

There was an immediate flurry among the witches. Half of them stood at one side of the fire and began a new and rapid incantation. The rest moved quickly, preparing their magic. Dusty powders were cast upon the fire and it blazed green and blue and violet, tinting the complexions of all with unnatural colors. Mystic words were spoken over a bubbling cauldron, and when it was stirred odd shapes rose from it in the steam. Misshapen figures, distorted faces, grotesque creatures, all vapors, rose agonized and lamenting into the air and vanished in the night.

At last the circle was formed again and another chant begun. Taash watched and listened to all that was done and said. He did not understand their ritual, the demonic monosyllables of their incantations or their evil magic. But he understood their purpose well enough.

They've stolen a child, he thought with horror. They plan to cast a spell upon it. Then they will make it king of this country and he will do whatever they ask of him! He shuddered to think of people being ruled by such creatures!

They must be stopped! But how? What could he do? There were so many of them and only one of him. And *they* were witches! How he wished Bargah had taught him some magic!

Now what were these horrible beings doing? They were circling the fire slowly and with a measured step. Their chant was a low monotone of magic words. As the circle moved from left to right, the tall witch with the baby in her arms began to move slowly around the outside of the ring in the opposite direction. When she had come a quarter of the way around the circle, she stopped, raised the sleeping child high in the air, and facing the east cried in a loud voice:

"Spirits and Demons of the east,
Attend this night!
Be there any from your domain
To halt this rite?"

All stood motionless and silent as she slowly lowered her arms until she held the baby straight out before her.

After a moment the circling began again, this time in the opposite direction. The witch with the child moved halfway around to face the west. Here she addressed the spirits of the west with the same question and with the same ceremony. Then she moved three quarters of the way back to the north and Taash heard the words repeated once again. Each time there was a breathless moment after her request; each time there was no sign; each time the circling began again as if on a given signal.

Now the moment had come for her to face the south. She halted and held the child in the air, directly before Taash.

"Spirits and Demons of the south!" she cried.

Taash, looking into her face, thought nothing in the world could have so wicked and cruel an aspect. Surely all that was hateful must be in this one woman at this one moment!

"Attend this night!
Be there any from your domain
To halt this rite?"

Her voice quivered with excitement and the smile on her lips was of an evil victor. Taash suddenly realized that this was the last request, the last chance for the child to be saved. The circling had stopped. The witch lowered the baby holding it at last straight out in her arms—offering it to Taash. He could see the child's face. A beautiful child it was, sleeping quietly. He glanced again at the wicked face gloating above it.

He could stand it no longer. Taash leaped to his feet, and dashing from behind the tree, snatched the baby from her arms. "Stop!" he shouted. "Stop! Stop! Stop!"

There was a wild shriek. The fire flared up in a monstrous white blaze. Taash cried out and closed his eyes against the brilliant glare of light. He clutched the baby tightly and waited for what felt like an eternity—waited for some horrible thing to happen to him.

Nothing happened.

He opened his eyes.

All was dark around him. The fire was gone, the witches were gone and the grove was gone. He stood alone beside a twisted ancient tree and held in his arms the still sleeping child.

A hot gust of wind like the breath of a sigh rose in the north, blowing across the desolate land. It touched his face then died away somewhere in the hills behind him.

After that all was still.

9

It was some time before Taash recovered himself. His legs were trembling under him and his chest hurt from holding his breath. He sat on the ground and filled his lungs.

He was safe and so was the little one in his arms. But what was he to do now? He was so weary and he had never felt such a dryness in his mouth. By the look of the fading stars morning was coming and with it would come the sun and the heat of the day. In all directions he could see no sign of shelter, not even another tree.

But there was nothing for him here. After resting a while he took up the child and set out once more toward the north.

He walked for perhaps two hours. The baby grew heavier with each step. The sun grew hotter. He was parched with thirst. Slowly he toiled up the side of a small knoll. He had kept toward the little mound ever since it had grown light enough to see, and he hoped that from this higher point in the now flat arid plain he would be able to see some sign of life.

When Taash reached the top the baby stirred and whimpered. He opened his eyes and when he saw Taash opened his mouth as well with such a wail that the boy was completely undone.

"There now," he muttered, "am I as bad to look at as all that? You're much prettier yourself when you aren't all puckered!"

He didn't know what to do with the howling child. It

refused to be comforted with any words. At last he put the baby on his shoulder, patted it on the back as he had seen the village mothers do and stood looking out from his hilltop for the first time.

"There!" he cried, his heart leaping up. "Will you stop your fussing and look at that!"

To his delighted eyes came the sight of a twisting line of green cutting across the brown plain. It was a river with trees growing beside it. Beyond, the grass was green and clumps of trees grew here and there.

Whether it was the tone of his voice or the patting on the back, the baby had cried enough. He stopped his noise as abruptly as he had started it.

"I'll keep you there where you can't see my face," Taash told him cheerfully. "That way you won't have it to complain about. We should have a nice drink of water before too long—and a bite to eat, if we're lucky."

Taash set off at once with the baby on his shoulder. Now it gurgled and jabbered happily and Taash made a one-sided conversation with the child.

"What's your name?" he asked. "And how old are you? What am I to say to folk when they ask about us? They'd never believe such a story as we could tell them!"

The baby waved an arm and gurgled.

"All right, if *you* think so. But what am *I* to say?"

"Mamamama!" said the baby.

"They'll never believe that either!" Taash laughed. "It's more likely I'd be your brother. Can you say brother?"

"Ba," said the baby. "Ba ba ba ba."

"We don't speak the same language," Taash told him, "but I don't think anyone will notice."

In a short time they came to the river. It was a shallow stream that babbled over a stony bed. Taash took a long drink and then tried to make a cup of his hands for the baby. But neither he nor the child were accustomed to such an arrangement. The baby's shirt was drenched and Taash had his finger bitten.

"Ow!" Taash shouted and snatched away his hand so quickly that the baby was startled and began to scream.

"Hush, hush, hush," the boy grumbled as he mopped the tears from the little face with the wet shirt. "I didn't bite *you*!"

The child was not convinced that some great wrong had not been done to him. He sniffled and snuffled. Then he got hold of the bedraggled shirt and began sucking and chewing on it. In a few minutes he was quite content.

Taash watched him for a while.

"I should never have thought of that," he said. He dipped the shirt in the water and gave it to the baby again. "But show me how you are going to get something to *eat* from it!"

He picked up the child and started following the river. They hadn't gone far when the baby began to fuss again. It whined and whimpered and squirmed so that Taash found it impossible to hold him. When he set him on his feet, the child sat down and howled.

Taash gazed at him in despair. At last he pulled out his flute and began to play. The baby stopped crying at once. Taash put aside the pipe and the child at once set up such a tune of his own that Taash hastily raised the flute to his lips again.

He played everything he knew and then invented more. So busy he was that he did not notice the boy on the opposite bank.

Taash grew tired at last and put down the flute.

"We won't get far this way," he muttered gloomily to the baby who had fallen asleep in the soft grass.

"Where are you going?" asked a voice.

Taash glanced up and saw the boy across from him.

"We have to find something to eat," he said. "The baby is hungry and so am I."

Taash looked at the boy. He was a shepherd for he carried a crook in one hand and a dog, ears pricked forward, stood beside him.

"I liked your music," the boy said. "I've never heard anyone hereabouts play like that. Where do you come from?"

Taash waved his hand toward the south.

"From the other side of those hills," he said. "We've been walking for days and days and we've run out of food."

The boy's dark eyes opened wide.

"Did you come all that way? Where are you going?"

Now Taash was convinced that the truth was too fantastic to tell. And so he did the best he could and hoped the boy would not question him too closely.

"I've come to find my sister. She married a man from the court of your King. Before our mother died she told me that I must take the baby and find her. We've managed to come this far, but I don't know where to go from here. Can you help us?"

The boy nodded.

"I can give you something to eat," he said. "And I'll take you home with me this evening. Will you play your pipe again if I give you some bread and cheese?"

Taash did not need to be asked twice. He took up the baby, waded across the shallow stream and followed the boy and his dog up into the green meadow. Under a big tree the boy spread out his lunch and divided it in half. Taash ate hungrily. The baby chewed on a crust of bread and drank milk from the skin the boy carried.

"Now play for me," said the boy when they had finished.

Taash again played all the tunes he knew and more besides. The boy would have him play all afternoon, but Taash grew so drowsy he could scarcely sit up. Finally, the baby having fallen asleep again, both Taash and the shepherd boy, whose name was Ral, lay down in the grass and fell asleep too. The dog was left to look after the sheep.

It was almost evening when Taash was awakened. Ral was shaking him.

"Wake up!" he said. "It's time for my brother to come out and watch the flock. We take turns. He's older than I am and he doesn't mind being out at night."

Taash rubbed his eyes and sat up.

"I gave the baby some more milk," Ral said. "Is that all right?"

"Yes, that's all right," Taash nodded, trying to sound as if he knew all about babies.

"There's my brother now."

Taash looked across the meadow. Coming toward them was a tall young man. He gazed in surprise at the children when he came to them.

"This is Taash and his baby brother," Ral told him. "They came all the way across the mountains to get here. They're going to the King's court to find their sister. I gave them something to eat."

The older boy was as astonished as the younger and just as friendly.

"Oh!" he exclaimed. "That *is* a long way you have come! How did you ever do it with the baby? What is his name?"

"His name is Teyal," Taash answered promptly. He avoided any explanation.

"You had better take him home with Ral and have a good dinner. Mother will know what to do for you."

Ral and Taash and the newly-named Teyal went to the shepherd's cottage together.

There were so many children in the family that Taash

could not keep them straight in his mind. There were three or four little girls and two older ones, several boys younger than Ral as well as a baby that was not yet walking. In spite of her large family the mother, a plump, bright-eyed, cheerful woman, immediately took little Teyal in her arms and hugged him and dandled him and exclaimed over the state of his clothes. She told the older girls to look to the supper and mind their own baby brother while she herself bathed and fed Teyal.

In no time at all, Taash found himself seated at the table with ten other noisy children eating boiled mutton and vegetables.

Later in the evening, Maro the father came home. After he had heard Taash's story, he sat smoking a pipe and thinking.

"Well, lad," he spoke at last. "You have come a long way and you have a long way ahead of you still. But you must stay with us for a while. When you and the babe are well rested we shall see how we can help you get to the court." He shook his head gravely. "But it is a long way to go!"

Taash thanked him for his kindness and then went to bed beside Ral on a pile of straw. The baby, wrapped in a blanket, was already sound asleep in a wooden box.

Taash woke late in the morning. Ral had left to take his turn with the sheep. All the older children were at work. Little Teyal had been given his breakfast and was dressed in borrowed clothes. He was cheerfully padding around investigating everything, delighted with the bustle and busyness.

There was spinning and weaving and sweeping and the clatter of dishes. In the yard the chickens were scratching and clucking, and everywhere was the incessant chatter of voices—talking, laughing, and sometimes squabbling.

Taash rose at once and went outside to wash. He tied his

shirt around his waist so that it would not get wet and splashed the cool water over his face and neck and shoulders.

As he rubbed himself with the towel Ral's mother brought him he thought she looked strangely at him. But she said nothing.

For breakfast she gave him a bowl of porridge.

"You and your baby brother look much alike," she said suddenly.

"Do we?" The remark startled Taash. "Well, yes," he stammered. "I—I suppose we do. I suppose we must. I mean—being brothers, that is."

He grew more confused under her gaze and was afraid he might say something foolish.

"Ay," she said simply. "Being brothers." And not seeming to notice his confusion she turned back to the wash tub.

While he ate his breakfast Taash watched Teyal. He was a pretty baby, a very pretty baby. But Taash could not see where they looked alike. They were both fair and their hair curled in the same way. Outside of that, however, Taash could not even imagine how a baby could look like a boy as old as himself. Grown people were always saying odd things like that. If it pleased them to see a resemblance, that was fine. It made his story the more easily believed. When he had finished his meal Taash offered to help with the work. Soon he found himself as busy as the rest of the family.

The day passed—then the next and the next. On the fourth morning Taash spoke to Maro.

"I must be getting on my way again. I don't really want to go. You have all been so kind to me—to us. But I must find my sister." And I must find where this baby belongs, he thought.

"Of course you must," the father agreed, "though we shall be sorry to have you go."

He thought for a while.

"I am taking some sheep into the village today," he said. "And I shall ask in the market place if there is anyone going to the north. Sometimes someone is traveling to the next village, sometimes farther. If we could arrange it, you might go along. From there you might find another who is going farther yet. In this way you might come at last to the court without having to face the dangers of so long a journey by yourself."

Taash told Maro that he would be happy to help drive sheep or tend a mule or load a cart, whatever work there might be for him to help earn his and Teyal's way.

So Maro left for the village. But things did not work out the way they had planned. And though Taash found a companion it came about in a very different way.

10

The family was at supper when Maro returned from the village.

"How late you are!" his wife exclaimed.

She turned to him then and, seeing his face, cried out.

"What is it? Come and sit down! Why, your hands are like ice! Ral, put your father's chair near the fire."

Ral placed the chair for his father. Mara looked anxiously into her husband's distressed face. Maro shook his head.

"I bring grave news, Mara. This morning there was a rumor that something had happened to the baby Prince. It was only a rumor, but as you know, strange things have happened before in the royal family, and any such talk makes everyone uneasy.

"Some said the child was ill. Others said they had heard he was dead. Still others said there was nothing to it but gossip. No one really knew anything certain, but talk had spread.

"It took a long time to sell the sheep. No one could settle down to bargaining. Then, late this afternoon, the tinker from Roon came to the market place. His horse was all of a lather, poor beast, but in no more of a lather than the tinker himself. He had the news that a body of the King's guard were on their way—not ten minutes behind him.

"It seems the baby Prince has been stolen away. He disappeared in the night. No one saw who took him or where they went.

"The King has sent forth his entire guard, and all the

knights and lords in the kingdom have joined in the search for the child. They have been sent in every direction to scour the land. Oh, it is a terrible thing! A terrible thing!"

"Terrible indeed!" cried the mother. "Oh, the poor child! Our poor King and Queen! Does no one know anything?"

"No one," Maro said sorrowfully. Then he leaned forward and spoke in a low voice.

"There are some who fear it is the work of the witches!"

At that, Mara began to weep.

"That would be too horrible," she sobbed. "Their first child—stolen by witches! They must be near out of their minds! Oh, Maro, how fortunate we are to have all our children safe around us. What a cruel thing it is to steal a child!"

"Ay," said Maro grimly. "But more, Mara my dear, for it is the Crown Prince they have stolen. It puts our country in danger."

Taash turned pale as he listened to Maro's story. Could Teyal be the stolen Prince? Had not the witches said he would be King? Should he tell them how he had found the baby? What if they didn't believe him! They might think he had lost his senses! Then what would become of Teyal—and him?

Even as these thoughts raced through his mind, Taash heard the sound of horses' hooves upon the road. Within minutes there was a knock at the door.

Maro rose and opened it. The children sat wide eyed, gazing at the man who stood upon the door step.

He was a knight, a hot, dusty, weary knight—but all the same, a knight. For he held himself straight and proud. At his side hung a long sword and in the crook of his arm he carried his helmet.

"I come from the court of His Majesty King Aciam," he said. "We are here in search of the infant Prince who was taken from his bed as he slept. It is five days now since he vanished. Will you permit us to search your cottage in the name of the King?"

Maro, too overcome to speak, nodded and waved his hand toward the humble room.

The knight's eyes swept across the faces of the children seated around the table. They touched upon the two babies playing upon the floor. Then he glanced around the room. He crossed to the opposite side and looked into the other room of the house.

"Are there any others in your family?" he asked Maro.

Maro nodded.

"One other," he murmured. "My oldest son who is out guarding the sheep."

He gestured toward the meadows. "You will find him there if you continue in that direction."

"Are there any more cottages beyond yours?" the knight inquired.

Maro shook his head. "Ours is the last before the river. Beyond that is the desert and then the mountains."

The knight nodded wearily. "The King has offered a reward of a thousand gold pieces for any word of the Prince and ten thousand for his safe return," he told them.

Then going to the door he bowed politely, thanked them for their service to their King, and returned to the others who waited for him in the road.

All the time the knight was in the room Taash's heart beat wildly. Here was the man to tell! He would know if Teyal was the Prince. He would take him safely back to the King! But the boy was so overawed by the splendor and noble carriage of the knight that he could not find his tongue.

When the knight turned to leave Taash quickly jumped to his feet to follow him. He *must* tell him, no matter what happened.

But even as Taash jumped up, so did all the other children. They rushed to the door to see the noble band mounted on their tall steeds.

It was a sight such as they had never seen. And though these men were tired and covered with dust, the magnificence of their armor and the rich colors of the trappings shone through. Indeed, the pride with which they carried themselves was enough to behold.

Taash found himself held back at the door by the rush of the others. And as he stood gaping with the rest he saw the face of one rider and his breath left him. He shrank back in fear, ducking behind the oldest girl.

It was a tall stern knight that he saw. He had a sharp nose, a dark brow, and a cold hard eye. He was a knight, he was a man, but *his was the face of the witch who had brought Teyal to the fire*! The very one from whose arms Taash had snatched the baby!

The boy was filled with consternation. Could the witch have changed herself into a knight? What other form might she take? Desperately he scanned the faces of the other knights. Good men they looked to him, and kind. But how could he be sure that he could trust them with such a one among them? Had this knight-witch seen him? Where would they be safe, he and Teyal?

Suddenly his eyes were caught and held by the gaze of another rider. They stared at one another and Taash's heart leaped up.

It was Kashka!

No! No, it was not Kashka. His heart sank again, but he could not take his eyes from the man. He looked so much like Kashka! Though now he could see that his eyes were brown and his face not quite as thin. Perhaps it was the clothes he wore, for he was dressed in hose and a tunic of the same cut as Kashka's. Still—it was more than that!

A great loneliness rose in the boy. How he longed to see Kashka! Tears came to his eyes and blurred the face before him. He looked away.

"Let us go on!" cried the leader of the horsemen. "We shall make camp in the desert. We must lose no time."

A solitary groan rose into the air. The man who so resembled Kashka slipped from his horse to the ground.

"I cannot," he moaned. "I cannot ride this beast any longer. I cannot bear to feel one more step of his jarring hooves!"

He stood half bent over and rubbed his thighs.

"It's all very well for the rest of you," he went on. "You're accustomed to such journeys. But I'm not! If I sit on that creature for one minute longer I shall be turned to butter, such a churning he has given me. And in this sun I should soon be rancid and of no use whatever. For who would beat rancid butter into their batter?

"Alas, Sir Andros, I am beaten, battered, bruised, and blistered. I beg you leave me here 'til I grow better!"

Smiles flickered across the knights' faces.

"Stay then, Piff, and rest," said the leader of the men. "It was your own idea to come. We warned you! I am surprised that a jester who is accustomed to sitting upon a cushion at the feet of the Queen should have lasted this long! I salute you, Piff! There is more man in that scrawny frame of yours than in many a hulk three times your size!"

"You are kind, Sir Andros. But flattery will never repair the damage done to that portion of me which is so accustomed to the cushion."

The jester winced.

"Alas, I fear I shall never again sit at the feet of the Queen! Henceforth I shall be her footman. A jester of long standing, I shall become a standing joke. Nay, perhaps I shall change my standards and become an upright citizen. Ugh! I must then take a stand upon all vital issues. Mmmm. The most important of these will be to purge the language of the verb 'to sit.'

"But let this be the end of my tale. For I fear that I take up precious time. Fare you well, Sir Andros, and may heaven smile upon your quest."

Laughing aloud, Sir Andros turned to Maro.

"Good shepherd, can you take this poor sack of aching bones into your house this night?"

As Maro nodded he turned again to Piff. "Wait for us here or return by yourself as you will."

"I shall walk," the jester groaned. "Nothing in the world will induce me to get back upon that animal!"

"Dance your way home, then," smiled Sir Andros. "We shall miss your glib tongue. Have a care though. The Queen would miss you if you should be lost. She takes great comfort in her favorite fool!"

With these words Sir Andros waved his banner and signaled the horsemen forward. Down the dusty road they went toward the river and the open desert beyond.

The children ran into the road and watched until the knights had disappeared.

Maro invited Piff into the cottage at once and offered him the most comfortable chair they had. Piff declined. He would join them in their evening meal for he was famished. But if they did not mind—please, no offense was meant—he would take it standing.

There was silence during the meal for the shepherd and his family were too shy to speak in the presence of the stranger. When they had finished Piff smiled and patted his stomach.

"Ah, little mother," he cried. "What a fine cook you are! I have never eaten so well at the royal court. To tell you the truth"—he dropped his voice—"I'm not well looked after for I must live by my wits and being poor in them, I have a poor living in return."

With that he took up a stringed instrument which he wore slung across his back, and strolled out into the warm evening air. He plucked the strings and began to sing:

> "Oh a king may sit on his throne
> And ring a bell for his servant to bring
> A sumptuous dinner of many a good thing.
> It may be a roast of beef or mutton
> On which he may dine 'til he pop a button
> Of silver or gold from off his vest;
> Nor can he tell you which dish is best,
> Be it humming birds' wings sautéed in butter
> Served up by a maiden whose eyelids flutter
> In such a way to make you stutter;
> Or a jeweled bowl of blushing berries
> Picked at dawn, dew-kissed by fairies,
> Served with the richest cream from dairies
> Of cows that dine on ripe black cherries.
>
> But a fool must sit on a three-legged stool
> And share cold soup with a stubborn mule!"

Piff accompanied his song with such droll gestures and grimaces that he soon had the whole family giggling and finally laughing aloud at the last sorrowful face.

"If you will pardon me now," he said. "I must attend to some important business. I have ridden four days and three nights on that miserable servant to man known as the horse, and my poor brains have settled to my toes. I must rearrange myself."

Without another word he stood on his head. He stayed there minute after minute until Lia, the oldest girl, gasped.

"He will surely injure his brain! Shouldn't we turn him right side up again?"

"Oh, don't worry about him," said Taash. "Jesters are very good at that sort of thing. I knew one once who could stand on his head for an hour at a time if he wanted to."

At these words Piff flipped to his feet.

"Did you now?" He eyed Taash closely. "And where did a shepherd's boy who has never been farther from home than the next village have the acquaintance of such a jester?"

Taash was too startled to answer.

"He is not our son," Mara explained. "He and that little one are brothers. They came from across the mountains but a few days ago and wish to go to the court where their sister lives. They have been staying with us until we found a way to help them on their journey."

"Ah?" The jester looked from Taash to Teyal and back again. "Brothers, are you? No, you don't resemble the others here. That's certain. And you want to go to the palace to find your sister?"

Taash nodded to both questions.

"Perhaps I can help you," said Piff. "What is your sister's name?"

Taash thought frantically.

"Tiliana," he blurted. It was the only name that came to his mind.

"Tiliana? Hmmm. Let me think. Yes, Tiliana! There was a maid of that name—a handmaiden to some duchess or other I believe. It may be the same one. Well, we shall inquire when we arrive. We may as well go together, don't you think?"

He looked keenly at Taash who nodded mutely.

"It's very kind of you," said Maro. "We thank you for concerning yourself with the lad. We shall miss him, but of course he must find his sister."

"Of course," said Piff and the matter was settled.

The jester then amused them with every manner of trick and stunt. He juggled Mara's dishes until she gasped with fear. She expected to see them lying shattered on the ground. But he never quite dropped one. He sang songs and played the lute, for so he called his instrument.

They told him how well Taash played the pipe and Piff suggested they play together. Taash became so excited at the wonderful sound of the two instruments together that he finally laid aside his flute, leaped into the air with a double click of his heels, turned his somersaults, did his handsprings, and ended with his flourishing bow, all in the best manner that Kashka had taught him.

Piff's eyes gleamed.

"Wonder upon wonder!" he murmured. "And where did you learn that?" he asked aloud.

"A jester taught me," laughed Taash so full of himself that he lost all caution. "The same who could stand on his head. I learned to play . . ." Then he caught himself. "I used to watch him," he stammered. "He came through the village now and then. I would watch him and listen to him. He— he was very fine. I cannot do a tenth what he could do."

Piff's eyes pierced Taash to the marrow.

"What was his name? Perhaps I know him."

"Kaa—Kaa—Kaachoo!" Taash sneezed violently. "It's the dust from the road," he said lamely. "I—I never knew his name. No one ever told me."

What have I done? he asked himself. What an idiot I've been! Another five minutes of this sort of thing and the whole story will be out! I must watch what I say. He may be helping the witches! He will have Teyal, and what will he do to me?

"No matter," Piff said casually. "But you have the making of a fine tumbler. I don't see how you taught yourself so well! And you play the flute well too. We shall make a pair on the road! The whole country will be talking of us by the time we get to the palace. I should not be surprised if the King himself might not wish to see you." He smiled to himself, then added. "That is to say, if the Prince has been found by then."

It was late now and all the children were sent to bed. Taash was glad to escape and he lay for a long time imagining questions Piff might ask and the answers he would give.

Piff and Maro and Mara sat up longer talking about the disappearance of the baby Prince. The shepherd and his wife were deeply concerned. Piff reassured them.

"They cannot help but find the child," he said. "There is not the least doubt of it in my mind. The best men in the country are looking for him. In fact everyone is looking for him because everyone loves King Aciam and Queen Ekama. Who could wish them harm?"

Who indeed? Maro and his wife shook their heads.

"It's a blessing the old King is dead," said Maro. "For having lost a son, how could he bear to have his grandson spirited away in so strange a manner? We have eleven and could not bear the loss of one of them!"

As they rose to go to bed the shepherd's wife touched Piff's arm.

"You will be good to the boy and his baby brother? We have grown fond of them."

"Of course," said Piff.

She lingered a moment longer.

"There is something else."

Piff waited for her to speak.

"There is something unusual about them, don't you think?"

"Taash is unusually quick-witted for so young a lad," Piff smiled.

"It's something else," Mara shook her head. "Perhaps in the country they come from it is not unusual. I don't understand such things. But I must tell someone. When I bathed the baby I tried to take the amulet he wore from around his neck. It's only a small stone on a silver chain but I could not lift it. It wasn't a heaviness—how could so small a child bear such a weight? But it reminded me of something. And now I remember what it was.

"When I was a child my father had a lodestone. It was a marvelous thing to us. It was like magic to see it draw bits of metal to it. One day he brought another lodestone and showed us an even more marvelous thing. If they were held in a certain way you could not press them together, no matter how you tried. I shall never forget how the stones felt in my hands. And that is how it felt to me when I tried to remove the amulet."

"That is very strange," said Piff.

"There is more," Mara said. "Taash wears one too, much like the baby's. I noticed it when he was washing his face. He seemed to have no trouble moving it around his neck, and I wondered . . ."

She paused and blushed.

"I—I managed to tangle a bit of ribbon from the baby's shirt in the chain. It was a little uncomfortable for him. I asked Taash to undo it. He—he lifted the stone easily. But when I tried again later, I could not raise it. Not an inch. It must mean something. Don't you think so?"

Piff lowered his eyes as if in deep thought, but in truth to hide the excitement in them. One thing upon another so fast it makes me dizzy, he said to himself.

"It may mean something, little mother," he said softly. "It may indeed. I shall take very good care of them."

With that they went to bed. The shepherd and his wife fell asleep at once, but Piff lay awake.

Ah, ah, ah, he thought to himself. Surely an astounding thing has happened. It is beyond my understanding and yet it is before my nose! We must proceed carefully for the boy is as skittish as a colt. He may try to run off. And we must be doubly careful, Piff. There are eyes and ears in the very dust of the road. There is no telling . . . But I *cannot* understand how it came about! He *couldn't* have known! Yet how was it Kashka let the boy go?

11

·———·

Taash was tired in the morning. The thoughts that whirled through his mind the night before had kept him awake until a very late hour. When he did fall asleep his rest was broken by strange dreams that woke him again and again. With relief he saw that the sky was finally growing light and in spite of his fatigue he was glad to rise and escape from the disturbing night.

Through breakfast he was quiet and thoughtful. The Prince's safety depended upon him. He must be alert every minute. He did not know what the witches might do, or when or where or how. Nor did he know who . . .

The boy could not look at Piff. To be reminded so of Kashka was almost more than he could bear. It was *not* just the clothes he wore, but his look and his manner that were like Kashka's. He was softer spoken and not so inclined to leap about, but the quick turn of the head and the sharp look that saw so much in a single glance might have been Kashka's own.

Taash scowled at his porridge. The cruel face of the witch swam before his eyes. It turned now to that of the knight, now back to the face of the woman. If she could change herself into a man, might she not be able to change one of the other witches into a jester who resembled Kashka? What if all the knights that had come were witches? What if they knew all about him and Teyal? What if Piff took them directly to the witches? Was it not a little odd the way he had suddenly decided to go no farther with the band of knights?

And how quickly he had suggested taking Taash and Teyal with him!

He jabbed his spoon fiercely at the face in his porridge. "Taash!"

When the time came to say good-bye and Mara had hugged and kissed little Teyal, she put her arms around Taash and with tears in her eyes hugged him too. Taash clung to her a moment.

Mara looked at Maro.

"That settles it," she said, and she held Taash close. "Lia must go along. *You* may think it is perfectly all right for these poor motherless children to go off with Piff, but *I* don't. Of course he is a man and he can protect them. I'm sure he is trustworthy. But protection is not enough. Can you imagine a court jester seeing to it that an infant is fed and clothed and properly washed? Lia is seventeen now and could take over a dozen babies if she had to. I will not let Taash and Teyal go without her!"

There was nothing Maro could say that would change her mind. As for Lia, she was so delighted at the thought of such an adventure she was beside herself. To go to the King's palace! To see the beautiful ladies and possibly to glimpse the Queen herself! She stuttered and stammered, turned pale and flushed. At last after Piff had added his assurance that no harm could possibly come to her, Maro agreed.

Lia shrieked with joy. She rushed into the house, snatched up her belongings, rolled them into a bundle, and joined the others on the road in exactly four minutes and twenty-three seconds. Piff remarked that this was most certainly the record time for a lady to prepare for so long a journey!

Half the world was suddenly lifted from Taash's shoulders. Without having to look after Teyal, it would be easier to keep both eyes open for the witches.

Maro hitched the mule to the cart. He took them as far

as the village, but he could not leave them. He must take them just a little farther. He had gone halfway to Roon and would have gone farther still if Piff had not reminded him that Mara would be worried if he did not return by evening.

Another good-bye was said and Lia cried a little when she realized that she was leaving her family. But she did not cry long. Everything was too new and exciting. Soon she was singing songs one after another with Piff and Taash.

Taash sang and played the flute but there was little heart in his music. As the afternoon passed his misgivings doubled and redoubled distorting everything in his eyes and ears. The rhythm of the music was broken and the melodies out of tune. The country around grew ominous until the simple caw of a crow brought a cold dampness to his hands and the sharp memory of the witch's face in the leaping flames.

Piff's every word, every gesture became in some way a threat to the boy, a hint to him of his helplessness. He felt more alone than he had ever felt when he lived with the woodcutter.

He must get away. How could he get away? But his mind was dull and his thoughts could not go beyond the question.

He was so tired.

It was late afternoon and they stopped to rest.

"I've been wondering," Piff said thoughtfully. "We are traveling under rather odd circumstances. Of course *we* know perfectly well why we are going where we are going in the manner we are going. But the explanation is a little involved. There might be some who would not believe us. There are people who invent their own explanations for everything. They spread tales that bring trouble. Do you understand?"

Taash nodded and sighed. Lia was not sure.

"I don't see anything wrong with the truth," she said.

"There is nothing wrong with it," Piff agreed. "The truth is usually right! But matters would be simpler all around if we traveled—let us say—as a family. Three brothers and a sister. No one would question a family traveling together."

"N—no," Lia said pensively. "But I don't see why we need tell a story. I don't feel right about it."

"It's only for our own protection," Piff said quietly, "and especially for yours, Lia. Young girls don't usually go off with strangers. There are always a few scoundrels, thieves, and gypsies on the road who might think you would be as pleased to go with them as with us. But with three brothers to protect you I doubt if the thought would enter their minds."

Lia blushed and tears came to her eyes.

"You promised Papa that you would see that I was safe."

"And that is exactly what I'm trying to do," Piff urged. "Is it so far from the truth to say that you have three brothers? It seems to me you have several more than that!"

Lia sniffed and wiped her eyes. "All right," she agreed. "If you think it's best."

She smiled a bit to think of Teyal protecting her.

Taash said nothing but his heart sank even closer to his shoes. He had not thought of any danger to Lia. Thieves, gypsies, scoundrels—and witches. Piff had not mentioned *them*! He felt more entangled than ever in this wretched net, and now he was drawing others in with him.

The sky had thickened and grayed through the afternoon. By evening a fine drizzle of rain was falling.

They stopped at an inn for supper. Taash had no appetite. He wanted only sleep.

They took a room for the night. Lia and the baby slept in the bed. Taash had a pile of straw to sleep on, and Piff rolled up in his cape and stretched out on the floor—across the doorway.

"No one can get in without falling over me," he said.

And no one can get out without falling over you, Taash thought. He had decided that he must take Teyal and run away with him in the night. Then Lia could go home safely. But now he could not get out without waking Piff.

No matter how he tried he could think of no way to escape. How his head ached! If only he could trust Piff— but he couldn't. No, not with the face of the knight-witch peering over the jester's shoulder! What should he do? Taash turned and turned again.

They were chasing him. He could not run. Now they were all around him. What terrible faces! They had built a fire and were pushing him closer and closer to it.

"We'll teach you to lie to us!"

The fearful heat of the fire seared his face.

Taash sat up trembling in the dark. He could still feel the heat of the flames burning around him though he was awake and they were gone. He lay down again.

What should he do? He must wait. They were waiting.

Why were they waiting? Why didn't they come? Why hadn't Piff taken him and Teyal to them at once? Why? Why?

The melancholy drip of the rain on the roof lulled him.

Chop, chop, chop. We are waiting for you. We are looking for you. Come to us. Chop, chop, chop. He was standing beside the black pool and the terrible silence again surrounded and pressed upon him. But now he knew what it was. *They* were there. They were waiting, waiting, willing him to come to them. Bit by bit they were drawing him closer to the black water. If he looked down into it he would see . . . he would see . . .

Again Taash woke with a start. He was drenched with sweat and shivering all at once. He had escaped them once more, but how long would it be before they found him again? How many times must he run out of the forest before they followed him? Where could he hide? Who would help him?

Where was Kashka?

He must find Kashka!

The boy got to his feet and tiptoed to the door. How simple it was. He was floating. He would walk through the door without even opening it. Piff would never know!

Piff sat up.

"What is it?"

"I'm going out," Taash said. His voice sounded far away in his ears.

Piff got up. He touched the boy's brow and started to take his arm.

"You had better go back to bed," he said.

Suddenly Taash grew furious.

"Let me go!" he said. "You can't keep me here!"

He pushed Piff away from him and leaped to the door. But he could not open it. Perhaps he pushed against it when he should have pulled. Piff was beside him again.

"What's the matter?" he asked.

Taash was desperate. He tried to push Piff away again but this time the jester was not taken by surprise. He held the boy. Taash struggled against him. A sudden burst of strength surged through him. He tore himself free, pushed Piff against the wall, and seized the latch on the door. But at that moment his strength left him as quickly as it had come and he sank to his knees.

Piff wrapped his cloak swiftly around the boy and carried him back to bed. Lia was awakened by the scuffle and got up.

"Piff," she whispered. "Taash, what are you doing?"

"Taash has a fever," Piff told her. "I have something here for him to drink. Perhaps it will help."

He had wrapped Taash in such a way that the boy could not free his arms, and he had not the strength to roll over and fight his way out of the cloak. He lay on his back and glared at Piff in the light of the candle that Lia brought.

Piff raised the boy's head and held a cup to his lips.

"Drink this," he said. "You'll feel better."

Taash turned his head away. He dared not drink it. He was taken again by a terrible chill.

"What's wrong with you, Taash?" Lia asked. "Piff is trying to help you."

"You had better go home," Taash told her rudely, "before he tries to help you too!"

Lia stared at him in amazement. "Is he out of his mind with the fever?" she asked Piff.

"I don't know," Piff said thoughtfully. "Go back to bed, Lia. I'll talk to him a while. Maybe I can persuade him to take the medicine."

Piff sat beside Taash and watched him for several minutes.

Taash could stand it no longer.

"Why are they waiting?" he burst out.

"Who?" Piff asked.

"You know very well who!"

"No, I don't know very well who!" Piff said firmly. "But I've been guessing. And now it's time to stop playing games."

"That's fine!" Taash said through his chattering teeth. "Call them in now and be done with it. But why don't you send Lia home? She doesn't know anything. Why should she be hurt?"

"No one is going to hurt Lia! Listen to me, Taash. If you'll tell me what happened I shall know better what we must do. You must trust me!"

At these words Taash turned to look at Piff. How dared he look so much like Kashka! But what did it matter? What could he do trussed up like a chicken ready for roasting?

"How can I?" he cried in despair. "I don't know you. I don't know what you are!"

"Can you trust Lia?"

"Ye—yes . . . No!"

"No? Why not? She's kind and good. She's like her mother."

"Because—because she *is* good! Because she's never seen such a wicked face. She couldn't believe such a terrible thing. She wouldn't understand. That's why I couldn't tell Maro and Mara," he added feeling quite drained of all hope and strength.

Piff turned his face away from the boy. When he spoke his voice was low.

"Then there's no one you can trust?"

"There are people I trust," Taash said slowly. "But they're far away and I don't know if I shall ever see them again. I don't know anyone here. I don't even know *where* I am!"

"What?" Piff was astonished. "But how did you find Teyal?"

"I saw the fire and the witches brought him. But you won't believe me."

"But I *will* believe you! How did you get him away from them?"

"I just took him."

"You just took him?"

Piff sat on the floor and stared dumbfounded at Taash.

"Of course you knew who he was?" he asked at last.

"No. Not then."

Piff held his head with both hands.

"I don't understand it! How did you—but you don't know *anything* about it! Why ever did Kashka send you?"

"Kashka?" It was Taash's turn to be amazed. "Do you know Kashka?"

"Do I know him? Do I know my own hand? We could not be closer if we were twins, and we are close to that! And that is why I can't understand his letting you come here without knowing anything!"

"He didn't let me come here," Taash said. "It was an accident."

Then Taash told Piff the whole story of Nanalia and the pool, the strange land, and the stranger ritual around the fire. Finally he told him how he came with the baby to the shepherd's house where Piff found him.

"I wish I had known this sooner," Piff said.

"I would have told you," Taash explained, "but I didn't dare."

He then told Piff of the resemblance between the witch and the knight. He described both of them as well as he could.

Piff whistled softly.

"No wonder you have a fever! Here, drink this and go to sleep."

"I feel better already," Taash told him.

"Ay." Piff smiled. "Let me worry now. We'll see if I can come up with something better than a fever!"

Taash fell asleep quickly. Piff sat down with his back against the door.

Well, Piff, he thought to himself, we were right about the Lady Ysene. And our hunch to go along with the great Duke of Xon was a good one. I'll wager he has a finger in it somehow. Why else would he have come to the south with Sir Andros? Ah, we have a formidable pair in those two! Stepsister to the Queen and she would do such a thing! She has the heart of a scorpion! As for her brother, he has no heart at all! A juggler's bag and a lute are poor weapons against such a pair.

The door was suddenly cold upon his back.

It won't be easy, Piff.

He pulled his cloak tightly around his hunched shoulders, rested his chin on his knees, and sat thinking in the dark.

12

By morning the rain had stopped and the country lay washed and sparkling in the sun. Like sheep running before a dog the few remaining clouds were driven across the sky by a fresh breeze. The air was so sweet each breath of it demanded another. Taash filled his lungs again and again.

"Do you know," said Piff lightly when they were well on their way, "that I have spent my last penny for our breakfast? From now on we must earn our way. It would do us no harm to practice a few songs together."

Nothing delighted Taash more than music and today it was more pleasing than ever. Soon they were playing tune after tune, piping, plucking, and singing.

"You've a fine ear," Piff said now and then. Or he would say, "No, you don't have that quite right. Try again—like this."

He would play the part over until Taash had it well in his head. He was every bit as particular and demanding as Kashka, but his manner was far more gentle.

"Kashka would never have been so kind about *that* note!" Taash said once, and he grinned sheepishly.

Piff yawned and stretched. Then he smiled.

"When Cousin Kashka was Teyal's age he sat down one day on an ant hill. He was given a profound lesson in impatience and learned at first hand how quickly a stinging bite brings the desired results. He took his lesson to heart and ever since he has been impatiently biting people."

He rubbed his nose thoughtfully and then added. "Or perhaps a few of the little creatures never left him. Something certainly keeps him from sitting still!"

Twice they were given rides that day. Twice they sang for their meals. At night they performed for their lodging as well as their supper.

The next day was much the same. The weather was fine and the country, golden under the late summer sun, was new and pleasing to Taash. The people were friendly and hospitable. No one questioned them or seemed in any way suspicious of them. Taash began to hope that the witches had lost them and that in good time they would arrive safe and sound at Nazor where stood the palace of King Aciam.

The third day, thanks to a long ride in a farmer's wagon, they arrived at the town of Gynnis. It was a fair town with the river running along one side and a stone wall surrounding the other three sides. The streets were narrow and the houses tall.

The market place was large and thriving with open stalls full of all kinds of foods and wares. Merchants and farmers, townsfolk and country folk—big and little—crowded the square. They milled among the stalls and the tethered animals. Horses, mules, cows, sheep, and all kinds of poultry added to the noise. Their quacking, cackling, bleating, and lowing mingled with shouts, laughter, voices sharp with argument, and the cries and calls of children. Ordinary speech was impossible, but that did not matter to Taash and Lia for they were quite speechless in the unfamiliar hustle and confusion.

Piff guided them to a corner where there was a bit of space, dropped his sack on the ground, and took his lute under his hand. Taash drew out his pipe and they began singing and playing once again. When enough of a crowd had gathered to satisfy Piff, he reached into his sack and brought out several balls which he began to juggle.

He started slowly and simply with a seeming indifference to what he did. Then faster and faster the balls flew into the air. Three, four, five of them danced up and down, to the side of him, behind him, and in front of him. Under one leg and then the other went the balls. Piff turned, spun, twirled—and never lost the smooth rhythm of the juggling.

Taash and Lia stood open mouthed when they should have been collecting coins for the performance. When he had finished his act Piff, with a laugh, snatched his cap from his head and passed it around.

"Here's luck!" he exclaimed after the crowd had wandered off. "There's more than enough for our supper and beds."

And it was indeed time to think of supper and beds for evening had come. The crowds thinned rapidly and the merchants packed away what wares remained to them. The farmers led off their unsold animals and in a short time the market place was deserted. The sun cast the last long shadows across the emptiness and darkened it. A chill wind swept the street and carried bits and scraps of litter whispering across the cobblestones like faint echoes of the cries and laughter that had filled the square so short a time ago.

Something in the sound made Taash shiver.

"There's an inn across the way," said Piff. There was an odd sharpness in his voice. He swung his sack quickly over his shoulder. "Let's see if they have a room."

But the innkeeper shook his head when Piff inquired.

"All the rooms have been taken by his lordship's party over there," he said nodding toward a group being served dinner. Then he looked at Piff from his toes to his cap.

"Though if you don't mind a bed of straw, I can give you the garret. Blankets. Half the regular price. Pay in advance."

"That may do," Piff nodded. "Show me the room."

The innkeeper motioned to a boy and gave him orders. The boy led them up a wide stairway to a second floor, down a narrow passage, through a door, and then up a steep narrow step. It took them to a room under the roof.

"There's straw in the loft next to this," the boy said. "I'll bring blankets and a pitcher of water. Will that be enough?"

"It will have to do," Piff told him. "I'll be down to settle with your master in a moment."

The boy nodded and left. Piff made sure he went down the stairs and then turned to Taash.

"There is something we must decide at once," he said. "Either we must tell Lia and let her decide what she wants to do or we must send her home now."

Taash stared at him. Had Piff felt it too, there in the market place?

"What are you talking about?" Lia asked looking from one to the other.

"Let's tell her," Taash said after a moment's thought.

"Lia," Piff looked into the girl's eyes. "Teyal is the baby Prince."

Lia gasped and turned pale.

"Hush!" Piff warned. "We've not stolen him. We're trying to return him to the palace. Listen carefully to me. I haven't time to tell you how Taash found him. But believe me, if we don't get him back to the palace soon not only he but the whole country will be in grave danger.

"Those who would do him harm are looking for him. They may know where he is—where we are. If you stay with us your life will be in danger. If you want to go back to your family I might find a way for you to go tonight. It's up to you, but you must decide now."

Lia listened to Piff in amazement.

"I shall stay with you of course," she said promptly. "I'll do anything you say. Who could want to harm so sweet a little one?"

"They are evil," Piff said quietly. "They have great power

and they want the child. They will do anything to get him—things that would freeze the breath in your lungs."

Lia lifted her chin, smoothed her skirt, and folded her hands together deliberately. "I shall stay with you," she repeated. "I am not afraid. But I do not believe anyone can be that wicked."

"You *must* believe it, Lia!" Taash broke in. "I've seen them and I know!"

But the girl shook her head. "I've never in my life seen such wickedness nor even heard of anything like it. It can't be true!"

"Have you ever seen the King and Queen?" Piff asked her.

"No," Lia answered.

"But you believe they are there, don't you, ruling the country?"

"Of course," said Lia impatiently.

"But you've never seen them!"

"But I've *heard* of them. And Papa once saw the old King before he died."

"If your papa told you there was such wickedness in the world, would you believe him?"

Lia thought for a moment.

"Papa would never lie. But he didn't say . . ."

"But he did!" cried Taash suddenly. "Don't you remember when he told your mother that perhaps the Prince was taken by witches, and how she cried?"

Lia nodded reluctantly. "Yes."

"Then don't you suppose they knew of such things, even though they never told you of them?"

"Are you trying to frighten me?" the girl cried.

"We only want you to understand what it is we must face, and that we must be so very careful," said Piff seriously.

She thought for some time then.

"Is that really why you lied about our being brothers and sister?" she asked at last. "And why you have been hurrying us so? And why you would carry Teyal until I thought your arms would fall off from being so tired?"

Piff nodded.

The girl stared first at Piff, then at Taash, and then at the sleeping baby.

"I still cannot really think that there are such horrid people in the world," she said slowly, "but I will do the very best I can. Tell me what I must do."

"There's a brave girl!" Piff smiled. "I can't say what will happen or exactly what you must do. But we must never tell anyone who Teyal is, for we don't know who can be trusted. And we must keep him out of sight as much as possible so that no one will recognize him. Perhaps you can make some sort of bonnet for him, Lia, to hide his face a little. There is a strong resemblance among those of the royal family. Someone might notice him and take a second look."

Lia nodded.

"And if anything should happen to me, you and Taash must get the baby back to the King and Queen. If anything should happen to either of you, the other must go on. Is that understood?"

The two children nodded.

"We shall have to get by on our wits," Piff warned. "We have nothing else to protect us." He paused and Taash wondered if Piff too were afraid. "And promise me that never, *ever*, will you leave Teyal alone!"

"I would never dream of leaving him alone!" Lia said at once.

Taash swallowed. *"And you must promise me that never, ever, will you go down that path!"* Kashka's words rang painfully in his ears. The boy nodded his head but he could not speak.

"I'll go down now and fetch some supper for the baby,"

Piff said. As he spoke he pulled off his cap and boots and slipped an old jacket over his shirt. He rumpled his hair and pulled on a pair of soft leather slippers.

Taash stared in wonder.

"You look exactly like Kashka now!"

Piff laughed. "It's not surprising. We're double cousins, Kashka and I. Our fathers were twin brothers and our mothers were twin sisters. We're that near twins ourselves!"

Then he held up a finger.

"Remember, take care!"

And he went down the stairs.

Piff was gone but a minute and Taash had begun to tell Lia how he had found Teyal when there was a commotion in the room below them. The children stopped talking. Voices came clearly through the floor.

"That clumsy, clumsy girl! Do you see now what I mean, you idiot! You wouldn't let me bring Nina. No! I had to bring that awkward stumbling Jia! Why, I don't know unless *you* had some reason for it. Now look what she has done! My dress is ruined, my hair has been an absolute fright ever since we left, and she can't even tend little Sibet. He cries every minute of the day and night until I am so exhausted with listening to him that I have *bags*! Yes, bags—under my eyes. But, no. It doesn't worry you that your wife, the most fashionable lady at court, has bags under her eyes. Not you! Of course *you* brought Jip along to see that your beard was kept combed and curled and dyed, but you have no consideration for me whatever!"

A man's voice muttered in answer. The shrill response of the lady soon made clear what he had said.

"Jip and Jia! Indeed! Who cares if they are in love? When has it mattered to you what the servants feel? Really! It is beneath your dignity to know they have feelings. Oh! I am humiliated! But wait a moment! I see it now! I see the whole thing. Jip wouldn't come unless Jia did, was that it? Or couldn't he keep his mind on your beard if she weren't around where he could roll those stupid calf's eyes at her. Oh oh oh! It is enough to make me want to go home to Mother!''

"Now, now, my dear," the man's voice rose. "I'll find someone to look after things for you. Let's not talk of going home to Mother!''

"No, indeed!'' snapped the lady. "Let's not talk of going home to Mother. And why not? Because if I were to leave I should take my fortune with me and you wouldn't have a penny, would you? That's why you married me, wasn't it? For my money? Well, let me tell you something, Lord Vayn! I married you for your title and your beard! Do you know that your beard was the rage at court seven years ago? Now, if I had my way, I would gladly pull it out whisker by whisker! You—you goat!''

"Hush, hush, hush," muttered Lord Vayn. "The servants will hear you and *you* speak of being humiliated! Hold your tongue!''

The lady was so angry she could only produce a kind of strangled noise. Then there was a knock at the door and the argument ceased.

"Good heaven!'' whispered Lia. "Is that the way lords and ladies talk? I'd rather be wife to a shepherd like Papa! He and Mama never have angry words. They're always kind and thoughtful!''

"I suppose there are kind and thoughtful lords and ladies," Taash answered. "But these two! Ugh!''

In a few minutes they heard Lord and Lady Vayn leave the room. Another minute and the quick light step of Piff was upon the stair.

"Here we are," he said. "Bread and milk for Teyal. I'll take care of him now while you have your supper. I saw no one I suspected, but keep your eyes open.''

Piff gave them several pieces of money and they went down for their meal. They shared a meat pie and found there was still enough to pay for an apple baked in sugar syrup. When they had finished the last bite they returned to the attic room.

Teyal was asleep. Piff had brought enough straw to make beds for all of them. Taash and Lia lay down to sleep and Piff went down to supper.

Taash lay on his back and stared at the rafters above him. Lia didn't understand. He knew she wouldn't, just as he knew she would keep her promise all the same. She would be very careful of Teyal, but she didn't understand the evil of them. But then, he didn't understand it himself, not really. The only thing he knew for certain was the terrible fear that rose in him whenever he thought of the faces of the witch and of the knight who was her brother.

But Piff would take care . . . Piff would . . . He turned over and closed his eyes. The fear slipped away from him. He was almost asleep.

What was that sound? He sat up. Was it the woodcutter's axe? No. It was the sound of horses' hooves on the stones of the courtyard. He lay down again but was now wide awake. The horses stamped and snorted and voices rose to his ears. The door of the inn closed and the sounds ceased.

Still Taash held his breath and strained his ears. Something else had come with the sounds. Something had arrived at the inn. Every nerve in his body grew taut, stretching, reaching, trying to sense, to measure the strength of the presence, to feel the pulse of it as it grew and spread with the very beating of his heart.

Suddenly he leaped to his feet. How long had he dozed before the horses had awakened him? Where was Piff? Why wasn't he back? Taash glanced quickly at Lia. She lay sleeping peacefully with the baby in the curve of her arm.

The boy ran to the door and down the stair.

Halfway down the second flight of steps he stopped, stunned.

Piff stood in the room below. He half faced the stair. And across the table from him—there was no mistaking them though their backs were to the boy—stood the witch and her brother.

Piff spoke to them. How easily he spoke, and with a smile on his lips!

". . . trust me!" Taash caught his last words.

Then, even as the boy stood rooted to the stairs and numbed by the sense of betrayal, Piff raised his eyes to meet Taash's gaze. There was no sign in his face that he recognized the boy. He returned his look to the two before him. A few more words came from his lips. Taash was too dazed to grasp the meaning. Then, with a sudden movement, Piff tipped the table before him and the dishes and crockery fell to the floor with a crash. The clatter shook Taash from his stupor and he came to his senses.

"Piff!" he cried.

But Piff seemed to have eyes at the back of his head. He had already leaped sideways and eluded the men who tried to seize him.

"Run!" he called to Taash. "Get out! Hide!"

Taash hesitated. He could not leave Piff.

"Run!" Piff cried again. He dodged the men once more and backed toward the door.

"Get the boy!" It was the knight who spoke.

Taash turned then and fled up the stairs. They must hide Teyal! He fairly flew up the second flight of stairs and burst into the room.

"Lia!" he cried. "Lia, quick! Wake up!"

There was no answer.

"Lia!"

She was gone. The baby was gone.

There were footsteps in the hall below him. Taash looked around quickly. Not even Lia's clothes were there!

He caught up his jacket and ran to the door of the loft. Perhaps Lia was hiding in the straw.

"Lia?"

No answer.

The men were on the stairs.

Taash pushed the door shut behind him and ran to the window. It was too far down to jump and the distance to the huge oak tree growing in the courtyard was enough to send a sharp throb through the palms of his hands. But there was no choice. The men were in the room behind him. Taash took a deep breath and jumped. He heard the door of the loft bang against the wall as he caught the branch. The rough bark scraped his hands, but he held on, swung himself up, and quick as a squirrel hid among the thick leaves.

"There's no boy here. There's no one here," said a rough voice.

"Look in the straw. They must be hiding there," said another.

Taash heard the crackling of the dry straw as they prodded in it and tossed it aside.

"What's in the other room?" asked one after searching a few minutes.

"Nothing. Oh, the juggler's bag of tricks is here. Nothing else. Doesn't look like anyone else has been here."

"They *must* have been here! Somebody must have warned them. Someone will be sorry for this!"

"Most likely you or me when the Duke hears they've gone!"

"Rather the Duke than his sister! But we'll look in every corner and closet in this place."

They went out of the room and down the stairs. Taash was able to breathe again. But where could Lia have *gone* with Teyal? And Piff? Even as he wondered, the door to the inn below him opened and through it was dragged a very limp Piff.

"Where do we take him?" asked one of the men who held him.

"The old mill," said the other, jerking his head toward the river. "It's solid as a mountain. Nobody can get out of it."

"This one won't be trying to get out of anywhere tonight," laughed the first as they hoisted Piff over the back of a horse.

"He'd better wake up by morning or he'll miss his own hanging!"

They both laughed then, and mounting horses of their own led the animal with its unconscious burden down the street.

13

Taash climbed cautiously down the tree a way and found a stronger branch to crouch upon. His mind was in such a whirl from the sudden turn in their luck that for a moment he did not realize what his eyes were seeing. Then he blinked twice to be sure it was real.

He was staring through a window at the back of a fantastic mass of plumes that nodded and trembled as the lady beneath it moved her head. Two unbelievably tall fronds resembling nothing so much as the feelers of some monstrous insect rose triumphantly from either side of the headdress. Beyond the quivering feathers sat Lia. Her voice floated through the open window to Taash's ears.

"I heard the poor little thing crying and I said to myself, 'It sounds like my own pretty one when his teeth are cutting through.' Ah, the poor dear must be in pain. Why should I keep this good herb all to myself when there is plenty for the both of them? My own mother gave me the herb for Pommy and you see how well he sleeps."

Lia nodded toward a corner of the room. Then her face vanished behind the plumes as crooning softly she bent over something in her lap.

"There, you see?" She popped up again. "He loves the taste of it too, and he's happier already. Aren't you, my dove?"

"It's a marvel!" It was the unmistakably affected voice of Lady Vayn. "The child has fussed the entire way until I thought I would go out of my mind. But you have quieted him in two minutes! Who are you, my dear? You must come with us. I'll make you the child's own nurse and you shall have anything your heart desires—if only you can keep him quiet!"

"That is very kind of you, Lady Vayn. But I must ask permission of my sister. You see, my own sweet husband died only three months ago. We were married but two years when he cut himself with a scythe while he was reaping hay. A terrible poison came into his blood and he died so suddenly!"

Lia paused and hid her face in her hands and sobbed.

"We were so happy together! But now I must stay with my sister and her husband. They do nothing but complain of what a burden we are to them, though I *do* try to make myself useful! Perhaps they would be glad to see us leave." Lia sighed and wiped her eyes. "But I must ask them for they decide everything I do."

"You must run, my dear, and ask them at once! Tell them I *command* it, if you must!"

"They aren't here just now," Lia told her. "They have gone to visit a friend in town. That's why I brought the baby in with me. There was such a to-do downstairs. I feared he might wake and find himself alone in the night."

"You dear sweet thoughtful thing!" gushed Lady Vayn. "I *must* have you! You will have no other duties than the care of the two babies!"

"I'll wait up for my sister and her husband," said Lia. "When they return I shall ask their permission. Now see how your precious one sleeps! I'll return to my own room."

The astonished Taash watched as Lia exchanged Lady Vayn's Sibet for Teyal, curtsied politely to Lady Vayn, and left the room.

At that moment the door to the inn again opened below

Taash, and a bearded man with a companion stamped across the courtyard.

"Not a trace of them!" growled the Beard.

"There'll be the devil to pay!" said the other.

"Better the devil than a witch!"

"Watch what you say!" The second man looked nervously over his shoulder as they went muttering around the corner toward the stable.

A moment later the witch and her brother crossed the courtyard. Taash held his breath and clung to the tree.

"They are here," said the lady. "Your men are clumsy."

"Your methods are not always successful," her brother replied coldly.

"They are still here," she insisted. "I can feel their presence."

She raised her eyes and looked around the top edge of the wall.

"They are very close. Did your men look on the roof? Are you sure they made a *thorough* search?"

"As thorough as possible, under the circumstances. We could scarcely search through closets ourselves, my dear Ysene. But perhaps you know of those who would be more thorough!"

His voice as well as the meaning of his words froze Taash.

"That takes time," she answered with some anger. "But yes. I shall call my sisters and *they* will find them. At least we have one," she added as the coach rattled around to the gate. "I'll see he doesn't escape."

The lady's murmured words were the last Taash heard for they entered the coach and drove away into the darkness.

"Taash?"

The whisper came from the loft window.

"Lia?" Taash climbed quickly up the tree again.

"I hoped you were there. I heard you go up the stairs and

I couldn't imagine where else you might be. I knew they hadn't found you. Those dreadful men searched everywhere except in Lady Vayn's chamber. They didn't dare look there!"

"You were terribly clever, Lia."

"Did you hear?"

"Yes, just outside the window."

"Oh Taash, I had to do *something* to save the baby!"

"I know. You did fine!"

"Thank you." She giggled. "But what shall we do now? Where is Piff?"

"They've taken him off to prison. They mean to hang him in the morning."

"Oh, they can't!" Lia gasped.

"Shhh!" Taash warned her. "We can't let them, but we can't take Teyal and go hunting for him either."

They fell silent.

"I can hear Lord and Lady Vayn talking," Lia whispered after a moment. "They're arguing again. Lord Vayn says Piff stole his purse because those men found it in his pocket. But Lady Vayn says that Piff never came near Lord Vayn so how could he have stolen it?"

"Lord Vayn is a little stupid!" Taash said.

"They're both a little stupid!" Lia said.

"What are they saying now?" Taash asked.

"Lady Vayn wants to leave tomorrow. She wants to get to Nazor in time for some ball or other."

"They're going to Nazor?" asked Taash thinking quickly. "Then you must go with them, Lia. You and Teyal will be safe with them even if they are stupid. Don't you see? They'll be looking for *three* of us. No one would ever guess that you and the baby were with them! And if I can find Piff, we'll join you farther on."

Lia nodded. "I don't see what else we can do."

"I'll go now," Taash told her. "There's not much time."

He hesitated, fingering the amulet he wore around his neck. Then he slipped the chain over his head.

"Take this. Put it on Teyal. It may help keep him safe." He tossed the amulet to Lia.

"But Teyal already has one," she said.

"I know. But he's the Prince and he needs all the help there is. Bargah once told me there was something special about mine." He paused. "You don't know how terrible and powerful they are, Lia. Put it on him and don't ever take it off. And remember, don't tell *anyone* who he is!"

Lia nodded and wished Taash luck. They said good-bye.

Making sure no one was in sight, Taash climbed down the tree and dropped softly to the ground. He must cross the town to come to the river, but where the mill stood he did not know. He did know that he must find it quickly.

The boy darted through the deserted alleys. It was a dark moonless night. The houses rose tall and somber above the empty streets. The hour was so late no light shone from any window. The flickering lanterns that hung on tall posts at the corners of the streets cast dancing shadows on the walls and the ground. They made the town seem all the more abandoned.

The night watch made their rounds. Taash had no trouble dodging the echoing footsteps.

He reached the river at last. This side of the town was poor. Decaying buildings, mounds of crumbled brick and rubble, a few hovels surrounded by weeds—all spoke mutely of spring floods.

A hard-packed narrow footpath ran along the top of the bank. To the north stood a few sagging docks. To the south, about half a mile from Taash, a dark mass rose against the stars. Taash set out toward it. It *had* to be the mill.

Though it was not far from the town the old mill stood apart and isolated beside the darkly muttering river. A tangled mat of creeping vines and young willows had sprung up around it shutting it off even more. Close to the walls a narrow path had been cleared so that the guards could keep watch.

It was an ancient edifice. The high stone walls were furry with moss and slippery with the damp night air. The wooden paddles of the huge wheel had rotted away and the iron shaft upon which it had turned had been removed and melted down for other purposes. But the stone of the walls was thick and solid. An indestructible air hung around the building as if neither flood nor earthquake could jar loose a single brick. The mill might stand forever brooding over the river and the wide field of weeds that separated it from Gynnis.

Taash stared up at the black massive wall before him. There was neither door nor window, no shadow of a recess nor glimmer of light coming through any chink in the rocks.

He crept softly along the side of the building stopping now to listen, now to look over his shoulder. Had the witch already summoned her sisters, or did she herself keep some lynx-eyed vigil here? What nameless thing might rise from the hollows where the river fog had collected? What malign spirits might lie hidden in the rank growth watching his every step? Were they waiting to seize him and throw him inside this moldering heap? The face of the witch formed before his eyes, took shape in the wisps of fog. Her evil smile added a malevolent air to the gloomy desolation of the place.

He had come to the corner of the building and was about to peek around it when someone sneezed in his ear. Taash flattened himself against the wall and held his breath.

"Cursed place!" a man's voice muttered. "I'll catch my death in it. Why do they buy a rope to hang a man when all they need do is throw him in this hole for a few days?

He'd die soon enough and with no cost to the town. But they must have a show!"

"What's that? Who's there?" another voice called.

"Never mind, never mind. It's only Jok. This place gives me ague and fever. Brrr!"

"It unsettles your mind for sure, if that's you talking to yourself. Cheer up, man! The prisoner'll be gone in the morning. If they don't find another you can stay home tomorrow night and toast yourself in front of the fire."

"Ay, and *he* can toast in one!" Jok jerked his thumb toward the mill and laughed bitterly. "I wish he were toasting there now. Then I wouldn't be wandering out here in the cold."

"Stop your complaining, old woman! Come in for a nip to warm yourself and your heart. Have pity on the fellow. He's a short enough time left him to keep cool! Come on, come on! There's no one'll come looking for this thief. He's a stranger."

Footsteps crunched away from Taash, scraped on stone, and ceased. A heavy door slammed. All was silent. Taash peered around the corner and along the front of the mill. There was no one in sight. He went softly down the path, tiptoeing past the door. He examined the wall, looking for a window or any opening through which he might crawl. But there was nothing except the door where the guard had entered. The third wall showed no more promise than the other two. Taash ran quietly along the south side of the mill.

There was now only the back of the mill along the river itself. Time was short. The yellow rind of the waning moon hung in the east. In a few hours the sun would rise and with it the people of Gynnis—and among them, the hangman.

It was darkest of all on the river side of the mill. The black water flowed swiftly by, gurgling and muttering. Deep and menacing it looked at night. Taash stared downward into the murky rapids and clung to the slimy wall. Water is water, he told himself. If I can swim in it in the day, I can swim in it at night. And so reassuring himself, he clutched the edge of a protruding stone and tried to study that part of the structure that he had not yet seen.

The stone he held was the end one of a ledge that ran the length of the wall. He boosted himself up and on to it, and began to edge along the fourth side of the building. It was a narrow piece of footing and here and there the brick had crumbled. Taash felt his way inch by inch, stepping across open places and testing each foothold before bringing his full weight upon it. Perhaps the mill was not as solid as he had first believed.

So he made his way carefully until his hand suddenly came to the end of the wall. Yet he was not quite halfway across it. He felt up and down the edge of stone, peering into the darkness of what appeared to be a gaping hole in the wall. What could it be? Of course! It was the opening where the huge shaft went through into the mill and connected the wheel to the gears that turned the millstone.

It was a large opening, large enough for him to stand upright. But once he had found a firm footing and gone into it he could not see a thing. It was pitch dark. No spark of light, no gleam of the moon or reflected bit of starlight penetrated the aperture. What Taash would not have given for a torch! He felt the walls with his hands. There must have been some sort of mounting here to support the shaft, but where had it gone through the wall and into the mill itself?

Suddenly there was a strange grating sound from the other side of the wall and a gleam of light shot through a crevice. Taash, moving quickly to the spot, climbed on a heap of rocks and put his eye to the crack between the bricks.

A torch held high in the hand of a guard cast a flickering light through a cavernous room.

"He's still asleep!" said the guard.

"He do be peaceful though!" The second guard stood behind the first.

"He hasn't moved once. Let's go back upstairs."

"Ay. But help me with the door, will you? Why don't somebody bring some oil for it? It's heavy enough as it is, but rusty and all it takes a man's full weight and strength just to push it open. And how a body is to pull it shut again nobody says."

"Ah, Jok, you should use your head!" said the other. "If we 'ud stick a torch there in the wall we could look in on him through the grating and not have to open the door each time we come down."

"Use *my* head, you say! Why didn't *you* think of it before?"

"Why didn't you?"

"Stop wasting my breath and fetch another torch. I don't fancy standing here. The place gives me the chills."

"There's more than one has had a case of chills from this place. But they're soon cured and are warm enough the rest of eternity! All right, all right, I'm going for it!"

The man vanished and in a minute returned carrying a second torch. He thrust it into a crack in the wall beside the door and looked around.

"There. That'll do 'til morning."

He walked into the room and nudged something with his toe.

"He might enjoy the light when he comes round—if he comes round."

"Not much chance of that by the looks of him," said Jok. "He needs the beauty sleep!"

They both laughed and went out then, pulling the door shut behind them. Taash heard the heavy bar slide into place. After that all was still.

Taash scrambled off the pile of rock. The ray of light came

through the wall just at the top of the heap and as Taash got down a number of stones rolled and slid under him. The beam of light widened. The boy began pulling at the rocks and lifting them away. Another ray of light came through the wall. There *was* an opening.

The hole had not been bricked up with stone and mortar. It had merely been filled with loose rock. As Taash worked dust, mortar, and bits of brick and loose stone showered down from the damaged wall. It was hard work. Some of the pieces were large and it was all the boy could do to pull and roll them aside. His back ached and his fingers grew tender and bled. But he kept at it until the opening was large enough. Then he wriggled through and dropped to the floor. He was in the mill at last.

Piff lay on the floor in the middle of the room. Taash ran to him, but even as he reached his side he heard footsteps and voices. The guards were returning to look in on their prisoner. Taash darted across the room to the door and pressed himself against it.

"You see? We've saved ourselves some trouble."

"Ay," Jok admitted. "But you should have thought of it sooner. He's still in the same place. That one's not very lively! We'll look in on him once more before morning."

They turned to leave.

"It's not the job I mind," Taash heard Jok saying. "But I don't like the night air here by the river. Makes my joints ache."

The remark was followed by another sneeze and the voices faded away.

"Piff!"

Taash knelt beside the jester and shook his arm.

"Piff, wake up! It's me, Taash!" He shook him again but Piff did not move.

The boy rolled him over and laid his ear against Piff's

chest. He was alive, but what a beating they had given him! His face was cut and bruised and swollen. Taash turned his head aside to fight the sickness that swept over him. Then he grew hot with anger. He tried again to rouse Piff, but the jester did not open his eyes.

Taash looked around hopelessly. He could not lift the man. He could scarcely drag him across the floor. And if he did pull him as far as the wall, he would never be able to lift him through the narrow opening. He must rouse him somehow. Then Taash saw the leather money pouch Piff carried on his belt. He took it, crawled back through the hole, and filled it with water from the river. Back he came again, poured the water over Piff's face and shook him and called to him.

At last Piff moaned and opened his eyes.

"Get up, Piff. Come on. We must hurry!"

Piff groaned.

"It's Taash," said the boy. "Me. Taash! Come on, Piff, try to stand up."

Piff drew a deep breath and groaned again. He struggled to sit up.

"Taash?" he muttered. "Taash? Oh, Taash! What is it? What do you want? Ooo, what happened?" He held his head with both hands. "It must have been quite a party!"

"We have to get out of here," said Taash. "Hurry, before the guards come back."

"Guards?" Piff looked up bewildered. "Let me think! There were two of them, and then I must have run into a brick wall!"

"There were four of them," Taash corrected him as he tried to help Piff to his feet.

"Where are we now?" Piff asked.

"We're in a prison. It's really an old mill and I've found a way out. But we have to hurry. Can't you walk?"

"Give me a minute! Where are Lia and the Prince?"

"They're safe. I'll tell you as soon as we're out of here."

"That can't be too soon," Piff muttered as he looked around again. "There, bring that piece of wood over there. Put it here where I was lying."

As Taash dragged the timber to the spot the jester struggled out of his jacket.

"How was it, so?" He put the jacket around the log.

"The other way," said Taash seeing at once what Piff meant. He arranged the jacket in just the way Piff had lain on the ground.

"Now pile some wood against the door," Piff told him. "It will give them a little more trouble getting in."

Taash had not noticed how much lumber was scattered on the floor. As he picked up the pieces he saw that the wood was old and decayed. He saw too that the timbers that supported the roof were rotted and full of worm holes. It was a miracle the place had not fallen in years ago!

"That's enough," Piff told him.

Taash gazed for a second at the wood stacked before the door. Then he pulled the torch from the wall and thrust it into the pile. In a few seconds smoke began curling up and he heard the crackle of flames. Quickly he gathered more kindling and stacked it against one of the huge posts that rose to the ceiling. He set the torch to that and then ran to Piff.

"This way," he said as the jester managed to get to his feet.

"Ah," Piff gasped as he leaned heavily on the boy. "I think they have broken every rib I have and a few I haven't!"

He put his arm around Taash's shoulder and took a few steps. The boy staggered and almost fell as Piff reeled.

"Steady now," Piff murmured between clenched teeth.

The room was filling with smoke and Taash's eyes and throat were stinging. He hadn't counted on Piff's being scarcely able to walk. Step by step they moved toward the wall.

The wood beside the door blazed up suddenly with a crackling roar and filled the room with a burst of heat and red light. Shadows leaped in all directions over the rough stonework, and there was a scurrying and squeaking as dozens of rats skittered through holes and cracks.

Taash and Piff paused for a moment. They had reached the wall and Piff, eyes closed, rested his head against the cold stones. By the dancing light Taash could see the drops of sweat glistening on the jester's forehead and he knew it was not the heat of the fire that brought them there.

"It's only a few more steps," he encouraged Piff. Hurry, he thought to himself. Hurry, hurry, hurry! The flames were biting into the ancient wood of the tall post.

"All right," Piff whispered as if understanding the boy's thoughts. "This time . . ."

"Fire!"

The shout came to their ears through the roar of the flames.

Two minutes later the ground shook and there was a mighty roar and crash. Smoke and dust filled the air as the old mill fell in upon itself, smothering the fire that had finally weakened the beams and burying the prisoner in the old jacket.

Or so went the guards' story when they told it to the mayor of Gynnis. For they had discovered the fire when they went to see to the prisoner's well-being. And though they could not enter the room for the heat of the flames, they had seen the man in the patched coat as he lay on the floor. He was unconscious, poor devil, from the smoke and heat. He had begged them, they said, to leave him a torch for he had a great fear of rats. It was their guess that he had gone to sleep and let the torch fall into a pile of wood stored there—oh the irony of it—against a chilly night!

They were filled with remorse over the catastrophe. Indeed they were so shaken and pale they could scarcely tell their tale. But the mayor comforted them. After all, the prisoner would have been hanged in the morning, and was this not a sign of unquestionable guilt? That when he stood upon the very steps of the gallows his life was taken by a power greater than the hand of man?

14

Far, far away from Gynnis on a dusty road that approached Nazor from the north, three weary travelers slowly made their way. An old woman and a little girl rode in an ancient cart pulled by a long-eared donkey. A young man who piped a tune with a smile on his lips but with worry in his eyes walked beside them. Evening was drawing on and the little group stopped in a grove of trees by the roadside.

"We shall sleep here tonight," said the young man. "In two days more we shall be in Nazor. Then I'll have a proper bed for you, old mother. This is no journey for one your age to be making."

"You needn't worry about me, Kashka," said the old woman. "I've taken many a walk in my day and I don't intend this to be my last. Besides, what is more pleasant than sleeping under the stars? We have enough to eat and drink. What more can one ask?"

Seeing the look upon his face she added, "You must stop blaming yourself for everything, Kashka. All this is not your fault. *You* didn't steal the Prince or push Taash into the pool! And there is no good in borrowing trouble by worrying about that which you cannot change. When we get to Nazor you must talk with Piff. Between the two of you the world cannot help but be set right."

"Yes, Piff! I can hardly wait to see my cousin, Bargah. I feel I have only half a mind when he's not somewhere about."

"Ay, the two of you feed on each other's wit. I can never decide which of you is the more clever. There is no one can play the lute like Piff, but then no one in the world surpasses you upon the flute. Who can match his juggling? But can even a madman tumble and leap as you do? Happily we need not choose. The world has you both."

"Perhaps," Kashka grew gloomy again. "But the world needs the young Prince more. Oh Bargah, this is too much! First Taash and then the Prince! The last band of knights we met *still* had no word and it has been over a week since he disappeared!"

"Kashka, you have done nothing but fret! Now stop a minute and think. Doesn't it mean anything to you that Taash and the Prince both disappeared on the same day? And what should it mean, you ask, except that *they* were twice as busy as usual? Not at all—and take my word for it, for I know something of the ways of witches! They wanted Taash, of course, but the Prince was enough to keep them busy that afternoon. *We* know what they had in mind there, for they've been up to such tricks before. And we know that if they had been successful no one would have known anything about it. They didn't intend to spirit away the Prince and have the whole country turned upside down that he be found again!

"No, something went wrong for them, and I have a strong feeling that that something was Taash. Who else could have done it? You were gone, I was certainly nowhere near, and, according to the Margrave of Tat when we met him, Piff had been sent off on some errand. I suppose that was a device of the Lady Ysene to get him away from the palace. But Taash might well have been nearby."

"But what could he do? He knew nothing about it."

"He didn't know anything, that's quite true. But there is a strange bond within the royal family." Bargah shook her head. "I've seen it at work more than once! Now think again! If Taash had found the child, what would he have done? Would he have rushed to the mayor of the nearest town to tell him what had happened?"

Kashka laughed. "Eh, old woman, Taash would never go to a mayor for help! No, he was always quick to discover an explanation that had little to do with the truth! I expect he might explain himself well enough. But if the witches have them both . . . ?" He shuddered. "Bargah, my blood freezes!"

"If they had them both, we would have had news of even greater tragedy within the royal family by now. They would not wait."

"You may be right, old woman," Kashka sighed. "Sometimes I think you know more than you tell me."

"Nay, you may as well admit it is so, dear boy!"

Kashka threw back his head and laughed his old laugh for the first time in many days.

"We'll start early tomorrow," he said. "I can't wait to see Piff. He has the ears of a fox and the eyes of an eagle, though he does put on the face of a sleepy idiot!"

Bargah smiled and then she sighed. She was tired, but the night seldom brought rest to her now. There were journeys afoot in the day but there were such journeys in the night one did not speak of. Her old eyes did not see well in the light. But in the shadows such visions rose before them as the clearest and the brightest eyes of youth would never dream of seeing. And though the lovely song of the lark rising above the meadow rang but faintly in her ancient ear, there were whispers and murmurs in the dark that none heard but she.

This night, as she had done for many nights now, she waited until Nanalia and Kashka were asleep. Then she drew forth from the bottom of a basket of winter clothing a small silver casket. She placed it before her and sat silent for several moments, her head in her hands.

After a time Bargah raised her head and opened the casket. Taking a thin white candle from it she fitted it in a tiny holder in the center of the box. Then she opened a small container and dipped her thumb and forefinger into a blue powder that it held. This she rubbed briskly just above the wick of the candle which glowed at once with a high narrow flame. Finally she plucked a clear stone—it had the appearance of glass—from the casket and held it before the flame.

"What is it?" Kashka cried as he leaped to his feet.

For Bargah, so startled that she had nearly dropped the stone, must have made some sound that woke him.

He stared at her and at the silver box and turned pale. For though Kashka knew well enough of Bargah's powers, he had never seen her put them to use. And he was as fearful as the next man of the practice of magic.

Bargah swayed forward and back, both hands clasped over the stone.

"What is it?" Kashka repeated, alarmed now by the look upon the old woman's face.

Bargah shook her head and moaned. Then seeing him and recovering somewhat she motioned to him to sit beside her. Kashka obeyed and Bargah once more held the stone before the wavering candlefire.

Kashka stared at her hand.

"Every night since Taash has disappeared I have looked into the stone," Bargah told him. "This one and his amulet are cut from the same jewel."

She sighed deeply.

"At first it was pale, a very pale blue. That was all right, for I knew he was far away. It has grown more brilliant as we came nearer, especially since we have crossed the mountains. Last night it fairly sparkled with a deep and beautiful blue.

"But tonight—tonight—" She could say no more but handed the stone to Kashka who held it between his eye and the flame.

The stone glowed a dark and angry red laced through with darker, almost black, jagged and irregular streaks.

Every trace of color drained from Kashka's face and his arm grew so heavy he could not hold up the stone. He lowered it from his eye and handed it back to Bargah.

"What does it mean?" he whispered.

She shook her head.

"Might he be dead?" His lips scarcely moved.

"I don't think so. But the danger is great. Or . . . or perhaps he has lost the protection of the stone."

"Then let's go on!" cried Kashka leaping to his feet. "Why are we sitting here?"

Bargah replaced the candle and the stone. Carefully she stowed away the casket while Kashka harnessed the donkey to the cart. With the sleeping Nanalia settled in the back of the cart he helped Bargah up onto the seat.

"Hi!" he cried and slapped the donkey sharply on the haunch. The little animal moved reluctantly, Kashka impatiently tugging it forward into the still dark morning.

It was two days later in the evening that they arrived at the gates of Nazor. Kashka took Bargah and Nanalia to a small house near the palace walls. He hurried then to the palace to inquire after the health of the King and the Queen and to look for Piff.

Kashka was told by the servants in the kitchen that the Queen had not left her bed for a week. The King, though tending to the affairs of the country, was distraught and unable to concentrate upon important decisions. Lastly, Piff had left with a party of knights who went to the south in search of the baby Prince. They had not yet returned.

After hearing all this and a few more bits of gossip, Kashka left the palace and returned at once to Bargah.

"I must be off," he told her. "Piff has gone to the south with Sir Andros and a party of knights. The Duke of Xon was one of them. I don't trust that man, Bargah, any more than I trust that venomous sister of his.

"Stepsister to the Queen!" he snorted. "If it suited her rank ambition she would corrupt the fragrance of a violet, use it to poison the air and by it spread a plague of hatred. And what loving thoughts do you suppose are behind those dead-fish eyes of the Duke? Why, he would put a dagger into his Majesty's back with no qualm whatever!"

"Be careful what you say, Kashka. They are powerful. You *must* hold your tongue or you will lose your head. Piff knows those two well enough. He'll watch his step."

"Ay, he soaks his head in a bucket of water every morning so that he'll stay cool! Don't worry, I'll watch myself. So, I am off. Take care of yourself and Nanalia."

"Must you go now? Wait until morning!"

Kashka shook his head. "I must find Piff. If I leave now I'll be that much farther on my way. Besides, he may need help."

Bargah did not protest more.

"Take this then," she said, and she hung a silver chain with the same clear glass stone around his neck. "I don't need this any more. It has served me, and now it will serve you—though differently. I don't intend that you close your eyes to danger simply because this lies under your shirt. There's nothing like a quick wit and a nimble foot to keep you from pitfalls," she smiled. "But sometimes there are matters that neither wit nor courage can overcome. This may be helpful then. You will know if it has served you."

She kissed him good-bye.

"Go now and find your cousin. Come back safely. We need you too, Nanalia and I."

Bargah shook her head sadly as Kashka went out the door.

She would trust Nanalia before she would trust Kashka to show prudence. Sometimes she did not know but that he was more of a madman than a madcap.

Let us hope nothing has happened to Piff, she murmured to herself. I don't think he could bear it. Poor Kashka! Either he was bounding through the sky touching the moon and the stars and burning himself on the sun itself, or he was suffering the despair of a condemned man. And yet— yet, though she did not want to admit it to herself, of all of them that she loved with her old heart, she loved him a little more.

Kashka walked rapidly for several hours. It was past midnight when he finally wrapped his cloak around himself and lay down behind a hedge that grew beside the road. He was up and off again before the dawn and traveled long and far that day. The next day he passed the country estate of Lord and Lady Vayn. He could have stopped there and asked for a meal in the kitchen. The servants knew him. But he did not want to. Lord and Lady Vayn were a pair of imbeciles and the servants were of the same cut as the masters. He could not bear the thought of listening to the shallow malicious gossip that would be the kitchen talk of the great house. And so he went on—and on, and on.

On the fourth day he encountered a band of knights traveling north. He scanned the group eagerly, but Piff was not among them. He would have passed them by with only a salute when he recognized the Duke of Xon. Their eyes met and there passed between them such a look as defies description.

You scoundrel, thought Kashka, and his eyes flashed. How can the King trust such a villain!

The Duke's stare was cold. It seemed to say, "Beware, young man! I'll see the day you are hanged!"

Kashka drew a deep breath and addressed himself to Sir Andros.

"Good day to you, Sir Andros. It is I, Kashka. Has your search been fruitful?"

"Ah, Kashka! I didn't recognize you. Alas, no. We've been far into the desert but have found no trace of our young Prince. We only pray that others have had more luck."

Kashka shook his head. "I've heard no good news as yet. By the by, I understood that my cousin Piff journeyed with you, but I don't see him. Did he fall asleep and tumble off his horse?"

"Ha! In a way he did! But rest yourself. He wasn't harmed. The truth is we left him at a shepherd's cottage just before we went into the desert. When we returned the good wife told us that he had left along with a part of the shepherd's family—a lad, a lass, and a babe. I could not quite make out what the story was, but the gist of it lay in their traveling to Nazor where the children were to seek out a married sister. With such a houseful I should think they would be glad to see them off! I don't know how the poor can feed so many mouths! At any rate, it seems Piff offered to accompany them and see that they arrived safely.

"We had word of them as far as Gynnis, but beyond that city they seem to have vanished into the air. Perhaps we'll have word of them again by and by."

Sir Andros then asked for news from the palace. Kashka told him it was not good.

Before they parted Kashka's eyes again found those of the Duke of Xon.

The smile of contempt on the knight's face made his message easy to read. *Find him if you can!*

"If you've harmed a hair on his head I'll strangle you with my bare hands!" Kashka's lips moved as his eyes blazed.

"As you hang from the end of a rope?" murmured the Duke pushing his horse against Kashka as the knights began to move away. "Good-bye, my dear fellow. We shall meet again soon."

The Duke's expression was all too plain in its meaning. The knights rode on.

After two steps Kashka sat down upon a rock by the way. His knees were trembling under him—not from fear but from anger. It took him a few minutes to get hold of himself and then he was able to consider the information he had.

Now why should Piff set out with a flock of shepherd children? Surely assuming such a charge had more in it than mere kindness. A lad, a lass, and a babe? Well, at least he knew what to look for. Such a crowd could not vanish into the air! He would go to Gynnis. He would find some trace of them. But what was behind those heartless eyes of the Duke? Kashka frowned.

When he came to the village of Sootyn Kashka stayed at the inn. He was completely exhausted and admitted to himself at last that he needed good food and a bed to sleep in. All the talk there was of Lord and Lady Vayn who had sent a messenger ahead to secure rooms for the next day. There was a great to-do and hustle and bustle for the finicky and querulous pair. The host was tearing his hair in an agony of overseeing everything to the final shining of the door knobs.

Kashka groaned. All the running to and fro wearied him all the more and he went quickly to bed. No one had been able to give him any information concerning such a party of travelers as he described.

Kashka was so tired that he slept all that night and well past noon of the next day. When he woke his body protested being moved and he was slow at dressing and dining. So slow he was that the worst of all possible disasters occurred.

He was present at the inn upon the arrival of Lord and Lady Vayn.

"My dears, what an exhausting journey! I shall never recover in time for the mid-autumn ball at the palace! Really, the heat was terrible. And those dreadful horses! They stir up so much dust and attract so many flies!" Lady Vayn ran off at the mouth. Kashka wished she would run off!

"Jana, my dear, fetch me my fan. Jana, my dear, have them prepare a bath for me. Are the children all right, Jana? Ah Jana, what *should* I do without you!"

Jana? Kashka did not recognize the name. Lady Vayn had *another* new maidservant! It wasn't surprising. And was this girl like all the others? He started watching from sheer boredom and saw to his surprise that the lass who quickly carried out all the orders of her mistress was a bright-eyed lively girl. She had an alert look about her that spoke of more than the usual intelligence one found among those of the Vayn retinue.

Where did she come from? Kashka wondered. Perhaps he did not realize how hard he was staring at her, for she turned suddenly and looked him full in the face. Not wishing to embarrass her he looked aside at once. So quickly did he turn his eyes that he did not see the faint start in her face.

The lord and lady finally retired to their rooms. Kashka, who had remained in a dusky corner that he might not be noticed, rose to settle his bill. When he turned to leave he was startled to find Jana, a child in her arms, standing at his elbow.

She bent her knee in a curtsy.

"Good day to you, sir, I hope you are well?"

She was from the south country. He could tell by her accent.

"Quite well, thank you, miss." He bowed with exaggeration, sweeping off his cap.

"My lady sends you her greetings. She would like a word with you, but she is so fatigued she begs to be excused."

"Indeed!" Kashka's eyebrows lost themselves under the fringe of his hair. Why should Lady Vayn deign to speak to one as lowly as a jester, favorite or no?

"Oh, yes, indeed!" Jana slipped an arm through Kashka's and walked with him into the courtyard away from the innkeeper and the servants who were rushing around faster than ever.

When they were quite alone the girl whispered. "For a minute I thought you were Piff!"

Kashka started.

"But you must be Kashka. I heard about you from Piff and Taash."

"Taash!" Kashka's heart leaped within him. "And Piff?"

"Yes. We were together as far as Gynnis where Piff was arrested. It was all arranged by *them*, I am sure! Taash went to find him and I haven't had a word from either of them since. You must find them. They may need help. I have the precious baby with me and he is safe and well and no one suspects in the least who he really is."

She shifted the child in her arms and it looked up at Kashka, smiled and then ducked its little face shyly on Jana's shoulder.

Kashka gasped. It was an olive-skinned child with short dark hair. But its eyes were a startling blue. It peeked at him again and Kashka stared and stared.

"I'm very watchful," the girl continued. "It's a great care but I'm sure nothing will happen to him. Do hurry and find Piff and Taash! We'll be here for a week and at the country house for four days."

"And that is her message, sir," the girl's voice rose to its natural pitch as a servant walked by them. "Good day to you, sir."

She curtsied again, turned and re-entered the inn leaving Kashka mute with astonishment.

This was the lass Sir Andros mentioned, no doubt of that! And Taash was the lad! And the babe—the babe— Why, she carried the Prince in her arms as easily as if he were her own child . . . out in the open . . . out in the air . . . for everyone to see! But who in the whole world would ever recognize him?

But what should he do? Should he stay and help watch over the Prince? What reason in all the kingdom could he give for visiting the estate of Lord and Lady Vayn? None! He knew that well enough and so did every servant of Lord and Lady Vayn! There would be something suspicious in it. No, the child would be safer with the girl alone. She seemed to have no fear at all.

Well, then he would go on. Piff and Taash were somewhere between Sootyn and Gynnis and he would find them.

The servant who had passed them was returning to the inn and Kashka stopped him.

"You're with Lord and Lady Vayn, aren't you?" he inquired. "I'm sure I've seen you about the palace."

The servant condescended to nod.

"Tell me, who is that young lady with whom I spoke just a minute ago? She brought me a message from Lady Vayn, but I've never seen her before. And whatever became of Jip and Jia?" Kashka leaned forward confidentially. "I understand there was all kinds of talk before they left the palace!"

The fellow thawed at once and told Kashka the whole story of Jip, Jia, and Jana and added several other choice tidbits. He might have gone on all afternoon if he hadn't been summoned by Lord Vayn. He left Kashka with a broad wink, and Kashka smiled knowingly.

Ugh! he thought afterward as he went down the road. What a walking journal he is! I wonder what he knows about me? Kashka had a few misgivings as he recalled several of his less mentionable escapades.

But the important thing is that they believe the girl's story, he told himself. And she had given them one they have swallowed with the bait and the hook still in the fish! Eh! But the Queen will have a fit seeing the Prince with his curls shorn and his hair darkened! Brave girl to do such a deed! Ah, but it will grow again—the hair. And he is safe. Who would ever dream of looking for him in the arms of a maidservant to Lady Vayn? Ho! Ho!

15

Satisfied that the Prince was in good hands and as safe as any circumstances would now permit, Kashka hurried on toward Gynnis. An almost unbearable weight had been lifted from his mind and the entire world looked new and fresh to him. He could scarcely keep his feet upon the ground. At last he pulled out his pipe and began accompanying his step with the most cheerful melodies he knew. He embellished them with trills and turns and mordents, piling note upon note in a way that would fill the greatest musicians of today with wonder.

In no time at all a farmer coming up behind him with a horse and cart hailed him and invited him to ride with him if he would just keep up the pleasant noise. The horse was young and full of spirit and Kashka, delighted by the prospect of a more rapid journey, accepted at once. Off they rumbled together.

He would not have been so pleased if he had known that just at the moment in an old fisherman's hut by the river and but a stone's throw from the road, a ragged and dirty boy had pricked up his ears.

The boy sat still as a post listening, waiting for the sound of the pipe. But it did not come again. Then he scrambled through the brush and up to the road but he heard no more and found no one. There was nothing in sight but the back of a farmer's cart vanishing in a swirl of dust around the bend of the road.

"Hello!" he called. "Kashka!"

But no one answered.

When they were rolling along at a good pace, Kashka took up his pipe again and charmed his companion with every known tune in the kingdom. The afternoon wore on. At last the farmer arrived at his own fields and invited Kashka to stay the night.

"Thank you, friend, but I have a long way to go in as short as possible a time. Thanks to you I am well beyond the distance I had expected to cover today. But I must take advantage of my luck and hurry on."

"And thanks to you," said the young farmer, "a dull journey has been made so pleasant I don't know where the time has gone."

They said good-bye and Kashka went on his way afoot.

Again he walked until midnight. Again he slept in a field and again he was up at dawn taking to the road. He was given two rides that day and though they were short ones, every minute saved raised his hope of finding Piff and Taash that much sooner. He should be in Gynnis the next evening. If he had luck, he might arrive before that.

He had walked for several hours the following morning when he heard the sound of horses behind him. This is no farmer, he told himself, nor is it a merchant. No one would drive their horses at such a pace except a nobleman who is in a desperate hurry. But what an hour for a nobleman to be upon the road! The matter must be urgent indeed! I shall have no ride from him.

But on both counts Kashka was mistaken. The coach whirled past him, then suddenly drew to a stop. A head appeared at the window of the coach. It was not that of a nobleman but of a noble lady. A voice called to him by name.

"Kashka! What a surprise! Won't you join me? I am going to Gynnis."

Kashka's heart turned to lead and sank to his feet. It was Lady Ysene, sister of the Duke of Xon, stepsister to the Queen!

What is she doing here, he asked himself, and what does she want of me? But he knew the answer before he asked himself the question.

"You are very kind, my lady." He bowed low. "But I am disreputable company for one so great."

"The great choose their own company, my dear Kashka. I should be delighted to have yours."

He did not have to glance at the coachman. He knew well enough his size and strength. Kashka shrugged, entered the carriage, and seated himself opposite the lady.

The coach started up at once. Kashka drew a deep breath, grated his teeth and then smiled.

"Would you have me pipe you some music, my lady?" he asked innocently. "A sprightly dance for so beautiful a day?"

"I don't care for trivial music."

"Ah. Would a dirge please you?"

"No music!"

"Then you have invited me to travel with you because of my wit! Good! I have a tale for you. . . ."

"No tales, Kashka."

A devil's tail for you, my lady, he thought.

"Then you must want to look at me! Ha! I've never been so flattered in my life—not by the King himself!" And Kashka brushed the dust of the road from his shoulders, leaned back against the cushioned seat, and smiled inanely.

"Don't play the fool with me, Kashka. I know you better. You have always been difficult. I shall never forget what you did some nine years ago. But time is running thin. I shall have my turn."

She smiled but her eyes sent a shudder down Kashka's

spine. His smile in return was as empty as before but he did not reply.

They rode for a long time without another word. Kashka's thoughts, however, were far from still. So she *did* know it was he who had snatched Taash from her! Of course he had always suspected that she knew, but it was nice to be sure of these things. Well, let her do what she would to him, she did not have the boy and if matters stood as he hoped, Piff would get him safely to Nazor. The infant Prince was safe too, and well on his way back to the palace. She held no high cards in her hand. Did she expect that *he* would slip her the Ace, King, and Queen under the table?

"I can offer you a choice," Lady Ysene broke into his thoughts.

"A choice?"

"You are a very wily young man. If I had dreamed at the start that I had such an adversary, I would have managed things differently. I cannot help but admire you, Kashka. It is really a pity to see you, shall we say, completely dropped from the cast of players? A person of your talents could well survive the last act if he chose the right part."

"A fool is a fool, my lady, whatever the play," Kashka answered lightly.

"How stubborn you are! It is just what I mean!" She leaned forward. "Then let me tell you, whether or not you choose to take advantage of it, that there will soon be a new ruling family in this country. Nothing can stop it now. I had preferred more subtle means and they would have been quite harmless to all concerned. But you interfered, Kashka. First you and then another. You will live to regret it—if you live!"

Kashka said nothing. Lady Ysene frowned.

"The Queen is ailing because of the loss of her child. After her death the King will fall ill and live but a short while.

My brother and I will not die of *our* grief however! Grief is for fools. Ah, not for jesters, Kashka—but for those who wallow in sentiment. They are the *real* fools on this earth! No, we shall accept our responsibilities—in deepest mourning of course—thoroughly alive!"

Lady Ysene leaned back against the seat of the coach.

"You're not surprised? If you had any notion of our plan why didn't you speak to the King?"

Kashka shrugged.

"Ah, of course! I am the Queen's stepsister. Such talk might be considered treasonous. And would the King take the advice of a fool? Ha! Besides, he is too busy with his concern for the poor, the ill, and the aged—and all the weak and useless creatures in this world! He thinks that by his devotion to those petty deeds of goodness such powers as mine will vanish of their own accord. His smug content has blinded him to the threat that lies upon his very doorstep. More—it has destroyed him.

"But, Kashka, if you will join *us* matters will change for you. We know what lies under that fool's cap and bells! With us you will be no mere prancing jackanapes, wasting your breath on a bog of dull-witted courtiers! Join us! And there will be a king upon the throne who will seek your advice!"

Kashka closed his eyes. His heart was pounding.

"You're tempted? That's good!"

Suddenly Lady Ysene dropped the cool tone in which she had been speaking. She sat forward, her eyes glittered and she hissed through her teeth.

"But there must be no mistake! There must be no chance for error! *There must be no pretenders to the throne!*"

She struck the palm of her left hand with the fist of her right.

"I must have those children!"

She fell silent then and turned her eyes to the passing countryside. After a while she spoke musingly.

"The boy would now be sitting upon the throne. Yes. And he would be mine. I've not seen him since that night nine years ago. How old was he? Two years? Three? But even so, I would know him now. I can see him balancing upon the thin wire of time between childhood and youth. It's a delicate time. A time to turn—to bend—to choose. But he would have no choice. He would be mine. Mine!"

Her voice grew more intense.

"His eyes would see as *I* would have them see. His thoughts would run as *I* directed them. He would look with contempt upon this cowardly race of men—weak in their effort to do good but afraid to turn to the dark knowledge that I have to offer. Well, *he* would turn! And what horror he would spread among his fellow men! And how much greater it would be coming from one so young, so fair, so seeming innocent! From those tender lips would fall such commands as would bring the most corrupt courtier, the most callous villain to his knees in terror.

"This was my desire!

"And I might have reached him still, but matters went awry." Her voice grew harsh. "I had to ask my brother's help. And now the boy must die. He and the infant—they both must die!"

Kashka stared into her face.

"I have come to Gynnis to look for them and I will find them. When I saw the old woman Bargah in the streets of Nazor I knew it all. *She* has had the boy all these years. It was *he* who took the infant from my arms. Blood to blood! My curse upon him and all the royal family!"

Her eyes grew wild as she spoke.

"And I will have them both! When they have been put to

death before my eyes, I will know there will never be a claim against the throne. Against *my* throne."

Kashka, mute with horror, sat as if turned to stone.

"And you, Kashka, can lead me to them. I know you have come to Gynnis on the exact same quest as I. And if you will bring them to me, you shall be prime minister!"

"You piece of evil!" Kashka cried choking on the rage he could no longer hide. "You heartless fiend! Monster! Witch!"

"You miserable fool!" she shrieked. "Die then!"

Kashka saw the knife gleam in her hand as she threw herself at him. He grasped her wrist and thrust her back upon the seat. With the other hand he flung open the door of the moving carriage and jumped to the ground, fell, and rolled in the dust by the side of the road.

The driver pulled at the horses so that they reared up and stood on their hind legs.

"After him!" Lady Ysene shouted to the driver.

But Kashka was on his feet and running, and no man in the kingdom was more fleet than he.

"Wretch!" she screamed after him. "You will never find your cousin. He is dead!"

He is dead! He is dead! The words rang in his ears as Kashka fled across the fields toward the walls of Gynnis.

16

The day had been oppressively hot. Scarcely a breath of air moved. In the narrow streets between the tall houses of the town of Gynnis life was hardly bearable. For several hours in the afternoon clouds had been building on the western horizon. Now, late in the day, the sun in an angry blaze suddenly dipped behind them. In the unnatural twilight flashes of lightning could be seen leaping in jagged streaks from cloud to cloud and cloud to earth.

The merchants in the square closed their stalls hurriedly, took with them what they could and covered the rest, tying down heavy oiled cloths and skins over their wares. The storm now approached rapidly. The mutter of thunder grew louder. A sudden twist of cold wind caught up and whirled the dust of the road into a skyward spiral. Mothers stood in doorways calling to their children and everywhere people scurried to fasten shutters and latch doors. Wagons were drawn under sheds. Horses and mules were driven into stables.

When the first heavy drops splatted upon the ground, the streets of Gynnis were deserted.

No. Not quite deserted. A lone figure, cap pulled down, shoulders hunched against the wind, dashed from a nook in the wall, ran down one street, turned into another, and just as the deluge hit, suddenly pushed open a door and disappeared behind it.

The innkeeper glanced up, gasped, and turned pale.

"Who—what . . . ? Oh, by heaven, you frightened me! I thought you were a ghost!"

"A ghost?" asked the stranger. "Why should you take me for a ghost? I'm made of solid enough flesh and bone."

"Ay, I can see that now, and I beg your pardon. But you have a sharp resemblance to him."

"To whom?"

"Oh, some poor devil who came this way a week or so ago. Just a common thief—begging your pardon, but it's the truth. They would have hanged him the next day if it hadn't been for the accident. Accident? More the hand of fate, I should say."

He filled a glass for his guest.

"Indeed? What happened?"

"Why, they threw him in prison—the old mill it was. Saved us the cost of building a new prison. Sound it was too. A good solid pile of rock. But somehow—even the guards don't know exactly how—a fire started and ate through the posts underneath. The roof collapsed with him under it all. Ah, it was a loss to the town. We'll have to build a prison now."

"The guards didn't get him out?" the stranger asked casually though his hand trembled in setting down the glass.

"A pair of drunken guards?" the host snorted. Then he leaned forward confidentially. "You know, I've not breathed a word of this to anyone, but there was the smell of pike about the whole affair!"

The stranger appeared to be interested, though not so much so that it closed the mouth of the innkeeper. The host's eye swept through the empty room and then he continued.

"Ay, it was a strange affair. The fellow arrived here with three young ones. A lass, and a sweet-looking one she was! About seventeen, I'd say. A fine age in a lass!" He smiled. "Fresh they are then, like the peaches in a lord's garden. The lad was a few years younger. And there was a babe. All handsome children, if a bit dirty.

"Took a room in the attic. Seemed to be glad for anything. They paid, mind you. Nothing wrong with the money they gave me. Had supper. First the lad and the lass, then this fellow. He was minding his own business. Very quiet, polite. You know. Shabby, but well mannered. I see all sorts and it's not always the best dressed that are the best mannered."

He rubbed his upper lip thoughtfully. "Ay, I've noticed that—about the manners, that is. Maybe it's why I remember him so well. Ah, no matter. What matters is that it was about then that a lord and lady came in at the door. Oh, they were a fine pair! Regal! That sort don't stop by here often. Nor did they stop by long that night!

"But for all their style, I didn't like 'em much. Looked through me with never a nod and went right up to the little fellow where he was supping.

"He spoke to 'em. Polished as a silver spoon, he was. And then these two hulks came in. They weren't from hereabouts. I'd never laid eyes on 'em before. Said he'd stole a purse, that little fellow, and were on him in a minute. Oh, he put up a fight. He was a quick one!" The innkeeper shook his head. "You don't see a man that fast very often. Built about like you. Maybe a shade shorter. Don't have a brother, do you?"

The stranger shook his head.

The host sighed. "That's good. It's really quite a likeness. Amazing!" He paused, scrutinizing the stranger's features. Then he continued.

"Quick he was, but no match for them when two more came in at the door behind him. Poor little fellow! Well, the long and short of it is, they took him off to prison and that night it happened. Probably never knew it himself; not by the looks of him when they carried him out.

"Hey! Here! Have another swallow of this! It'll warm you. Sit down there. Better now? Tired, eh? And I stand here gabbing!"

The innkeeper left the room and came back in a minute with a steaming bowl of soup.

"Drink this. You'll feel better. Do you mind my talking? This whole thing's been eating at me all week. I'm an honest man and there was the smell of pike about it. Dead pike! And I'll tell you why. First, I don't believe the little fellow took that purse. Never came near Lord Fuss and Feathers. Then the young ones—all three of them—vanished! Melted! Not a sign! Nothing in the room, nothing in the whole inn. Two of them big fellows stayed behind. Turned the place upside down looking for 'em. What should they want with children? People didn't like it. Bad for business. But there wasn't a trace. Not a whisper."

He stopped talking and pursed his lips. Then drawing up a chair he sat down at the table.

"But here's something to chew on." He leaned forward and dropped his voice. "Them two guards—the ones from the mill—was in here last night. Drunk again they were, though they'd vowed never to touch a drop again as long as they'd live.

"Seems that there were more to it than just a fire. Seems that there were something else that night at the mill. Seems that . . ." He stopped speaking suddenly, poured a drink for himself and downed it quickly. When he spoke again his voice was lower still and it trembled.

"I seen them two when they brought the news the mill was afire, though by then everyone had heard the crash of it when it fell. Their eyes was popping out of the sockets. Their helmets was teetering atop their hair, so stiff it stood on their heads. Nor could they say a word that made sense. Jabbering they were. Teeth chattering, tongues clacking like bits of dried leather flapping in the spokes of a wheel. Eh! Well, we laughed at 'em for too much of a good thing from the bottle. And everybody rushed off to have a look at the mill—or what was left of it.

"So nobody give it much thought, I no more than another, 'til last night when they was in here, like I said. Nobody here but me and them. They got talking about it all.

" 'It wasn't no man lyin' there,' says the one. 'It was plenty light with all that fire. I *could* see. Didn't look like no man.'

" 'Was it one o' *them?*' asks the other grabbing quick for the bottle and drinking straight from it. 'Do you think they was inside too?'

"The other pours himself a quick one. 'I didn't see none inside,' he says. 'Wasn't one o' *them.*'

" 'Well what *did* it look like?' asks the other. 'Must have looked like something!'

" 'Looked like his jacket layin' there,' says Jok (he's one of the guards). 'Looked just like his jacket wrapped around a log.'

" 'Couldn't 'a been one o' *them*, then, says the other. '*They* didn't look like no logs.'

"You know, his hand was shaking so he spilt his drink down his shirt.

" 'Do you suppose they took him out first and then set the place afire? Or do you suppose maybe he was one o' them?' says Jok. 'All that fire—somebody had to start it. Had to pile the wood in front of the door. It weren't that way before!'

" 'If he was one o' *them* they could 'a had him out and no fire needed.'

" 'Then maybe there was another body? Some one else?'

" 'Aagh, Jok, you make me go cold as death! Will you

stop talkin' of it? He's gone. They're gone. Let's forget the whole thing like it were a bad dream.'

" 'That were no dream outside,' says Jok. 'I can still feel the cold fingers of 'em on the back of my neck. Cold as death, you say? My blood turns colder than death froze stiff every time the sun goes down!'

"They really fell to emptying the bottle after that. But they was through talking. Drank themselves under the table and slept there all night. To tell you the truth, I hope there *was* someone else. I took a liking to that little fellow. Full of fight he was. Carried a lute too. Must have been a musician. Pity. I like a good tune myself. Fact is, it was the only thing I found in the room."

The stranger looked up.

"The lute?" he asked.

"Ay. Hung it on the wall there. Thought one of the young ones might come back. . . ." He turned in the direction he had waved a hand, and both he and the stranger stared at the wall. No lute hung there.

"Now by . . . ! I'm an honest man, or why should I have said the lute was there? Someone's stole it. It was there—let me see! I can't remember. Now who'd 'a done that?"

"Very curious!" said the stranger.

The innkeeper turned to look at his guest. Then he leaned back and smiled.

"Feeling better, eh? That's good soup. Made it myself. Cook went home with a toothache this morning. Not many people traveling now. Last week was about the end of it. Winter be in soon and then business is poor. Listen to that thunder!"

"That was a most curious story," said the stranger. "You say there was no trace of the children at all?"

"Not a sign. Not a hair."

"Surely there was some evidence of their having used the room! A bed slept in? A pin or ribbon from the girl's hair?"

"Not a footprint! It was the attic, two flights up. There was straw for beds on the floor from the loft next to them. I hadn't no other room and they seemed pleased enough with the arrangement. No, there weren't nothing in that attic but straw and the lute."

The stranger shook his head. "That is certainly strange. But I am tired. Can you give me a room tonight?"

"Oh, ay!" The innkeeper picked up a smoking lamp and they went up the stairs. He pushed open a door. "This be all right?"

"Quite!" The stranger entered the room and glanced around. Everything was in order.

"Tell me," he said suddenly as the innkeeper was about to leave. "Where is that attic room? I know it's not any of my affair, but something about the whole thing has caught my fancy, particularly since you say I resemble the unfortunate fellow. Don't show me if you don't want to. It's really none of my business."

"No trouble. You can look for yourself. There's the door to the stair." The host nodded down the hall. "Hup! I hear the door below. I'll have to go down. What a night for travelers! There's your lamp lighted. Take it with you if you want a look."

The innkeeper turned to the stair going down and the stranger turned to the stair leading up. The latter had just opened the door at the foot of the step when a hoarse shout from his host made him pause and turn.

The innkeeper was pushed roughly aside by two men who then rushed down the hall toward the slender stranger. One glance was enough to send the guest bounding through the door and up the stairs.

In the garret he glanced quickly around, set down the light and jumped toward the door of the loft. The ruffians were only ten steps behind him when a gust of wind blew out the lamp. The men hesitated for a second and then a blinding sheet of lightning filled the attic with a white glare. In the instant of the flash they saw him—the stranger—silhouetted in the window of the loft. They lunged at him. But their hands touched only the drenching rain. The stranger had leaped into the thin air and any cry he may have given as he fell was drowned in a tremendous clap of thunder.

The pair stood a moment, dumbfounded. They turned then and groped their way down through the darkness.

"We'll pick him up outside. If he ain't dead, *she'll* get something out of him. If he is dead, we're in for trouble."

The man with the beard and the low heavy brow frowned as he spoke.

They brushed past the trembling innkeeper and dashed into the stormy night. No torch would stay alight in so violent a downpour but the constant flickering of the lightning was enough to illumine the courtyard. It was enough to show that there was no crumpled body beneath the high window.

The wind howled, driving the rain crosswise and whipping and lashing the branches of the great oak tree in the yard. A huge limb snapped and fell near them. But there was no man. No stranger. He had vanished as completely as had the three children before him.

After a hurried word between them, the two men set off at once and were swallowed up in the rain.

The innkeeper, pale and shaking, bolted the door, poured a drink for himself, sat down at one of his own tables, and suddenly burst into tears over the fright he had had.

Kashka's leap was an act of desperation. He was not at all sure that his hands would find the swaying branch he had glimpsed in the sudden glare of light. But he knew that his life in the hands of those who sought him would be short enough. So he had plunged into the darkness. His hands touched the wet bark, slipped, grasped, and held on. He was down and out of the tree quick as a cat, dropping to the ground just seconds before the two men rushed out to search for him. It was a simple matter to duck behind a wall and vanish into the rain.

There was no light in the streets except that which came from the blinding flashes of lightning. He needed a place to wait out the storm. It could not last long. When it eased a little he would continue his search.

Kashka slipped into a doorway and wiped the water from his face. He was wet through to the skin and as he stood there a chill went through him. While he rubbed his arms to warm them he listened, trying to hear if there might be some other sound than that of the pounding rain. There was nothing—no call of voices, no footsteps.

And then another chill passed over his body.

There was something in the coldness of it that was not brought on by the wind or the clammy shirt that clung to his back. It was a presence that chilled him, that froze him. No, it was more an absence of any warmth, an emptiness in the very air that left a black and frigid void.

Even as the sense of this horror grew upon him something touched his face and neck. It had the feel of wet clay and sent goose flesh over him from his scalp to the soles of his feet.

Kashka leaped into the street. The night rain upon his back was like a hot shower of water after the intolerable cold of the doorway.

They're on to me, he thought as he ran. His feet led him more by instinct than any reasoning of his mind. Down an alley, under an archway, over a wall. There must be some way, some where, some place they could not follow him.

Now he had lost his own direction. Panting, he flattened himself into a niche in a wall. He could not see in the dark. He could recognize nothing in the rain.

But the rain was growing fitful. One moment it would slacken to a drizzle. Then there would be another flash of lightning, a clap of thunder, and a momentary cloudburst. He waited for the deluge to pass, and even as it grew quieter he became aware of a different tapping sound that filled the street. It was a soft quick rapping that came from everywhere and nowhere at the same time. It grew in intensity until it beat upon him, and even though he covered his ears with his hands he could not shut out the sound of it. Where was it coming from? Was it out there in the silent street, echoing and re-echoing between the dark still houses? Or was it within him, in his mind, taking possession of him, beating him to his knees?

Up and off with you, Kashka, before you are completely maddened by the unbearable din! Run! Run! Run! Not that way. Not this way. There! Straight ahead!

There was the patter of feet behind him, on this side of him—that side too. There was no other way. He knew at last where he was and in what direction he ran. Gasping for breath he ran as he had never run before. He ran for his life.

And there it was—the wide empty stretch of grass beside the river. Another flash split the heavens and revealed the coach of Lady Ysene looming in his path. Kashka swerved to one side, wrenched himself free from grasping hands and leaped for the second time that night, leaped for his life, leaped far out into the dark swirling waters of the raging river.

Behind him a shriek of anguished rage mingled with the thunder, and Lady Ysene stood upon the bank of the river, arms outstretched, hair streaming in the rain, her drenched cape whipping around her in the wind.

"All the curses of Hecate upon you!" she screamed. "Die! Die a thousand deaths, wretched mortal! If you dare to live

I will seek you out! I will hound you to the end! I will not rest until I drench the earth with your red fox blood! You shall never escape me!"

Her fury was so terrible to behold that even her sisters shrank back from her, trembled with fear, and threw themselves face down upon the earth.

At last she dropped her arms to her sides and standing on the bank of the river stared silently out over the dark waters. In a low voice that made the hair rise on the scalps of those who heard, she began a weird and terrifying chant. When she had finished, she turned, entered her carriage and, with a single word to the driver, was whirled away into the now mist-filled night.

The menacing waters closed over Kashka's head and he went down and down. He held his breath in lungs already painful from lack of air. Boots, he thought, or I shall be dragged to the bottom and drowned like a cat in a sack. He pulled at them. One gone, now the other. Still he went down. His cloak! He fought with the clasp. He could not last much longer.

The river, swollen from the intense storm that had raged along its course for many hours, dragged him in its swift current. He struggled upward at last. Oh, the blessed air! He gulped it, swallowed it, drank it! And all the time he was being carried down the river, swiftly, swiftly.

Free at last of the terrible menace that had hunted him through the town, Kashka began to feel the fatigue that was creeping into his arms and legs. This is a quick way out of town, he thought. It may well be as quick a way out of the world! I must get to shore.

He pulled to his right but his arms were heavy. The water washed over his head. He caught half a breath, then sank. Once more, a breath, and he was sinking again. Does it matter, Kashka? Lady Ysene's smiling face rode with him under the water. I will have you now or later! Her voice hissed in the boiling current. You've done your best. It simply wasn't good enough. You've nothing to regret!

Nothing to regret! A thousand regrets! He fought the churning water with the last ounce of his strength. His outstretched fingers touched and closed on something less elusive than water. He pulled himself up and clung to the large branch of a tree, his head above the swirling waters at last. He filled his lungs again and again.

Down the river they were whirled together, man and branch. I thank you, leafy friend, please believe me! Kashka addressed the limb. I would as lief hold on, if you will but give me leave. If you cared a twig, you would leave me upon the shore. I'm growing quite water-logged. Kick, Kashka! And save your breath. You've little enough of it! Welcome moon, and good-bye again. Don't be so hasty next time. I need your light. Kick! I must be near the shore. Aha! Here is something more attached to mother earth. I shall take this branch of the river. Good-bye, leafy friend. I take my leave of you! There we are, safe and sound!

Kashka pulled himself up out of the river, stumbled up the bank, and fell face down in the sand.

The last bits of shredded clouds passed across the night sky. The flashing constellations took their westward paths until at last the morning star hung bright in the east. The sky grew light. Birds began to sing, and finally the sun rose with its gifts of heat and light and life and touched upon the sand and the river and the man who lay upon the beach.

17

Of late so many things had been happening at the palace that those who enjoyed wagging their tongues had grown hoarse. They were obliged to continue their conversations in whispers. The most wild of rumors flew around in the most wild of manners. An army was gathering with the Margrave of Tat at the head, ready to take over the government in case of the King's death. For the Queen was dying of grief at the loss of the young Prince, and the King was dying of grief at the Queen's grief. Had the Prince been found after all? And was he being kept hidden? No, the Prince had not been found but was still hidden! The Prince might well be dying at the grief of his parents.

There were many fools in the palace who believed everything that was told them. But they did not bear the name of fools. The two whom everyone called fools were not there. No one knew where either of them was, but who had time to worry about fools when there were so many better things to worry about?

Ah, but there were some who were concerned about the two fools. The Queen from her bed asked again and again for her gentle Piff. She longed to hear his sweet songs and the lovely sound of his lute. The King, pacing his chamber from end to end, sighed and murmured, "Ah, if only Kashka were here he would have some mad word for me that would carry off this burden for a moment. Then I might come back to it and look upon it afresh. Some new thought, some new idea might then come. Heaven knows, it is no time for jesting, but I am sore in need of his jests!"

The Duke of Xon, who had a suite in another part of the palace, fumed and fretted over a message he had received concerning a fool.

"That miserable dog! He *must* have drowned! How could he survive such a night? But it is as Ysene says, one can never be too sure. He is forever popping up like a jack-in-the box with his silly cap and his silly flute and blowing all our carefully made plans to the four winds! If I ever get hold of him, I shall throttle him!"

He clenched his fingers around the empty air.

Unable to bear the confinement of the palace any longer, he sent a note to the King that he was joining the search once more for the Prince. He immediately set out on his horse and went toward the south. He left some very strange instructions for his attendants to attend. Very strange they were indeed for one so devoted to his King and Queen!

Last of all, there was Bargah.

The morning after Kashka left she took Nanalia and went to the house of an old friend. The two old women talked long of this and that and at last it was decided that Nanalia should stay with the friend's daughter for a few weeks. There were many grandchildren in the daughter's house—dark-eyed, dark-haired little things. Girls, boys, puppies, kittens—one more child among them would scarcely be noticed! And how all those children loved exciting stories! They would adore Nanalia with her tales of the forest and the marsh and the long journey to Nazor!

But—and Bargah drew Nanalia aside—Taash must never be mentioned. Was that understood? Nanalia nodded and hugged a little wooden doll that she carried. Tears came to her eyes.

"Don't cry, little one," Bargah told her. "There is still a

chance that we shall find him." She smiled. "I'll tell you a secret. Kashka has gone to look for him! Now, see? You are all right again! But if you speak of him we may lose him forever. There are those who would be happy to have him dead."

Nanalia's eyes grew large and round and she promised. And she knew in her heart that it was one promise that she would keep!

With this arranged Bargah busied herself for several hours and then visited the palace. She didn't enter through the great gate at the front, but at a small door in the wall of the garden at the back of the palace where the river ran. The door in the garden wall was overgrown with vines, and so long it had been since anyone had opened it that no one even remembered that it was there.

Bargah had some trouble with the lock. And the little door complained when she pushed it open for the hinges were rusted as well. But she managed at last and slipped into the garden. It is odd that no one saw the old woman walk past the beautiful green hedges and the well kept beds of late blooming roses. The gardeners were busy taking up old summer plants and storing bulbs and preparing the grounds in general for the oncoming winter. Still, it is odd that with such a staff of gardeners, not a one saw her smile over the chrysanthemums and admire the stately walnut trees. But not a one did.

Perhaps what is stranger still, no one saw her enter the palace. She did go in by a little used kitchen entrance. Perhaps that explains why. And she went up an old and narrow back stair that no one ever climbed. She had to pause upon the stair for she lost her breath easily. She shook her head.

"It has been close to ten years," she murmured to herself. "And I've grown no younger!"

But up she would go again until at last she came to a

third door. This she opened with a key she chose from a ring of keys that she carried in her pocket. No one had given her the ring for no one in the palace had seen or spoken to her. Yet the key fitted perfectly and opened the door as nicely as you please.

But what was this? The door opened upon a wall! Wait! It was not a wall, but a curtain of some sort, a heavy thick back of a tapestry to be exact. And the door was covered completely by the hanging cloth.

Bargah paused and listened. The sound of someone weeping came to her ears.

A latch clicked.

"Did you call, Your Highness?" asked a voice.

"No," was the reply. "I wish only to be left alone."

"It is almost time for your medicine, Your Highness. I shall bring it in a few minutes."

The latch clicked again.

Bargah stepped from behind the tapestry into a beautiful room. The walls were pale blue and covered with fine tapestries. Several handsome chairs stood upon the thickly carpeted floor. A warm fire blazed in the fireplace at one side of the room and at the other stood a handsome bedstead intricately carved and ornamented. In the bed, behind curtains of silk, lay the Queen.

Bargah approached the bed with no hesitation.

"Your Majesty," she spoke softly.

The startled Queen turned and stared at her. Then a look of surprise and recognition came into her eyes.

"Bargah!" she cried joyfully. "Where did you come from? They told me you were dead! You haven't been here for years and years! Ever since—ever since—! Oh Bargah!" and she fell to weeping so that Bargah could not comfort her.

"There there, my dear," the old woman tried to soothe

her. "Don't cry. You must listen to me for I have some important things to tell you. Quickly now, dry your tears and listen. But wait! Someone is coming. Is it the nurse? You must not take that medicine! Put her off somehow. I shall hide here by the bed behind the curtain. Give me the medicine and I shall take care of it. Quickly now!"

The old woman had barely time to hide herself.

"Here you are, Your Highness."

"Leave it beside the bed, there on the table," said the young Queen. "I'll take it in a few minutes."

"You must take it now," said the nurse firmly. "The doctor's orders are very strict."

The Queen sighed and took the glass in her hand.

"Very well. But will you give the fire a shake? I'm chilly again." Her teeth chattered.

The nurse turned to poke the fire. A hand came from behind the curtain, took the glass, and in two seconds time returned it full to the brim.

"There," said the nurse turning again to the Queen. "What! You haven't taken it yet? Now let me see you drink it. Naughty child!"

The Queen dutifully drank the medicine, shuddered a little, and lay back upon the pillow.

The nurse smiled. "You will be over this illness in no time at all, Your Majesty. You must stop fretting. I am sure we shall have good news at any moment now."

"Thank you. You are so kind," murmured the Queen. "But I am tired. Please let me sleep now."

The nurse continued to smile as the young Queen's eyes closed. She tiptoed out of the room, pulling the door softly shut and locking it behind her.

The Queen opened her eyes. Bargah smiled down at her. And how different her smile was from that of the nurse!

"Do you feel better now?" asked the old woman.

"Oh, yes," said the Queen. "Before when I took the medicine, I felt as if I could scarcely move and I would fall asleep at once. And what terrible dreams I have had since I became ill! Oh, Bargah!" and she began to weep again. "My baby has been stolen away! I am afraid I shall never see him again. I wish I were dead!"

"I know all about it," said Bargah patting the Queen's hand. "I have come to see what I can do to help find him. You must not give up hope. *I* am a long way from giving up hope!"

The Queen stopped crying and gazed at the old woman. The color rushed into her face and she sat up.

"Have you heard anything?"

When the old woman shook her head the Queen grew sorrowful again.

"But that isn't all, Bargah," she sighed. "The King is angry with me. He has not spoken to me since our little Prince disappeared. I am sure he blames me and hates me. He has not been in to see me since I became ill. He keeps the door between our rooms locked and has taken away my key. At least I have not been able to find it."

"Hmmpf!" snorted Bargah. "We shall see about *that*!"

She went to the door that separated the Queen's chamber from that of the King. There she stood listening with her ear to the panel. What she heard, the Queen did not know, but after a time Bargah turned and smiled and nodded to the Queen. Then she again drew forth her ring of keys and searching among them with a frown on her face tried first one and then another.

"Ah, this one! Of course! It has been so long I had forgotten!"

She slipped the key into the lock and turned it. The Queen gasped, but Bargah touched her finger to her lips for silence, pushed open the door and entered the King's chamber without so much as knocking.

The King was pacing again. He reached the far end of his chamber, turned, and started back. When he suddenly came face to face with a little old woman his jaw dropped.

"What? How did you . . . ?" And then, "Bargah! Bargah—you—you old witch!"

He seized her and hugged her.

"Now now!" she gasped. "Stop it! You've broken all my ribs. There, let me look at you. Tsk, tsk. It has been almost ten years, hasn't it? And neither of us is any younger!"

The King laughed. "You make it sound as if I'm in my dotage!" Then he grew serious. "Ah, Bargah, such terrible troubles have fallen on us this past fortnight I have aged a hundred years. The Prince has been stolen. The Queen lies dying and they will not let me go to her. They say she thinks I have done away with the child through my jealousy of him! Me, his father! How could such a thought have entered her mind? It's madness! But they say I will drive her even more mad if I go to her."

The King had scarcely finished speaking when he gasped as if in pain.

"What is this?" asked Bargah sharply.

"Nothing," said the King after a moment. "It is just the worry plus a new cook who has a passion for serving rich foods."

"Nonsense!" snapped Bargah looking closely at him. "I can see that it is something quite different. Now, you do exactly as I tell you and matters will improve. First of all, you must go to the Queen. The door is open and she is waiting to see you. Go and tell her that you love her. Then I shall tell you what to do next."

The King obeyed somewhat fearfully, and tiptoed into the Queen's chamber. She had been anxiously watching the door and when she saw him and the look of tenderness upon his face, she stretched her arms toward him.

Bargah busied herself examining the needlework in one

corner of a tapestry while the young King and Queen opened their hearts to one another.

"Very well," she said briskly after a few minutes. "That is enough sentimental talk for now. The watered silk is absolutely weeping and will make a puddle on the floor if you don't stop all this mish-mush. I should think that after five years of marriage you would be a little more sensible."

The King grinned and looked a little foolish. The Queen laughed aloud.

"But I am serious about *this*!" Bargah took a new tone. "You must not either of you eat anything except that which I bring you myself. I had a feeling something like this was going on and I brought along some good bread and cheese and fruit, just to be sure. You may both dine like peasants from now on until this matter is cleared up. I think, however, that you should pretend to grow weaker.

"You, my sweet Queen, must appear to be unconscious from time to time. And you, you overgrown Prince—ah, you do look like your father!—you must have one of those uncomfortable spasms at a council meeting. Now I must speak to your husband in private. Do you mind, your Royal Highness?"

The Queen shook her head and Bargah drew the King back to his chamber and closed the door. She had a long talk with him. Then she returned to the Queen, kissed her, and left by way of the little door behind the tapestry.

If only they had known in the kitchen what had just taken place in the royal suite there might have been a shocked silence. But they did not know, and so they kept on talking.

18

Lord and Lady Vayn and their entire train of servants departed from Sootyn two days earlier than they had intended.

"It's all your fault!" the lady accused her husband. "You should never have spoken to Lady Ysene in such a way. You think I don't know about that little conversation? Well, I do! I know every word you said to her. What kind of an idiot are you? A woman of her position—and a fool like you would have to say such things!"

"And I suppose *you* thought you had caught the fancy of the Duke of Xon? What did *you* have in mind, my fair lady birdbrain?"

"I had nothing in mind at all!" she replied frigidly.

"That is your usual condition," remarked my lord.

"Lord Xon paid me a compliment," she said coldly. "Why shouldn't I smile at him? He is very gracious—more gracious than the King himself!"

"Do you think so, my pet?" Lord Vayn leaned close to his wife. "And do you also think he might prove to be a better king than the King himself?"

Lady Vayn regarded her husband with some curiosity.

"What do you mean?"

"Only what is common gossip. Do you know, my dear, we might stop this quibbling and take stock of the world. Without the young Prince and with both the King and the Queen ailing, we might do well to be—ah—*friendly* to the Duke and his sister. Who but the Duke would be in line for the throne? Think of that, my sweet, and let us consider carefully."

"Perhaps I have underestimated you," Lady Vayn smiled. "Just what was it that went on between you and the Lady Ysene?"

He shrugged. "Only that she desired us to return to Nazor somewhat earlier than we had planned. It was to look as if I had insulted her, she would snub you, and you would wish to leave here at once. But is it possible that she and I have underestimated *you*?"

"Mmmmm," Lady Vayn mused. "If we do have a new king there will be important appointments to be filled. The Duke is not at all fond of the present council."

Lord and Lady Vayn looked into each other's eyes and for once there was perfect understanding between them. They prepared to depart at once. They stopped at their country home for only one night and then hurried on to Nazor.

Lia, or Jana, was kept so busy fetching and carrying, packing and unpacking, looking after babies, and tending to all the hundred and two errands Lady Vayn gave her she scarcely had time to think. But the girl heard many things. The servants filled her ears with all manner of gossip. No one expected an innocent country lass to have any interesting gossip to relate so her silence was easily understood.

Lady Vayn herself found it difficult to carry secrets of such great doings all alone. This sweet child was so discreet! Lia was told many things. And the more Lia was told, the less Jana spoke.

The Duke of Xon, after a long conversation with his sister, set out once again from Sootyn on the tiresome journey to Gynnis. He inquired at every hut and hamlet along the way after a young man of such and such a description. If anyone asked why he was wanted the hint escaped the Duke that there was a connection between him and the lost Prince.

If anyone were to see this man, word should be sent at once to the Lady Ysene at the inn at Sootyn. By no means was any hint of this to be given to the young man himself. He was dangerous. It was difficult to say what he might do.

And far up the river Kashka woke, stretched himself, and sat in the sand holding his head in his hands. He had lost his boots and his cloak, and he had lost the silver chain with the clear stone which Bargah had hung round his neck. When this had happened he did not know. Perhaps it was when he fought with the clasp of his cape. Perhaps it had become entangled in the twigs of the branch to which he had clung and had snapped in twain when he changed one limb for another. Or perhaps the silver, which had been wrought with something more than the art of the silversmith, had been drawn finer and finer under the imprecations of the Witch Ysene and had at last broken and been carried to the bottom of the river, the stone heavy with the dreadful curse.

Whatever the fate of the stone was, Kashka did not know. Nor did he have time to concern himself over it. He must get back to Sootyn. The Prince was there and he must see that no harm came to him.

But they will be combing the bushes for me, he thought, those gentle sisters of the Lady Ysene. I haven't a chance if I take the road. He shuddered. I was an imbecile not to go along with the dear lady's scheme. She would have had me watched at every move, but at least my neck would not be in the noose this way.

He shook his head ruefully. Bargah was always right, the old witch! Why couldn't he keep his temper and his tongue? But Lady Ysene! Ugh! What a horrible creature! How dared she propose such a fiendish thing to him! The memory of her words set his blood to boiling so that he picked up a rock and hurled it over the water.

"You've a strong arm, friend," said a strange voice behind him.

Kashka leaped to his feet and whirled around.

"Eh! You're a bit jumpy, friend. I'm not the King's watch nor the Queen's guard—nor even the mayor's friend, though I've had some distant dealings with him. So sit down and throw your stones in comfort."

Kashka eyed the fellow with suspicion. He was rough, but he did not look like one of the Lady Ysene's companions.

"Hmmpf!" said Kashka, and remained standing.

The stranger laughed easily and seated himself on the sand.

"Life isn't a bed of goose down for all of us," he remarked as he chewed a blade of grass. "But there's no use beating your head on the cobblestones just because you don't lie on feathers! Look at me, would you. I picked up a small gift for a friend and kept it carefully for him. But he never came to get it and because of him I nearly lost my life. How was I to know the Mayor intended giving it to his wife to cover some little misdoing of his own? Someone told him I had it and the guard was after me in no time. Now here I am, lucky to have my life and my boat. You'll not find me begging the mayor for a feather bed!

"No, now that I'm this far down the river I may as well keep on. Why should I go back to Gynnis? They'd celebrate my coming with a party and I'd be the guest of honor. But I don't fancy their games. Head on a block, they'd play; or try the rope for size! No, even when the fellow with the hood explains the rules in his pleasant way, I don't fancy the games." He spat. "Never lose your head—that's my way of thinking!"

Kashka had to laugh.

"Now that's better!" The fellow squinted up at him. "I was ready to think you were one of those long nosed fellows who drapes everybody with shrouds and black ribbons.

Heh!" he laughed genially. "I don't fancy them neither. I sat the storm out just up the bank a way. When did you wash up?"

Kashka shook his head. "I'm not sure. It must have been near the end of the storm."

The new acquaintance whistled.

"Now who would go a journey on the river in a storm like that?"

"I didn't go *on* the river, friend," said Kashka adopting the same easy tone. "I went *in* it. And it was no scheme of mine to go! You might say I was sent on the journey. I was helped along. To tell you the honest truth, I didn't have any choice in the matter!"

The man eyed him for a few seconds and then burst out laughing.

"I like you more and more!" He slapped his knee. "What do you say we go on together? At least as far as Sootyn? With that current out there we could make good time if we took turns through the night with the boat. We'd be there by tomorrow morning. Will you join me?"

Kashka saw no other possibility. It might be one of the few chances he had left. And then—then—there was a chance of another kind, a hope small but persistent, a whispered possibility that someone else might have made his way to Sootyn. For someone had taken the lute from the wall of the inn. And whoever had taken it . . . But who else would take it?

Who else?

No one else, if Kashka had in mind a certain dirty, ragged barefoot boy who had gone in the dead of the night to the inn two days after the fall of the mill. The boy had quickly scaled the wall and found his way to the roof. From there he entered the inn by the open window of the loft.

The loft window had not been latched for there had been

no one in the inn who would venture into the garret room to latch it. Something to be feared lay in the garret. Something to be feared had roamed through the inn for two nights so that the guests moaned in their sleep, shivered in the hot night, and drew blankets over their heads. They were quick to take their leave in the morning.

But the third night the garret was empty of all but the stuffiness of a late summer heat. The boy searched the room quickly and then went down the stairs. Down another flight he went and by the flame of a bit of candle looked around the wide room.

After a moment his eyes grew bright. He ran to the wall and lifted the lute from the nail where it hung. Then he went to the door, unlatched it, unbarred it, and went out.

That the landlord had felt his knees turn to water when he found the door he had so carefully bolted the night before now wide open in the gray of the morning was no surprise. But he breathed nothing of it to anyone and the next night he double and triple locked the door with bolt, bar, and chain.

Taash, the lute in his hands, hurried through the dark streets and came once again to the river's edge. This time he turned away from the ruin of the mill and ran lightly along the bank until he came to a sagging hut. In he went, lit the candle end once more, and then went to the corner of the room where Piff lay.

Taash knelt beside him and put the lute in his hands.

"Here it is, Piff. It's safe and sound."

He drew his fingers across the strings.

Piff muttered and turned his head, but he did not see the boy. His eyes burned with a strange brightness and his words made no sense.

Taash folded Piff's hands around the instrument and sat on the floor beside him until he fell asleep.

When the boy woke in the morning Piff's breathing was even and his forehead cool. The jester slept through the day until late afternoon.

"Good morning," he said to Taash who was struggling to break a chunk of dry bread into pieces.

"Good afternoon," Taash replied.

"Is it now?" The jester looked around the room, then returned his gaze to the boy. "I suppose it's a long story?"

"Oh, not so very long. Three days."

"Three days!" Piff pursed his lips to whistle but no sound came from them.

Taash gave him water in a piece of a broken bowl.

"You're not much of a housekeeper," Piff told him as he looked around once more. "Where's Lia?" he asked suddenly and raised himself on his elbow.

"On the way to Nazor," Taash told him.

Then handing Piff a bit of bread and some more water to soak it in, he sat down beside him and told him what Lia had done.

Piff shook his head in wonder.

"Lia surely is a treasure! And to think I was going to send her home! From all the to-do she made about telling a harmless little story a few days ago, I never would have thought she could carry off such an act! Well, she and the babe are in safe hands, if rather foolish ones. Lord and Lady Vayn! Who would guess! Ho! Ho!"

He lay quietly for a time, chuckling now and then at some private thought.

Then, somewhat puzzled, he asked, "But how did we get here? I seem to have dreamed of a fire."

"The mill," Taash nodded. "It fell in, but we got out. I pushed you into the river and—well, we managed to climb out just down the bank from here."

"We?"

Taash grinned. "You weren't much help."

Piff rubbed his brow, then brought his hand down on the lute. He raised it in both hands and looked at it carefully, turning it around in his hands.

"How did you keep this from getting wet?"

"You left it at the inn. I went back for it."

Piff frowned. "You should never have gone back."

"There was no one there to see me."

"How can you be sure? You took too great a risk."

"But the Prince is safe, and who would recognize me?" He glanced down at his torn and soiled clothes. "Besides, you needed it."

Piff gave him a strange look. After a while he said, "If your flute ever needs to be rescued, I'll see to it. Especially if it's around your neck at the time."

Taash laughed aloud.

Piff felt the side of his face tenderly. "I wish I had an idea of what we should do," he said, "but my mind seems to be as bruised as my face. Ooof, and I'm stiff as a hickory staff!"

"There's a boat tied to the dock just below us," Taash told him. "It had water in it but I emptied it and it floats well enough. Can we go down the river?"

Piff nodded. "Sootyn is on the river. Lord and Lady Vayn are sure to stop there. Perhaps we'll find Lia there."

Then he added wistfully, "If there's anyone we need now, it's Kashka. I wish he would come swimming down the river with a fish for dinner between his teeth and a plan behind that knavish grin of his! There's no one who can get out of a scrape as quickly as he. He can get out of one almost as fast as he can get into one!"

And so that night a small boat was pushed away from the shore and in the darkness started down the river toward Sootyn.

* * *

In two days Piff was quite himself again. Taash awoke in the morning to find him up. He was looking through the small window of the abandoned fisherman's hut where they had spent the night. He motioned to Taash to be still and continued to watch the river. After several moments he turned to the boy.

"Good morning. Did you sleep well?" he greeted him.

"Much better than the night before," Taash told him. "I've never seen such a storm as that!"

"All the furies were loose in it," Piff agreed. "And the river is still running high. It brought some interesting things with it this morning."

"What sort of things?" Taash wanted to know.

"A man in a boat, for one," Piff told him. "I didn't like his looks. But he has gone on by. For a minute I thought he was looking for something—or someone. Perhaps he was just keeping a sharp eye out. He looked like the sort. Shall we breakfast on the rest of that fish?"

Cold fish was not the most appetizing of breakfasts, but Taash was hungry enough to be glad he had it. When they had finished eating he was ready to go in search of Lia. For they had learned that Lord and Lady Vayn were at the inn in Sootyn.

"Remember," Piff warned Taash, "be seen as little as possible. I would go with you if I thought no one would recognize me. Let's hope they don't recognize *you!* We don't know who is about. All the same servants were at Gynnis."

Taash nodded and off he went.

A ragged dirty boy was not such a rarity in the streets of Sootyn that anyone bothered to give Taash a second glance. He tried not to hurry, not to do anything that might attract attention.

At the inn there was very little doing. A stable boy groomed a horse, a servant drew water at the well, and smoke rose slowly from the kitchen chimney. There was none of the bustle that Taash had expected. Did the servants of Lord and Lady Vayn sleep as late as their master and mistress? It was indeed very quiet.

He went down the street and came back through the alley behind the inn. Taash glanced up at the windows, wondering where Lia might sleep. Then he had a thought. It was so simple he almost laughed that neither he nor Piff had thought of it before. He would pipe a few bars of music, a tune Lia knew well and would recognize at once. All she need do was come to the window and he could wave and leave at once. She would know then that they were nearby.

He pulled out his pipe, wet his lip, and leaned his back against the yard wall. Keeping his eyes on the row of windows he blew into the pipe.

It was a well known melody, a tune Kashka had taught him. But the way he trilled and embroidered the simple line was unique and he was sure that Lia would know it was he.

He finished the phrase. No face appeared at any window. He raised the little flute again to his lips, when to his amazement, he heard from the other side of the wall the next phrase of the music. He held his breath as he listened to the elaborate sweet sound and he knew that there was only one man in the world who could play in such a manner.

"Kashka!" he cried joyfully.

He heard the well known laugh and over the wall bounced his old friend. The only words in their greeting were Kashka's. He complained of dust in his eyes that made them water. Taash wiped the dust from his own eyes and wondered how he could begin to tell Kashka of all that had befallen him. Then from around one corner of the inn there came two men, and from the other direction, two more.

Before they could take a step, Taash and Kashka were seized, dragged into the inn through a side door and shoved up a flight of stairs. Through a door they were pushed and then another door was opened for them. There, hands bound behind their backs, they found themselves face to face with one whom they both knew.

19

Fateful melody! How could Taash have known that the ears for which it had been meant were miles away. And of all the ears for which it had not been meant, those of Lady Ysene were present.

"Ah, Kashka, so we meet again! And you have a young friend with you. How charming. I don't know what possessed you to serenade me in so delightful a fashion at this early hour, but I wanted to thank you personally. I could not help but recognize the tone and skill that only you possess. I hope you have not been too shaken by the enthusiastic welcome? Sometimes my aides are a little over zealous.

"And now, won't you introduce your young companion to me?"

"His name would mean nothing to you," Kashka spoke casually. "He's merely a pupil of mine whom I came across by chance. You have me now. Let the lad go."

Lady Ysene laughed, but it was not a pleasant laugh.

"Really, Kashka, you try so hard! And I admit that sometimes you succeed. But you cannot expect me to believe *that*!"

She stared at Taash.

"What miserable care you've taken of him, Kashka. Or did you think that dirt and rags would disguise him? That face? Those eyes—that mouth—I know who this boy is! You cannot deny it!"

Taash did not understand. He looked up into Kashka's face, a question in his eyes.

Kashka said nothing, but the look he returned to the boy was one of such despair that Taash was only more confused. The fear that had started up in him at the sight of Lady Ysene grew.

Lady Ysene burst into a harsh laugh.

"Kashka, you amuse me. You are more of a fool than I had thought! You put your heart where your head should be. I made you a perfectly beautiful offer only a few days ago and you turned it down. Why? The answer is written all over your face! Such devotion to your royal family! How can you be so stupid! You make me positively ill!"

Kashka said nothing.

Lady Ysene sat down and leaned back in her chair. She looked from one to the other thoughtfully. At last she spoke again. "I know that Piff is dead. That is one bit of fortune. Now I have you two. There is only one to be found. Matters are going well!"

Taash closed his eyes. Piff, he thought desperately. Piff, help us!

"I shall have to discover from one of you where the Prince is hidden. I cannot do anything until I have him. The only thing I must decide is which of you will be more inclined to tell me."

"You don't know where he is, Taash," Kashka said. "So you cannot tell her."

"Be quiet, Kashka!" Lady Ysene warned. "I have several pretty thoughts concerning your future, but I shall doubtless be able to think of something better yet if you force me."

Taash's heart was beating hard and his mouth was dry. What would she do to Kashka? He could not bear to think of it!

"So you are called Taash?" Lady Ysene turned her attention to the boy. "Hmm. Well, I suppose that name is as good as any. Are you fond of your companion here?"

Taash did not answer. Nor could he bring himself to look at Kashka again. If only he had not played his flute they would not be in the hands of this terrible woman. It's my fault, he thought. She will kill Kashka, and it's my fault.

"Oh, come now, you needn't look so miserable! All I want is the answer to a very simple question. If you give it to me, it will save you and your friend here some rather painful moments. Where is Prince Bai?"

Neither of them spoke.

Lady Ysene seized Taash and forced him to look into her face.

"Answer me!"

Taash stared directly into her eyes.

"I have never heard of any such person," he said firmly.

"Bah!" she snorted. "You will sing a different tune soon enough. Turgo!" she addressed one of the men who stood inside the door to guard it. "Have my carriage prepared. We will take a short journey. You there," she said to the other man, "keep a close watch on these two while I change my dress and tend to some other matters. And be careful. This fellow is slippery as a fish!"

With these and one or two other orders, Lady Ysene left the room.

"I'm sorry, Kashka," Taash said.

"What for?" asked Kashka.

"If I hadn't played the pipe we wouldn't be here."

"You didn't know," Kashka tried to comfort him. "And I was careless. I've been careless all along. Don't blame yourself."

Taash said nothing for a few minutes. Then he asked, "What will she do?"

"I don't know. We'll see soon enough."

Taash fell silent again. Perhaps Kashka would think of something. Perhaps Piff would come looking for him. But what if they should catch Piff too? Then they would all be lost—all except Lia and the Prince. But could she get him back by herself? What if someone were to recognize the Prince . . . ?

Lady Ysene returned.

"Let us go."

Taash and Kashka were taken down the same way they had been brought in. No one at the inn saw them. Lady Ysene's coach was at the door and they were pushed into it. She got in after them with two of her guards. The other two mounted the box beside the driver and they set off at a brisk trot. The curtains on the windows were drawn shut. Taash knew that they left the town by the sound of the wheels, for at first they drove over cobblestones and then they came onto the hard packed earth of a country road.

The boy sat next to Lady Ysene. Kashka was seated between the two burly guards. There was nothing they could do. No one spoke a word. After perhaps half an hour the coach slowed and then turned sharply. Another half hour went by. Again the coach slowed and this time it stopped.

A guard opened the door and Lady Ysene stepped down. Taash and Kashka were pushed from the coach. The four guards and the driver stood beside and behind them.

"I will take no chances this time. You have managed to escape me more often than I care to admit," Lady Ysene said to Kashka. "We shall put you away and keep you safe for a while. I wish to have my brother with me when we decide what exactly is to be done with you. He has some plans for you too, Kashka.

"I've already sent for him. It won't be long before he returns. Still, I don't doubt but that you will both be a little hungry and a little thirsty before he does get here. What a pity! You may wish to tell me a few things by then."

Taash looked around. They were on a road that had come

to an end in a wood. The trees were tall and grew close together. He could not tell whether they were in a forest or merely a grove of trees. From the end of the road beyond the coach a path led away into the woods.

Down the path Kashka and Taash were taken. It wound around among the trees until it came into a small glade. There stood the remains of a house: a few boards and a crumbling brick chimney.

Lady Ysene walked toward the ruin. Stopping halfway to it, she looked down into the tall grass and nodded.

"This will do very nicely. Bring them here."

Taash was pushed toward her. Kashka made a sudden jump to the side, but he was quickly caught and given such a blow on the side of his head that his knees bent under him and he fell to the ground. Taash cried out. A huge hand covered his mouth at once and his cry was smothered. He struggled against the man who held him but he was no match for such strength.

"Be quick about it!" Lady Ysene snapped. "Put the boy down first. The other one will wait."

A rope was lowered into what Taash now saw to be a sort of well. Were they to be drowned in it? Then one of the men climbed down and it proved to be dry. The rope was wrapped around Taash, tied securely, and he was lowered into the hole. The man undid the knot and Kashka was sent down in the same fashion. Finally the man climbed up the line, the rope was drawn up, and Taash and Kashka were left in a well about fifteen feet deep.

"I shall visit you this evening," Lady Ysene called down to them. "And we shall have a little talk then. Do you hear me, Kashka?"

But Kashka neither spoke nor moved from the place they had let him fall.

"Have a pleasant day all the same," she added.

Then she and the guards left. Taash heard nothing more.

* * *

Taash could not free his hands. The rope was tied tightly and his wrists grew tender from the chafing as he twisted and turned them. The more he pulled and strained the tighter the bond grew.

In a little while Kashka groaned and sat up.

"What have we fallen into here?" he asked when his eyes and his mind had cleared.

"It's some sort of well," Taash told him. "But it's not an ordinary one. I've been trying to find a brick or stone on the side to rub against the rope. But the sides are smooth. They're smooth and flat all the way around."

"Uh," Kashka grunted. "Our fine lady would never use anything so common as an ordinary well. I'll wager she had this dug for her own private use. Here, turn around and put your back to mine. We'll see if I can untie that knot."

It took Kashka a long time of picking and pulling at the rope. At last he worked it loose and Taash, his hands free, quickly untied the bonds that held Kashka.

They stood and rubbed the numbness from their wrists and arms. Then they examined the walls of the well more closely. Taash had been right. The walls were of stone that was smooth and polished. The pieces were fitted together so exactly that there was no chink or cranny in which they might so much as slip a fingernail.

Kashka measured the distance to the top with his eye and shook his head, murmuring, "No, you could not reach it even if you stood on my shoulders."

He cupped his hand around his mouth.

"Halloo!" he shouted. "Hello! Hola!"

They heard a crackling in the dry grass above them. Kashka listened intently, counting half aloud.

"You down there!" Taash looked up at the man silhouetted against the sky. "You keep still!"

"Would *you?*" Kashka asked.

The man grunted. "I would if I knew what would happen if I didn't!"

"Come now," Kashka laughed. "You know as well as I do that it doesn't matter *what* I do now! You heard Lady Ysene's words."

"You stop that shouting or *I'll* take care of you," said the man.

Kashka shrugged. "If you put it that way!"

The guard stared down at them for a minute, then disappeared. Kashka again listened carefully as the steps retreated. When the sound had stopped he spoke in an ordinary tone of voice.

"Guard, what *will* you do if I shout?" He listened and then raised his voice. "Aren't you afraid she might not like it?"

Again he listened. There was no response.

"Does a blackguard like you enjoy working for a witch?" This was louder still. "When will the monster be back?" It was near a shout.

"Hey!" at the top of his voice.

"I said keep still!" The answering shout was not loud in their ears.

Kashka smiled at Taash. "We can talk at last. He's at least at the edge of the clearing. Still, sound sometimes carries strangely. I wanted to be sure. Now, start at the very beginning—when you fell into the pool."

Taash did. And Kashka heard the whole story. When he had finished, Kashka told him how he and Bargah and Nanalia had come to Nazor and how he had come to the inn at Sootyn to look for the girl and the baby just in time to hear Taash's piping.

They sat quietly then, thinking, wondering, waiting, and looking up now and again at the little circle of sky above them.

Their thoughts were alike. Where were Lia and the Prince now? And what of Piff? And what fate awaited them at the hands of Lady Ysene?

What will they do to Kashka? Taash wondered. It was clear enough that Lady Ysene had something dreadful in mind for him. Recalling the face of her brother, Taash did not doubt that he had an even more cruel turn of mind than she. I'll never be able to bear it, he thought. I don't care if they kill me, I will never tell. But if they should torture Kashka? No, no. I could not bear that!

And Kashka thought. Whatever she has devised it will be the work of a fiend. But there will always be the end of it. Life is a frail thing. All I need do is hold out to the finish. But if she should start on Taash! He shuddered. I really do not believe I could stand that. Yet we can gain nothing by breaking down—only a quicker death, and even that is not certain. She must not have Prince Bai and Lia as well. We must hang on.

"Taash," he said at last. "Unless a miracle happens we are both in for a very bad time. You understand?"

Taash nodded. Kashka continued.

"She is a witch—she is a fiend of the worst sort. And her brother is no better."

Taash shivered. He could not help it.

Kashka put his arm around the boy's shoulder.

"Before it grows any later there is something you must know. Or has Piff told you who you are?"

Taash shook his head.

"You are a royal prince. You are the King's brother."

Taash looked at Kashka to see if he were joking. There was no gleam of teasing in his eyes.

Kashka chewed his underlip, then went on.

"Nine years or so ago, through no particular cleverness of my own, I stumbled onto Lady Ysene. She was up to tricks very much like those you found her playing with your baby Teyal. She had much the same plans then as now, only it was for *you* that she planned. I had a piece of luck, and with Bargah's help that luck has held until now. Lady Ysene has hunted for you in a thousand places."

Taash could not help but feel that there was more than luck in Kashka's doing.

"The old woman who was to take care of you died," Kashka went on. "And we lost you to the woodcutter. We had hoped—but I hadn't been quick enough, Taash. There was some witchery to be undone. Bargah knew that. It was *time* we had to have, and we had to give you up or lose you. You know well enough how Bargah got you back again.

"We couldn't tell you right away who you were. You weren't ready to know. And we couldn't take you back either. There were goings-on that made it difficult and dangerous—nay, impossible—to take you back at once. Lady Ysene is a restless witch! And so Bargah gave you some of the education you needed. We had decided to take you back next spring. Then this happened . . . and here we are."

After a long time Taash spoke.

"But supposing I am not the King's brother. Supposing the Witch Ysene did find him and changed him for me—or me for him? Perhaps she's just pretending—to make you tell her where she can find Prince Bai.

"All that time I lived with the woodcutter . . . how can you be sure you know who I am? Maybe I *am* only Taash!"

Kashka smiled.

"I know who you are because I know! Believe me! And when the time comes there will be a way to prove it."

He looked at Taash and suddenly his smile vanished. His face became grave.

"Where is the chain, the amulet you always wore?" he asked.

"I gave it to Lia for Prince Bai," Taash told him. "Bargah once said . . . and I thought that if it protected me it should protect him. It was more important for him . . ." Taash didn't know what more to say.

Kashka said nothing for a while.

Taash turned over in his mind what he had been told. It was more than he could believe. He, Taash, the brother of the King? No, he did not feel like any such person!

After a time Kashka spoke again.

"Taash, Prince Taash," he smiled a little. "There are a few things that you must try to understand. I serve you as I serve all the members of the royal house. Whatever happens to me, I will bear for the King, for Prince Bai, and for you. Do you realize that if some terrible catastrophe should befall the King and Prince Bai, you would become King? And so I serve you as I would my King." He was quiet for a moment, then added softly. "But if you were not a prince, it would make no difference to me. I should bear it then for you as I would for a brother."

Taash said nothing for a long while. Then he spoke slowly and thoughtfully.

"You mean too that whatever they do to you *I* must bear because it is also for the King and Prince Bai that I bear it. And if it is true that I am a prince, I must behave like one."

"That was well said." Kashka's voice was quiet.

"But oh, Kashka," Taash wailed suddenly. "No, no, no! I will not be able to stand it!"

Kashka shook him gently. "Yes, you will. Now let us be quiet, for someone is coming."

20

 "Good evening!" the voice called down to them. "I
hope you are comfortable?"

They did not answer.

"I suppose you are a little hungry and thirsty, but in such
an out-of-the-way place it is impossible for me to supply you
with the small necessities of life."

Taash found that he was hungry and not a little thirsty.

"I have planned a diversion for you this evening. Nothing would please me more than to give you directly into
the hands of my brother along with the final object of our
search. And so, as a modest trial of my power, I shall have
you tell me of the whereabouts of Prince Bai of your own
free will."

The shadow that had come over the top of the well vanished. Taash glanced up and saw that the sky was darkening
rapidly. It would soon be night. He yawned. Kashka laughed.

The shadow fell upon them again.

"Do not try me, gentlemen! I am not famous for my patience!"

There was something strange going on above them. The
air was filled with rushing sighs and weird whispers. The
sounds came down to their ears as words heard in a half-
sleep when only the shape of them enters the mind and the
meaning is lost.

"What is it?" Taash asked in a whisper. A chill had gone
down his back.

"I'm not sure," Kashka whispered in answer. "But what

was it you said you did when you wanted to join the witches in their dance around the fire?"

"Numbers," Taash told him promptly. "You multiply all the numbers you can. Then you do them over. And again, if you have to."

"Multiply!" Kashka's voice held a tone of dismay. "I can scarce add my fingers to my toes! Numbers and letters were never my meat and drink. I left such matters to Piff. He can do sums in his head faster than I can find my fingers. And he can write in any hand he chooses." Kashka chuckled. "He's pulled more than one prank with his forgeries!"

"But you *must* do it!" Taash insisted. "It's not hard. You say to yourself, eight five times is forty. Eight six times is forty-eight, eight seven times is fifty-six . . ."

"Bargah has taught you well," Kashka muttered. "At least I suppose what you say is true. But she never had such luck with me. I could never sit still that long."

"Then add *one* to every number you know!" Taash was convinced that there was something magic in numbers, and that if only his friend could put them together in some sort of way, he would be able to defy the spell. For by now they both realized that Lady Ysene had summoned her witches. Above their heads the same chanting voices and the same rhythmic beating of circling feet that Taash had heard in the desert waste had begun.

"Ay," Kashka said. "That I can do. Add one." He pulled at his lip. "I might even manage two if I add them one at a time."

"And then try three!" Taash said eagerly. He himself started at once with one, one time, is one. One two times is two.

Heads bowed, they sat back-to-back at the bottom of the well. The night was dark but the glassy sides of the well flickered and shimmered with a thousand tiny lights. The air was heavy with a sweet odor that dulled the senses. A soothing pulsing sound of far away voices crooning caressed their ears. The long seconds, minutes, and hours of the night began.

Five times five is twenty-five . . . Six times three . . . is . . . three times . . . is eighteen. Yes, eighteen. Six four times is twenty-four. Seven nine times is . . . seven nine times . . . Taash breathed deeply, evenly. Seven . . . He raised his head. His eyes were heavy. He couldn't remember. Did . . . it . . . matter . . . what seven taken nine . . . times . . . over . . .

His head fell back against Kashka's shoulder. How comfortable he was. How warm he was, and sleepy! Someone was calling him. Taash, Taash! Come with me. Come with me. Chop, chop, chop. No! Seven nine times . . . Come now.

He was falling, falling. He caught himself. Kashka! Seven times nine . . . Taash, Taash, let go! Seven . . . and . . . nine . . . Come and see what I have to show you. Taash . . . Taash . . . That was not so difficult, was it? Come along now. There is a world here. A whole world for you alone! A world of things you've never seen, of dreams you've never dreamed. Here lie the powers of night. Look . . . here . . . see . . . see . . .

And he sank into a darkness of a kind he had never known.

"Stop it! Taash! Wake up!"

"No no. Let . . . go!"

"Taash! What is it if you add four numbers in a row to four you have already? Tell me!"

"There's a world . . . I must . . . there's something here. No . . . no numbers . . . let go."

"Will you stop mumbling and tell me! I am going mad with ones and fives and sevens running all over my brain! I have come around to four." Kashka shook the boy again. His head fell back, his eyes, half open, looked dark and strange in the weird and flickering light that danced around them. Kashka stared into them horrified.

"Do you hear? Taash? But I can't keep track of them when I have four and I add one and another one . . . Taash, I will beat you if I must! That cursed witch! What is four and four again? Is it nine? Is it seven? Is it three and twenty? Answer me!"

"Bargah will turn you all into fat piggies if you shake me again! The whole village! A whole village of fat piggies!"

"Taash!"

"Three and twenty? Nothing is three and twenty. How can I think when you shake me like that?"

"Ah," Kashka sighed. "What is four and four?"

"Four . . . ? You have eight. That's simple."

"Perhaps for you," Kashka grumbled.

"I can't remember seven taken nine times," Taash said.

Kashka spread out his fingers and muttered to himself.

"It can't be done. If we had a hundred stones or more we might count out seven and seven more and seven more until we had nine rows of them. Then we could count them all and we would know."

Taash laughed. "That's a long way around! It's much easier to remember it."

"Of course," Kashka agreed. "But if you forget?"

"You don't forget. It's three and sixty."

Kashka drew a deep breath. "There's a battle won!" he muttered. "Listen to me," he said to Taash. "I can't do this any more. We must try something else."

"What can we do?" Taash was not sure that they should abandon the numbers, though the numbers did seem to be abandoning them.

"Let's sing a round," Kashka said. "There's nothing more difficult than singing when other music is being performed. Though I can't honestly call that stuff up there music! But you must keep your mind on what we're doing. Don't listen to anything from up there."

Kashka began and at the nod of his head Taash entered with the second part. They sang through it three times, and then started another one.

"I could go on all night," Taash said at the end of the fifth song, "if I had a drink of water."

"We shall probably have to go on all night, water or no," said Kashka. "Let's try a new one."

Phrase by phrase, words and melody, Kashka taught the boy a new song. When Taash could sing it through with no mistakes they tried the parts together. Now and again the wailing from above would come to their ears, but they plunged at once into another song and erased the sounds of the chanting and moaning. The hypnotic beating of feet and hands went on and on, circling around and around over their heads.

Kashka covered the boy's mouth with his hand. Taash had not noticed the stillness above them.

Into that stillness came the voice of the Witch Ysene. The sound of it chilled the marrow and made the scalp prickle. Taash covered his ears.

"She is conjuring all the demons and evil spirits of this world and the other!" Kashka shuddered and grated his teeth.

They could not shut out the cry, the evil summons of dark forces. Kashka's tongue failed him. There were no words that could dispel the awful visions, the terrifying shadows, the demonic shades and images evoked by the voice of the Witch Ysene.

Taash nudged him. Kashka looked at the boy. Hands clapped to his ears, Taash sat grinning. He's gone mad! Kashka stared at him in horror. But Taash nudged him again, raised his hands a hundredth part of a second, then pressed them again tightly to his head. He was almost laughing aloud! Then Kashka knew. His hands went to his ears, and they sat there listening, grinning and reducing the fearful invocation to a meaningless 'wow wow wow'. Rapidly, slowly, hands cupped, hands flattened, they alternately pressed their palms and released them again from their ears.

What evil thing can stand against laughter?

All night the ritual went on. Hour after hour Taash and Kashka fought the dark powers of the witch. The jester performed for the boy as he had never performed for the King. With the art of the mime he brought before him swift and startling images of friend and foe alike. Taash had to guess. It was Piff—Lady Ysene—the baker—the Duke of Xon— Lady Vayn—the woodcutter—the mayor—the King?—nay, he could not guess—Kashka himself! Over and over the boy stuffed his sleeve into his mouth to keep his laughter from rising to the ears of the witch.

The boy's head nodded. Kashka dragged him to his feet and danced him around and around, stood him on his head, his hands, his feet. He taught him the proper manner in which to bow before his King. And Taash, usually so nimble, at last found himself so fumble-footed with fatigue he scarce knew left from right.

Now they stood still and listened. The night was filled with silence, the silence of waiting, the silence of many beings listening. The air itself waited, listened.

"Sleep!"

The voice of the witch broke the stillness.

"Sleep and come to me. Let your thoughts come to me. Let your thoughts be mine."

The silence grew again, a silence that pressed upon them, suffocated them.

"Now speak," she crooned. "Tell me. Tell me what you

want to tell me, what you have been waiting to tell me. Tell me that I may help you, that I may help Prince Bai. Tell me where I may find Prince Bai. Tell me. Tell me."

The voice died into the waiting stillness.

Kashka sighed.

"My dear Lady Ysene, you ask too much! You have kept us awake the entire night with a lovely performance by your handmaidens. But to be honest, it has been very tiring. Even if we tried ever so hard neither of us could remember where the Prince might be. Besides, we don't know where he is! That is the absolute truth. How can we convince you of it?"

Lady Ysene drew in her breath sharply. Then in tones of silk she spoke again.

"Taash, my dear boy. My Prince! Tell me, where is your brother's son?"

"I'm sorry," Taash said. "I would like to help you. But I can't. I don't know my brother, and I don't know my brother's son, and I don't know where either of them are!"

They didn't *know* what passed through the mind of Lady Ysene for the next several moments, but they could guess. For when she spoke at last she was near strangling with fury.

"Wretches! Dogs! How dare you! How could you!"

Kashka's voice was all innocence. "Have we disappointed you, dear lady? I am truly sorry. The performance was magnificent! It really was! We have been an appreciative audience. Please believe me. I beg of you, do not be so distressed!"

"How could it have happened!" She was talking to herself, but leaning over the well as she was the prisoners within heard every word.

"Never before has even half such a spell failed!"

"Perhaps you are losing your powers, dear lady." Kashka's tone was of the purest politeness, respect, and sympathy.

"Miserable man!" she shrieked. "You will regret—you will—I will tear you to pieces with my own hands!"

"Leave something for your kind brother, dear lady. He must have his share!"

"I will scratch out your eyes!"

"Alas, am I never again to look upon your sweet and gentle features?"

"I will tear out your tongue!"

"I'll not tell a soul you did it!"

"Aaagh! You wait! You wait! You will be sorry!"

So enraged she could neither speak nor think the Witch Ysene straightened her back, waved her arm in a furious circle dispersing her sisters in a blinding burst of white fire, turned on her heel, and left the side of the well.

To the ears of the prisoners came her sharp commands.

"You shall stay here, all four of you. You shall stand guard in turn. Two shall sleep and two shall watch. Every four hours you shall change places. Do not move a step from your posts until I return. If anyone other than myself comes down that path, kill him! Do you hear? *Kill him!*"

The sky grew light. The sun rose. All the world roused itself and set itself to doing. Ah—not quite all the world. Two of its children, gray-faced with exhaustion, slept at the bottom of a well in a glade. A strange glassy-sided well it was, surrounded at the top by a circular path worn in the grass by the shuffling feet of yet stranger beings.

Ten paces distant from the well on all sides grew a thick grove of trees. A little path wound among these away from the place and out onto a road. By the side of the path where it left the clearing stood two giants of men. Two others slept nearby. They were oddly silent. Not a one moved or spoke. They scarcely breathed.

The sun rose higher and the day grew warmer. The sleepers awoke. The ones in the grass stood and took up positions by the sides of the path. Those who had been standing lay down in the same grass and fell asleep at once. No greeting was exchanged. No look passed between them.

The sleepers at the bottom of the well also roused. They stood, stretched, and yawned. Nor did they exchange words, but a look passed between them that said a thousand things. After a bit they slept again. It was past noon when they awoke for the second time.

"How shall we ever get out, Kashka?"

"Lady Ysene will see to that."

"I don't mean that. We must get ourselves out before she comes back."

Kashka's laugh was short. "Have you any suggestions?"

Taash gazed at the walls for the hundredth time and shook his head.

"There's only one chance for us," Kashka said. "And that's a slim one. You heard what she told the guards? We'd better not hope!"

"I hope he doesn't try," Taash said. "They would kill him."

Kashka agreed. "It would be best if he went to help Lia." They sat for a while in silence.

"The guards are so quiet," Kashka thought aloud at last. "But they can't have left. Hello! Guards! Hello!"

There was no answer.

"I don't understand it," Kashka was puzzled. "Hola! I have something to tell your mistress! Ah," he muttered. "My voice is gone. All that singing and not a drop to drink! I am parched. They must not hear me."

The thirst was worse than the hunger that gnawed at them. Hour after hour they sat with mouths of dust.

Once the dry grass crackled as if several people walked about in it. The noise stopped as suddenly as it had begun. All was still again. They could not think what it was.

Kashka drew out his pipe and began to play. The music poured from the instrument. The sweet fluting rose into the air with all the rich embellishment of the melody that only Kashka's skill could give it.

They were not the happy lilting tunes that he chose. The music that floated up and out of the dismal prison was wistful and mournful. Kashka the jester, so quick with the light quip or the unconcerned shrug, could not help but pour his feelings into the music. The melody rose and fell, tender, sorrowful, and weary; and around it he wove intricate patterns and the beauty of variation that was his own gift to the art.

Taash listened with his eyes closed. The music spoke to him of things for which he could not find words. New feelings and old ones that had slept in him forgotten, mingled within him. He could not stop and ask himself what they were, for the music was insistent. It would not let him go, but pulled him on through a tapestry woven of sound and feeling.

The last note from Kashka's flute died away in the lonely wood that surrounded the lonely prison. The silence grew and grew and Taash thought of a different silence he had known.

"Kashka," he said at last, "there was a minute last night when I dreamed."

"I know," said Kashka.

"I wish I hadn't. It was a—a bad dream."

"You couldn't help it. We all have those dreams—and with no such forces of evil to drive us to them as you had last night."

The boy sat with his chin on his knees, his arms wrapped around his legs.

"When I lived with the woodcutter he used to beat me every day. I hated him. I hated everyone in the village. But when I went to live with Bargah things were different. I didn't hate everyone any more. I began to think the rest of the world might be good. That perhaps the people in the village were the way they were because there was something wrong there—something in the forest, something in the sound of the woodcutter's axe—I don't know what—that made them so."

"They were an ignorant lot," Kashka told him. "They were afraid of you because they didn't know how you came there. Ignorance and the fear that comes from it—these are our greatest enemies. They make us hate all the wrong things.

"The village people were no different from any one else. They feared what they didn't understand. It made them brutal. But I expect they loved their own children—even the mayor that red-haired bully of his!"

Taash nodded.

"When I came here I was afraid," he said. "After I'd seen the witches I didn't trust anyone—Maro or Mara—not even Piff!" He smiled ruefully. "Can you imagine not trusting Piff?"

Kashka lifted one shoulder slightly. "You didn't know who he was."

"No, I didn't. But afterward I did." He paused. "And then something terrible happened."

Kashka waited for the boy to go on.

"When they caught Piff . . ." Taash couldn't find the words he wanted. Finally he burst out. "It wasn't the same as when the woodcutter beat me! They needn't have beaten him that way!"

Kashka turned his face away.

"No," he said harshly. "They needn't. But it's another part of it—to give pain for the pleasure of giving it. You have to watch out for that. It's not a long step from pulling a cat's tail to twisting a boy's arm to beating a man."

They were silent then for a long time. Finally Taash said in a low voice, "But the worst was last night."

His eyes had a sadness in them that the jester had never seen. Kashka could have wept for his young Prince.

"I didn't want to tell you," said the boy. "But after you played your flute I knew I could—that you would understand it. I wanted you to know."

The jester passed his hand over his eyes.

"There has always been evil in the world," he said. "We have to know it or we cannot choose . . ." He smiled crookedly. "It works both ways! We have to know what music is, for the Witch Ysene would have us hear it all untuned. What a horror that is! Ay, and she would turn all the shades of red—of roses, of poppies, of sunsets—to the red of blood. She would make the soft velvet of night into a shadow to hide monsters of terror. There would be no stars, no moon in her night! And the sun that gives us life would be a cruel fire searing our eyes and driving our minds to madness.

"Yet she offers them to us with such honeyed words that we think they are precious gifts—the gifts of hatred, brutality, fear, and ugliness!"

The boy stared at the jester.

"How do you know the dream?" he asked.

"I've been in that other world," Kashka said quietly. "One night some time ago—but I had forgotten. Bargah saw to that. Last night I remembered. I went with you. I had to bring you back so you would know . . ." Kashka paused. He stood up. A quick anger rose in his voice. "I wish you hadn't seen such things!

"Damned serpent!" he shouted suddenly. "To put them to a boy when a man would find it hard to choose! And to make that choice *your* way or death!" He slammed his fist against the side of the well.

Taash stared at Kashka. Nanalia's face came to his mind. "I don't like Kashka to be angry," she was saying. "He frightens me then."

Kashka looked down at the startled boy. "But what can I offer you? Ha! A temper as bad as the Witch Ysene's, but no magic powers to summon up visions of all that is opposite to her!"

His wrath died as quickly as it had flared. He knit his brows.

Taash didn't know what to say.

"But, Taash"—and the jester looked into the boy's eyes— "you've seen how deep her hatred of men goes. Now you know how strong your love must be to tip the scales against her. You've seen how she distorts and deforms all that is fair. But the more you are touched by beauty the more revolting this ugliness will be to you. To know that such ugliness exists is hard to bear. Some find it harder to bear than others. But no matter how hard it is you can't give up—you can't give in."

Taash nodded then. "I know," he said. "It was in the music that you played. I knew it then."

"You're all right then?" Kashka asked.

"Yes," said Taash. "I'm all right. She tried, but she can't touch us. I know that. I'm not afraid of her.

"And we won't let her have Prince Bai, will we? Even if she kills us!"

"No," Kashka said. "We won't."

The jester stared up at the high smooth sides of their prison, his eyes searching, seeking.

"And we won't let her have you," he whispered. "We *must* get you out!"

21

A pebble dropped into the well. It fell between them and Kashka picked it up. He turned it over in his fingers. They looked up, but there was nothing to be seen except the blue sky. The grass rustled faintly. Then there was nothing.

They waited. Another sound came to their ears, a faint metallic click. Again, no more. It was odd.

They looked at each other, heads cocked, ears strained.

An owl hooted.

Taash's jaw dropped. Kashka came alive. He raised his flute to his lips and a wild tumble of notes leaped from it. He stopped playing. They listened.

Suddenly there was a piercing shriek. Taash was turned as if to stone. He grew cold all over and his hands were wet. Kashka, his face white, moved his lips. Piff, they said, but no sound came from them.

Then there came a low laugh and the sound of a chord being struck from the strings of a lute. A voice sang.

> "A lovely lady loved her lord
> And oh she loved him true!
> She kissed his lip
> And filled his cup
> And held it up
> For him to sip;
> And this she'd ever do.
> The Lord was young,

The lord was brave,
Yet sickened he, and died.
The lady with her grief did rave,
And peeled onions 'til she cried!"

"Piff!" Two voices shouted in unison and two faces looked up into the smiling roguish eyes that peered into the well.

"Good afternoon, gentlemen! I was strolling in the wood nearby, and thinking you might be home decided to drop in on you. I always enjoy a visit with old friends. Tsk tsk! You have no stair to accommodate me. How thoughtless of you! How do you get in and out of your house? Do you fly? What a singular structure!"

All the while that Piff was chatting and teasing he was letting down a rope which hung in a coil from his shoulder.

"So you will not let me enter, but must come running up my ladder like monkeys on a pole! Such lack of hospitality!"

Then such an embracing there was! Taash didn't know whether it was Piff who tossed him into the air and Kashka who caught him, or the other way around!

Suddenly Taash froze, then cried, "The guards!"

Kashka caught sight of them at the same moment. He leaped backward, stumbled, and fell over the two others who lay sleeping in the grass. He was on his feet quick as a cat, ready for anything that might come.

Piff doubled over with laughter. "You should see your-selves!" he shouted. "I've never seen such faces!"

Taash and Kashka stared at him as if he had gone mad. Then they gazed with equal astonishment at the motionless guards.

"What's the matter with them?" asked Kashka.

"I'll tell you presently. But let's get away now and not press our fortune. Lady Luck has been kind, but she may soon tire of showing so favorable a face. Ah, not there, this way!"

Piff led them around behind the ruined chimney and through the trees. For some distance they scrambled through dense undergrowth. Then the trees thinned and they came out of the wood into a meadow. Beyond lay the plowed fields and thatch roofed cottages of the tilled countryside.

Piff pointed to a small tree-covered hill some mile's distance. Keeping their heads low and out of sight, they hurried along the hedges that divided the fields one from another.

In half an hour's time they found themselves in a small shelter of the kind that serves hunters in stormy weather. They were well hidden by the trees and the hillock afforded them a fine view of the country around.

Piff had brought bread and cheese and a skin of water for them. While they ate and drank he told them how he came to get them out of the well.

"The minute Taash was out of sight I knew I never should have let him go," he began. "It's not that I don't have the greatest respect for your ingenuity," he said to the boy. "I owe you my life. But a witch like Ysene is not a force to underestimate. I went after you, taking a different way around to the inn. I was just in time to witness a most tender and sentimental meeting between you two and a number of thugs.

"I would have joined the happy party but I had a painful sliver in my thumb and by the time I had stopped and removed it, you had gone into the inn and left me alone. Happily I didn't have to wait long before you came out, charming lady friend and all. 'Now they'll invite me,' I thought. But you didn't. Everyone hopped into the coach and dashed off in such a hurry that no one so much as looked around to see if anyone else wanted to go.

"Now I was really angry. A high ranking lady, a prince, a court jester, and a number of devilish looking rogues—it spelled out one thing. Fun! And I was being left behind! Of course I would have preferred having several more lovely ladies present, but I shouldn't have reckoned without the hostess. She provided more than enough of *them* in the evening.

"But that comes later. I was determined not to miss any of it even if it meant hanging on the back of the coach for an hour. Well well, one doesn't often have such a pleasant ride through the country . . . and at no charge!

"When the coach stopped I felt a little shy. After all, I *hadn't* been invited, though I probably would have been welcomed! I thought I would wait until things warmed up before I asked for a dance. I watched your hostess furnish you with your dwelling in her usual gracious manner. I knew you would be in trouble if you accepted her offer, but I forgave you your foolishness because I know how persuasive she can be. I was taken in by her charms too—only last week!

"I stayed a while after she left to make sure you had not succumbed to the blow on your head. Of course, when I saw how irritated the guard became I knew, though I didn't hear what you said, dear Kashka, that your brain had been spared any great injury. Perhaps it had even been improved!

"Then I took a walk. Lovely weather, lovely countryside— perfect for a stroll. I came here and enjoyed the view. At nightfall I went back to the woods. Lady Ysene had promised you a visit then and of course the *best* parties are held in the evening. I wouldn't have missed it for the world!

"It *was* a piece of entertainment! As a matter of fact, I did miss quite a bit of it. I hate to admit it, but it was a little strong for my stomach. I did want to keep track of the goings on, though. I hated to think of what might happen to you if you got too involved with the lovely lady. After all, you are my cousin and the family reputation must be looked after. And when you drag the King's brother with you on your escapades, Kashka, you're treading on thin ice. I wish you'd learn to be more discreet!

"Aaah! I'm footsore! Back and forth I went. Back and forth all night long. I'd catch the beginning of one act or the end of another. I never could stay for a single scene straight through. I must have walked twenty miles keeping up with the plot. I was in time for the last act of the play, though. Ugh! But it was by far the most interesting of anything I'd seen."

He paused, then added, "Of anything I've *ever* seen."

Piff suddenly closed his eyes, drew a deep breath and blew it out in a low whistle. His words lost their flippancy and in utter wonder and admiration he asked, "How did you do it? How ever in the name of all that is sacred did you resist that terrible spell? I tell you my heart was in my boots when that witch looked down the well and asked you where Prince Bai was. I never dreamed but that you would tell her! I knew that as soon as you said those words I would have to leave you there and find the Prince before she did.

"By heaven, Kashka! Can you imagine how I felt? To know that I must leave Taash and you in such hands!"

"By heaven, Piff!" Kashka smiled crookedly as he mocked his cousin's words and voice. "Can you imagine how I felt when I heard you had been buried beneath ten tons of rock and rubble?"

"Huh!" Piff's tone grew light again. "Well, you are a very thoughtless fellow. I almost lost my footing and fell out of my tree when I heard your answer. And where would we be if I had?

"Fortunately I can keep my wits about me. I don't go leaping over walls into Lady Ysene's arms! Nor out of trees either.

"Eh, the rest was simple. I caught a ride back to Sootyn with the lady. I wrote a letter or two there—I was behind in my correspondence with a certain lady and had to write a letter of explanation to her brother too. Then I bought a piece of rope . . . and here we are!"

Kashka smiled and sighed. "I particularly enjoyed the happy ending," he said. "For a while I was worried. I never did care for tragedies."

Then Taash asked, "But what of the guards? Why didn't they stop you—or us?"

"Ah!" Piff exclaimed. "I forgot to explain what I think must have happened. You see the guards were there all night. They didn't miss a thing. Imagine what a state of mind a person would be in after that when he didn't have much mind to begin with! Our dear witch was so upset after her conversation with you that she couldn't see straight before her. I saw her face. The sight of it was enough to slay an executioner! She was so blind she didn't see that her own guards had fallen under the spell."

"But she told them to kill anyone who came near!"

"Aha! But she didn't! I was a bit cautious at first," Piff admitted. "But after I had watched them a while I knew something peculiar had happened. They moved—but they were insensible. I threw some rocks at them to see what they would do. They didn't even notice they had been struck!"

"You mean you did hit them?" Kashka asked. "I'm amazed! Your aim is so poor one of those stones fell on us!"

"I hoped so. I wanted to be sure you knew something was going on. It was only a pebble. Did it hit you?"

"No. I said your aim was terrible. You missed."

"Then I shouted," Piff continued.

"Shouted! You near killed us with fright! I thought a pig was being butchered!"

"I tried to startle them," Piff laughed. "I couldn't understand it. Even when I stood in sight of them they didn't move. Then I remembered her exact words: *'If anyone comes down that path!'* They were obeying her to the letter! Let's hope it doesn't occur to *her* what she told them."

"And what of Lia and Prince Bai?" Kashka asked.

"They have left for Nazor," Piff said. "I had it from the stable boy. There is some connection between the Duke and Lady Ysene and the Vayns. I don't think we can get to the palace fast enough!"

"You're right, Piff. Let's be off!"

22

My lord, the Duke of Xon, arrived in Sootyn late in the morning. He was dusty, weary, and out of humor. He had received a short note from his sister urging his immediate return. She stated that she had the greatest piece of good fortune in being hostess to a member of the royal family and to a fine entertainer. She begged him to come at once and join her in the pleasure of their company.

The Duke was tired when he received the note. He had been in such a hurry to hunt up an old acquaintance that he had taken only two hours' sleep in two days' time. Now he had to hurry back. All had been for nothing, for he did not doubt but that it was the man he sought who now visited his sister. It put him out of sorts.

When he arrived in Sootyn he was told that the Lady Ysene was resting. She had spent an exhausting night and had been so ill and nervous the next day that she had been unable to rest. Indeed, she had not fallen asleep until this very dawn. They hesitated to wake her.

The Duke of Xon shrugged. His sister's nerves were not his affair. He went to his room.

He washed and observed himself in the glass. The lines of fatigue in his face were becoming to him, befitting his future position. Then he noticed a folded parchment tucked behind the corner of the mirror. He forgot his kingly aspect for the moment and drew forth the paper.

It was a sealed letter with his name written on it. The

Duke raised his eyebrows. He recognized the hand but could not imagine why he should receive a communication from that source. He scarcely glanced at the seal. It was familiar enough to him.

He broke the seal and read:

My Lord the Duke of Xon. Dear Friend:

I hope this finds you well. I cannot speak for my own health.

Strange events force me to communicate with you in secret and I must forebear from signing this. I hesitate to make matters known to you in such a manner but as you have ever been devoted, I feel I must warn you.

My news is unhappy and touches on one close to you.

I speak of your sister. Beware, my lord. Be on your guard. She is an ambitious woman and nothing is too sacred to her to stand in her way. Not country, nor King, nor brother!

Your devoted friend of many years.

The letter was unsigned. The Duke turned it over and over. The writing was unmistakable. The seal he had broken, but it certainly was the one he had thought it to be! But how ... what did it mean? He reread the letter and read it over and read it again. Each time he had the same questions. Each time he came to the same conclusion.

Was it a trick? Or had the King heard something concerning only the Lady Ysene? It was after all no more than a warning.

Had she plans of her own? The Duke of Xon flushed and

then turned pale. The agreement was that *he* would be king! But she was a strong and ruthless woman. Were her ambitions greater than she pretended? He would not put it past her. She and her weird sisters! How far could you trust a witch?

He had been warned. He would watch her closely.

He destroyed the letter, lay down upon his bed, and fell asleep.

Lady Ysene was furious at having been allowed to sleep. She had wanted to see her brother the moment he arrived. She sent for him at once.

"Why didn't you wake me?" she fumed.

"I thought you had left orders not to do so," he answered calmly. "I presume you have everything in hand?"

"Well enough!" she snapped. She was still smarting from her defeat and the sleepless time she had passed had not improved her temper. She had spent it devising the most cruel and fiendish forms of torture imaginable for Kashka and Taash. Recalling several of these now she managed to smile at her brother.

"You must forgive me. I had hoped matters would be even better when you arrived. I wished to present you with the entire cast for our little drama. But I am sorry to tell you that one of the members is still missing. You must help me discover his whereabouts.

"I know how eager you are, dear brother, to obtain the information yourself from one of the players. I cannot blame you. He is the most obnoxious person in the world and nothing will give me more joy than to see what we together can arrange for his discomfort."

The Duke of Xon did not smile. He did not like to show emotion.

"Have them brought before us then."

"I cannot do that, brother. We must go to them. Let us leave at once."

Shortly the coach of Lady Ysene was on its way once again to the wood.

"You know the place," the lady said to her brother as they rode. "I had to take extra precautions."

"Of course," he agreed.

She looked at the Duke narrowly. There was something in his tone that she did not like.

At the end of the road the Duke let himself out of the coach, nor did he wait for his sister whom the driver handed down the step.

"Wait here," she told the driver and hurried after the Duke who had disappeared down the path. She was angry with him. How dare he treat her so! He should know with whom he was dealing. Who caught these two? Who had the other one destroyed? Who would find the Crown Prince at last? Him? Ha!

A shout and the sound of the clashing of arms caused the Lady Ysene to break into a run. What in the name of the other world was it? There at the end of the path were the two guards and they had set upon the Duke of Xon! Or had he gone out of his mind and attacked them? She could not tell which.

"Stop!" she screamed. "I command you to stop at once!"

The guards put up their swords. The Duke sheathed his own. He faced her with blood running down his cheek. His eyes were smouldering.

"Had you planned this for me, my dear?" he snarled.

"What do you mean?" She stared at him angrily. "And what is the meaning of this?" she demanded of the guards.

"They were your orders, my lady. We were to kill anyone who approached on the path except yourself."

"Bah! You fools! You know my brother, the Duke of Xon. Do you think I want him killed?"

"They were your orders."

The guards stood strange and stiff, staring straight ahead.

Lady Ysene glared at them and then realized what had happened. Even as she snapped her fingers and muttered the words to release them from the spell, a fear chilled her and she rushed to the well, the Duke following close behind.

An icy silence filled the coach. Lady Ysene, pale, eyes burning, sat rigid. Only her hands twitched now and then. The Duke of Xon, his face grim, sat opposite studying his sister's features. They were dressed for traveling and the coach lurched and bumped as the driver whipped the horses to an ever faster pace.

"You seem to be peculiarly adept at failing your part of the agreement," the Duke addressed his sister at last.

She did not answer him.

"Sometimes I wonder if you hold your trust with me or with another. Perhaps you have other plans for the future reign of the country?"

Still she said nothing, though her black eyes flashed.

"Hmmm. Well, we shall see what the state of being is at the palace. *My* arrangements have been made carefully and thoroughly. My latest messenger tells me that the Queen is unconscious most of the time and that the King collapsed at a council meeting. My men hold every guard's post throughout the palace. There is no jester can stand against the power of the Duke of Xon!

"I see no reason to worry. It is merely an inconvenience that you have not been able to take care of your share. I shall see to it of course. I shall solve these petty problems. But I must say, I find it annoying to have to see to everything myself."

The Duke of Xon buttered no words. Feelings were not important to him. Matters were. Though he was not a sensitive man, he was not without emotion. He could hate. He even found a certain pleasure and satisfaction in hatred.

How he despised such and such a one! What a pleasure it was to contemplate by what means he would destroy that person! What a comfort it was to know that he could give himself so completely to his hatred and yet never lose his temper. It gave a fullness to his life.

It must be confessed that Kashka actually gave the Duke the greatest pleasure of all. There was no one he hated as completely as the jester, no one for whom he fancied such terrible torture. It is quite understandable that he should be annoyed with his sister for losing so juicy a plum. And he took no pleasure in annoyances. Of course he would soon catch the fellow himself. But to have had his throat in his hands, so to speak, and then to let him escape! Aaagh!

"How could you be so stupid!" he snapped at his sister.

"You helped dig that well!" she blazed at him. "You tell me how they got out!"

The Duke's smile was bleak. "Well, my dear, do not be so upset. I am sure you did your best though you have permitted both of them to escape you twice. Are you really sure that other one—what's his name—was in the mill when it collapsed?"

After saying this even the Duke of Xon realized that he was treading on treacherous ground. He fell silent before his sister's unspoken fury.

The coach swayed and jolted as it drew ever nearer the city of Nazor. There were still many hours of travel ahead on the road, but not another word was exchanged between the brother and sister until they passed through the gates of the city. Then the Duke curtly outlined his plans to the Lady Ysene. Shortly afterward they entered the palace and went to their separate chambers.

23

The walls of the palace kitchen vibrated with the bibble-babble of tongues. No one knew anything for sure, but everyone had heard something from someone who was an absolute authority on the subject. Voices were loud. Arguments were frequent and heated until a point came between the fourth cook and the seventh-doorkeeper-in-charge-of-the-east-wing-keys when they would not speak to each other or even acknowledge that the other existed. A pity that such old friends should have a falling out! Strange—so many authorities in such complete disagreement!

The latest rumor had the King dead. He had not been seen in three days—not since he had so startled his council by unexpectedly falling to the floor in a faint during an important discussion. Some said it was his heart, some said his brain, some said his liver. The seventh-doorkeeper-in-charge-of-the-east-wing-keys said it was doubtless his stomach because the fourth cook had prepared the soup that noon. Of course no one could say for sure, but everyone was sure that a public announcement would soon be made.

But an announcement of what? Of the death of the King? Or of the Queen? Everyone knew that *she* lay at the door of the next world. Or might it be the discovery of the death of the Prince? Or perhaps all three?

The kitchen was plunged into an uproarious wangle of shouting and gesticulating until the place resembled more a madhouse than a palace kitchen. Even the newly hired scullery boy, fresh from the country, was asked what he thought the situation to be. When he admitted that he didn't know, he received a box on the ear from the fourth cook who was smarting from the words of the key-keeper-of-the-east-wing.

If the kitchen was a bedlam, the rest of the palace was strangely quiet. There was little doing in the absence of the King and Queen. The only excitement had been caused by a small accident that had occurred that afternoon. The Queen's nurse had somehow tripped and fallen down three steps. She was not much hurt but the twisted ankle would not bear her weight.

Lord Vayn hastened with the news of it to his lady. He cleared his throat.

"Ahem, my dear, do you know what this most unfortunate accident means to us?"

"I don't see that it means anything to us," replied Lady Vayn who was occupied with a new hair style.

"But, my dear, who will take the place of the Queen's nurse?"

"I haven't the least idea. I know nothing of nurses. You must find that out for yourself and you had better do it quickly, or the Duke of Xon may be more than displeased."

"Yes, of course. And what I am trying to say is that there would be no one more suitable for the position than the little maid you picked up in Gynnis."

"Jana! How can you imagine such a thing? I cannot live without her!"

"But you have Nina now. She always looked after things for you before."

"I want Jana," Lady Vayn pouted.

"Think of it, my dear," Lord Vayn pleaded. "A personal servant girl—your very own—dutifully given to the highest possible position of trust and secrecy! The Duke will be pleased with your sacrifice!"

"I don't care for sacrifices."

"We must think of the future. And there simply is no one in the palace that can be trusted. The child is so innocent and so devoted. She will carry out every order to the letter."

Lady Vayn sighed. It was really too much to ask. One's country should not be so demanding. But there was the future to consider.

"Very well," she agreed. "If it isn't for too long a time."

"I'm sure it will be only a short time," Lord Vayn comforted her. "They say the Queen is sinking very fast."

Jana curtsied politely when Lady Vayn called her.

"I shall do anything you say. And it is a great honor. But . . . but . . ." her voice faltered.

"Yes, yes?" Lord Vayn asked impatiently.

"May I keep my baby near me?"

"Of course, of course, of course. You will have a room next to the Queen's own and you may have your child with you. His cries can scarcely bother her."

Poor Queen! She lost consciousness and heard nothing for hours at a time. There was nothing the court physician could do. What a tragedy to befall so young and beautiful a Queen!

The day had begun as a warm, slightly hazy, autumn morning. It promised to be fine weather—a true Michaelmas spring day. But in the afternoon a change had taken place. The haze thickened and grayed. And as the sun faded into the gray a sharp wind from the north cut across the land and scattered leaves which only the day before had been gold and scarlet but now were brown and sere. Low clouds driven by the wind scudded across the sky and the smell of snow was in the air.

Capes were pulled tight around hurrying figures. Doors were slammed and unfastened shutters beat against the walls of cottages. Curtains were drawn across windows and extra logs were thrown on fires. The smell of freshly baked bread and of soup simmering in the kettle brightened eyes and whetted appetites made keen by the first cold breath of winter. Night pressed hard the day and darkness crept over the land and into all the corners and crannies of men's building.

Through the now nearly deserted streets of Nazor clattered a coach pulled by four foaming horses. It dashed around a corner and up to the gates of the palace. The gates swung open and the horses leaped forward. The carriage rolled to the main door. Two figures descended from the vehicle, passed through the massive doors before they had fully swung open and were swallowed up in the maze of halls, waiting rooms, chambers, and suites that made up the great palace of King Aciam.

If the wind had grown more boisterous outside the palace, matters within the walls had quieted. The evening meal had been served from the kitchen to all the occupants of the palace. The lords and ladies who attended the court and were given the King's hospitality had retired to their own quarters. The arrival of the coach and its passengers brought on a slight flurry but that soon died away. With lights blown out here and there the restless inhabitants settled into the arms of sleep. Or so it seemed.

In the kitchen the fire burned low. A log crumbled. All was deserted now. No, all was *not* deserted! For there in the corner sat a boy sniveling.

It was the new scullery boy who had suffered the blow at the hand of the fourth cook. He rubbed his hands (which smelled strongly of onions from his evening chores) across a much besmirched face.

A door opened and a hardy, grizzled man with a kindly face entered the kitchen.

"I thought you might be here," he said. "Here now, what's the matter?"

"How was I to know anything about what's going on here?" whined the boy.

"You wasn't to know," the man comforted the lad. "That cook has a mean temper. Besides, I don't trust him nohow. Come here, lad, and wash your face in the bucket. It didn't hurt that bad, did it? Seemed to me you ducked the worst of the blow. You're a quick one! Now, isn't that better? Here's a towel to mop up. Let me look at you. I haven't had a good look at you since you came. I like to know the look of everyone who . . . Bless us, lad! Who are you?"

The man, Doro, an old and robust servant in the palace had taken the boy's face between his hands and turned it toward the fire that he might see it better. Suddenly he let his arms fall to his sides and dropped to his knees.

"Whom do you serve?" the boy asked as he looked straight into Doro's eyes.

"I serve the King," Doro whispered. "I served his father and I serve him. And from what I hear, if heaven don't be kind, I'll serve his son—if he be found. I'd give my life for both—or either."

"The King needs your help," said the boy. "He may need your life."

Doro nodded. "Ay, strange things are happening. I've tried to find out, but so many lies lie in fools' mouths I could learn nought. Lies there are in the air . . . and ghosts!" he added, still staring at the boy.

"Stand up," said the boy, lending his hand to the old man. "Is there anyone you know you can trust among the servants?"

"Ay. Two, for certain. The court fools, Piff and Kashka. But who knows where they are?" He spoke bitterly. "Those that are faithful to the King have disappeared of late. There's them I know as would like to see the jesters dead. Maybe they are."

"Never mind them," the boy told him. "There must be others who would serve their King."

"Ay," Doro mused never once taking his eyes from the boy's face. "There are others. What do you want of them?"

"Gather them here in the kitchen. Now. As quickly as possible. But be sure of them. We cannot take a chance that those who are against us find out what will be said here tonight. When you come back with them someone will be here to tell you what to do."

The old man nodded. "But lad, tell me," he pleaded. "Who are you?"

The boy shook his head. "I don't know who I am tonight. Tomorrow I will be somebody—or I will be nothing."

"Ay," whispered Doro. "It's in the air—tonight will tell a story. But there's only one you could be and I see him here now!"

Then he bowed, turned away, and vanished in the darkness of the passageway beyond the kitchen.

In the rambling palace of King Aciam and Queen Ekama there was a forgotten door at the foot of an old forgotten stairway and a forgotten door at the top of it. For many years neither doors nor steps had been used. But within the past week they were much used by an old lady. She went up and down the stairs and through the doors several times each day. No one ever saw her except the Queen, and no one knew the Queen saw her except the King.

The door at the top of the stairs led to the Queen's chamber. The door at the bottom of the stairs opened into a short passage which in turn led to the door of a room. It was in this room and another tiny one that adjoined it that Bargah set up housekeeping.

Does it seem odd that several rooms and a staircase should be so completely overlooked? The fact is, the palace was such a huge sprawling affair and had so many times been added to that no one knew for certain how many rooms there were or where they all were. Some wings of the palace were in constant use. Others stood empty year after year, doors locked, furnishings draped, dust gathering. So it is not surprising that such a corner as Bargah had should be forgotten.

On this night Bargah made her way up the stairs with extra haste. Things were about to happen. It was in the air. Bargah felt it. She had cleaned and polished every inch of her humble quarters for she intended to invite a royal guest to share them with her until that which was about to happen had happened.

Bargah slipped from behind the tapestry and smiled at the Queen. But they had no time for words. There were footsteps in the corridor outside and Bargah hid at once in the curtains by the side of the Queen's bed.

"Here you are," said a voice from the other side of the door. The latch clicked.

The Queen fell back on her pillows and closed her eyes.

The door opened.

"You might have trouble rousing her again," the voice went on. "Shake her hard until you do. Those are the doctor's orders. It's what he told me. Then see that she drinks the medicine. It's the only thing will save her. You do your job well and you'll see your Queen well."

The door closed again.

Bargah peeped from behind the curtain. It was not the usual nurse but a slender young girl who tiptoed to the bedside.

"Your Majesty!" the girl whispered.

The Queen sat up. "I'm so glad it's you again," she answered in a whisper. "I want you to meet a friend of mine. Bargah, come out now. It's quite safe."

Bargah, very astonished, stepped from behind the curtain.

"This is Lia," the Queen told her. "I have told her about

you. She came to me just this afternoon. I know she will help us. She warned me not to take the medicine."

Bargah frowned. Was this some new trick?

"So you are Bargah!" The girl smiled. "I heard so much about you from Taash."

Bargah sat down quite suddenly, right on the royal bed.

"And now that I have finally found someone I know I can trust, I must tell you something before it is too late."

There was a knock at the door.

"One more moment," cried Lia. "She is just wakening!"

She ran to the fireplace and emptied the contents of the glass onto the blazing logs. They hissed and sputtered. Then in whispers she exchanged a few hasty words with Bargah, ran to the door and called. "It is done now. You must let me out."

The door opened and the girl disappeared.

Bargah seated herself again beside the Queen and took her hand.

"I have a surprise for you, my dear," she said gently. "Do you think you are strong enough to come down the stairs with me?"

"I shall try," said the Queen. "I'm very tired of my own room anyway."

Bargah helped the Queen put her feet into her slippers and then threw a warm robe around her shoulders.

"Now, slowly and carefully. Hold my arm—so."

They moved across the room to the tapestry. A moment later the fire cast its flickering light upon an empty room.

24

Lord Vayn stood before the Duke of Xon. He had been reciting in detail all that had occurred since he and Lady Vayn had come to the palace. His recital was lengthy, but he finally had arrived at the very afternoon of this very day.

"We were terribly concerned," said Lord Vayn, "because the Queen's nurse had a nasty fall and couldn't wait upon her Majesty. But we had a girl—Lady Vayn had her—who is an absolute gem. The child is the soul of discretion, clever, intelligent, quick to learn, and slow to speak. Most unusual in a female. It was quite obvious that she should take over that important duty. I suggested her myself."

"Indeed?" The Duke raised his eyebrows, then frowned. A servant who was too intelligent might be more of a threat than an asset. "How do you know you can trust her?"

"Oh, she is the image of innocence! We found her in the country—in Gynnis to be exact, at the inn there. She is a young widow with a child. A very young child—about the age of our own child. But the girl has a magic touch with children in spite of her own tender years. Why, she can turn a howling monster into an angel in an instant. Lady Vayn is so . . ."

"A girl? With a babe?" The Duke interrupted the chatter of Lord Vayn's tongue. "Where did you say you found her?"

"In Gynnis, my lord." Lord Vayn was delighted that at last the Duke was showing some interest in his tale. "She came to us at the inn at the height of a nasty row they were having in the dining room. A miserable affair. I won't go into it now. But it was a marvelous piece of luck for us that she dropped into our laps as if by . . ."

The Duke heard no more. He smiled. At least there was a faint twitching about his mouth. Was it possible, he thought. But it *must* be they! That was why they couldn't be found! What a piece of fortune *this* was! But what cheek! It was almost admirable! Except, of course, now they had lost.

"Bring the girl here," he ordered. "And the child too. I am interested in them."

"What? Well—but it will take a few minutes," stuttered the surprised Lord Vayn. "She is lodged next to the Queen."

"What!" The Duke jumped to his feet. "Go and fetch her at once! Don't stand there gawking like the idiot you are! Get out of here!"

Lord Vayn bowed and left. But he was huffed. Who was he to run about after servant girls? Let the Duke send one of his own servants—or go himself, if he wanted her so badly! But as he recalled the look on the Duke's face he turned in the direction of the royal suite. Still—it was beneath his dignity to hurry.

At the door of the Queen's chamber a guard challenged Lord Vayn.

"I have not come to steal the Queen! Ha! Ha!" Lord Vayn was pleased to think he had made a joke. "The Duke of Xon wishes to interview that servant girl who took the nurse's place this afternoon. He wants her to bring the child with her. You are to fetch her at once and see that she goes to him."

With that, Lord Vayn turned on his heel and departed. He disliked talking to anyone beneath him except his own manservant Jip. It was beneath his dignity to talk to unfamiliar servants.

The guard curled his lip.

"Who does he think he is?" he snorted to himself. "It 'ud be a pleasure to push his nose in the mud afore the stables! Nor 'twouldn't be hard neither. He looks down it such a distance it's halfway there a'ready!"

"Here! You!" he called a page to him. "Go fetch that girl what took in the Queen's drink tonight. Tell her the Duke of Xon wants her and her brat too. She's in the room around the corner. Step lively there. See that she gets to the Duke. Them's orders!"

To himself he muttered. "That's the day I never thought I'd live to see. The great Duke of Xony Wony himself running around looking for babies! Ugh! I wish the King 'ud get well. Queer goings on around here. Me called up of a sudden by old Tat himself. Said the regalyer guard had a touch of 'digestion. Hmp! They live high here in the palace. 'Drather be back in the soldiers' quarters. Simple clean living there. Who's to do the Queen harm that she needs her door locked and a guard at it?"

"There are those who would, my man," a voice spoke in the soldier's ear. "And that is exactly why you were called tonight. Don't let a soul past that door, do you hear? Orders of the King!"

The soldier straightened to attention and saluted. "Ay, sir. Yes, sir, M'Lord Margrave of Tat, sir!"

"Old Tat is it? Hmmpf! Do your duty, my man. Guard that door with your life!"

The Honorable Margrave of Tat padded away down the hall muttering to himself.

The page returned to find the soldier standing stiff and red-faced.

"She's not in her room," said the boy. "Nor the baby neither. Nobody's there."

"Then go look for her," snapped the guard, "and when you find her take her to the Duke or you may well lose your head!"

The page scurried off not knowing in the least where to seek for the girl.

The kitchen had come to life. Or more exactly, life had come to the kitchen. A score of servants were gathered in the dim light of the dying fire. There was none of the uproar that had made the ceiling tremble earlier in the day. Now the talk was done in whispers and a feeling of wonder and expectancy pervaded the air.

Old Doro shook his head again and again and answered for the seventeenth time that he did not know what it was all about. He only knew that he had orders to gather them here and now. He almost wondered himself if he had not dreamed he saw the face of the lad and heard his commands.

Suddenly the door at the far end of the kitchen opened. Someone was coming. It was Kashka and the scullery boy! A murmur went through the kitchen and the servants pressed around Kashka to greet him and question him. Where had he been? The King had asked for him time and again. What was going on? What was this all about?

Kashka shook his head and held up his hand.

"Friends," he said. "The King!"

All turned to the door.

"The King! The King!" the hushed words sprang from astonished lips and as one man they fell to their knees before the young monarch. He stood before them, grave and pale. Every eye was fixed upon him. Never in the memory of even the oldest of them had a king visited the kitchen!

"Faithful servants, dear friends," the King addressed them. "It is the duty of the King to protect his people. But I have come to you tonight to invoke your help in protecting your King. It is not for myself that I ask your help. It is for the crown that I ask it. For my crown, my country, and my people.

"We have learned of a plot which would destroy your

King and the entire royal family. The plan has been long in the preparation and we believe that the attempt to carry it through will be made this night. Its success or failure rests with you and your like. There is little I can do by myself. The fate of your country as well as my life, the Queen's, and that of the Crown Prince lie in your hands."

The King gazed upon the faces of the men kneeling before him.

"It is only fair to give you your choice in this matter," he told them. "It lies between myself and the Duke of Xon."

The silence in the kitchen was like the silence of death so startling were the King's words. It was broken at last by one who murmured in disbelief.

"The Duke of Xon!"

"Scoundrel!" said another.

"Traitor!"

"Long live the King!"

"Long live Aciam!"

The face of the King brightened. He smiled and held up his hand.

"Thank you, friends! Now there is work to be done. Kashka here will give you your instructions. Good night to you all and good luck this night. If we meet again, it will be under different circumstances."

He turned then and left, and those in the kitchen saw that Piff accompanied him. The jester waved a hand in greeting and then vanished like a shadow to his King.

Kashka remained.

"Are there no more who are faithful to the King than this handful?" he asked looking around at the scant twenty men assembled.

"There are probably many more," Doro answered him. "But of these I had no twig of doubt."

"Very well," said Kashka. "Here is what you must do."

He dropped his voice and they huddled together listening,

questioning, making sure. Within five minutes the kitchen was again deserted.

The Duke of Xon waited with a smile on his lips. This was better than anything he had expected. Even Ysene would have to admit to his superiority. He would *enjoy* the look on her face when she found out.

He waited several minutes. He waited several more minutes. The smile vanished and was replaced by a frown. Three minutes more. That would be sufficient even if the girl had to dress herself and the child. Four minutes passed.

That idiot Vayn! What was he doing? Bah! He should have gone himself to fetch her. Vayn—that dolt! He may have given the whole thing away. If the girl were half as clever as he had said she was she might escape him! What a fool he had been to send that imbecilic self-loving fop!

The Duke rang for his manservant.

"Bring Dugor to me," he ordered. "Tell him to arm himself. Fetch four of my bodyguard as well. Give orders for the rest to be armed and ready. Take messages to Lord Beor, Lord Sec, and the Count of Mido. And to the Lady Ysene too. Tell them the hour has come and to prepare themselves accordingly. Be quick about it!"

The servant bowed and left.

The Duke of Xon donned a vest of mail. Around his waist he clasped his belt from which hung his long sword. Then he thrust a dagger into its case and fastened it at his side. Now he was ready.

There was a knock at the door. Dugor and four armed men were awaiting him.

"Excellent," said the Duke. "Follow me and be ready to strike. I do not expect any resistance but it is well to be prepared."

They moved quietly down the heavily carpeted halls. Once the Duke held up his hand. They stopped and listened. He had heard a rustle or whisper or footstep, he wasn't sure which, but it made him all the more careful. There must be no alarm.

They turned at last into the wide passage that led to the royal suite. The guard before the Queen's door called out to them to halt.

"It is I, the Duke of Xon."

"The Queen is not to be disturbed."

"I have not come to disturb the Queen. I am looking for the maid who replaced the nurse this afternoon. Where can I find her?"

"Her room is around the corner," the guard told him, "but she isn't there. I sent a page to look for her. He was to take her to you at once, my lord."

"Ah, but he hasn't. The girl is wanted for treason. She is suspect in the disappearance of the Prince."

The guard's eyes widened.

"But she's been in twice to the Queen herself!"

"Indeed!" The Duke bit his lip. "We must search the girl's room at once."

The guard let them pass and stared after them.

The door to the girl's room was unlocked and a glance inside was enough to assure the Duke that she and the baby were not there.

"Who was that guard?" he asked. "I didn't recognize him."

"He's not one of our men," Dugor answered.

The Duke frowned. "Take care of him on the way back. We must pay a visit to the Queen.

"You were quite right," the Duke told the guard as he passed again. "The girl was not there. I am sorry to have bothered you."

As he held the attention of the guard a sudden blow brought the soldier to the floor without a murmur. The Duke searched the pockets of the unconscious man, drew out a ring of keys, and found the one that fitted the lock of the Queen's door. He pushed open the door.

The room was empty.

The Duke stared at the tumbled bedclothes in disbelief. Then his glance leaped to the door that led to the King's chamber. Two steps brought him to it. He turned the knob. It was unlocked. His face grew black with anger. His orders had been to keep the door locked!

Well then, if the Queen were with the King, he would kill them both. Now.

In his fury he kicked the door open . . . and found himself face to face with the King.

It was an angry King he faced. It was a strong, upright, healthy, angry King. At his right hand stood the Margrave of Tat, at his left were Lord Ramul and Sir Andros. And in a corner, draped over a chair—lounged Kashka.

"You choose an odd time and manner in which to pay us a visit!" The King's eyes flashed.

The Duke of Xon was livid. Now the secret was out! But he would still win.

He leaped back and motioned his men out of the Queen's chamber and down the passage. His forces were ready. They would turn the moment to their advantage.

The Lady Ysene slowly mounted the stairs of the tower that rose above the east wing of the palace. The clash of fighting came faintly to her ears.

"So my dear brother had his part of the affair completely in hand! I cannot quite believe *that*!" She spoke aloud though she was alone. "I too have my forces to call and we shall see who succeeds in the end."

She glanced at a letter she held in her hand.

"In any case, if this speaks true, we shall have an accounting—the Duke and myself." She smiled. "*I cannot help but win for I have the trust of the Queen. She cannot have been as ill as the Duke was led to believe, else how could she have written this? I know her hand as I know my own!*

"Here—she writes of his ambition that threatens my safety! Ha! We shall see! If he wins, I shall bide my time. If he loses, I shall be innocent of his affairs and handle the rest my own way. Either way, there will shortly be a queen rather than a king upon the throne.

"Then shall my sisters and I rule! Yes, such an arrangement is much more to my liking."

By this time the Lady Ysene had reached the top of the circular stair. She opened the door on the landing with a key unknown to the seventh-doorkeeper-in-charge-of-the-keys-of-the-east-wing or to any of the other six doorkeepers. And there in the little room at the top of the tower Lady Ysene, undisturbed, turned her will to the exercise of her dark powers.

The King had leaped into the fray at once and every blow he struck had been a furious one. He stood now, out of breath and slightly wounded on the brow. He faced the Duke of Xon.

They had met on the high balcony that ran the length of the great council hall and ended in the wide descending staircase. The Duke took the measure of the King with a cool eye and felt content in the strength of his own arm. He came to the contest fresh.

"I have been waiting for you, Your Majesty," said the Duke.

"I see that you have not wearied yourself in protecting your own!" the King observed.

"Why should I?" asked the Duke. "There is only one death here that matters. With yours, I am victorious. I am at your service, Sire!"

The King struck the first blow. The Duke warded it off.

Another blow fell, and another. They circled, thrust, parried with no seeming advantage for either. One for one, blow for blow—every play of the sword was that of a master of the art of death.

Until this moment the two had never matched blades. No one doubted the ability of the King. But there was not a man in the country or out of it who did not quail before the sword of the Duke of Xon.

The Duke began to press the King more closely. He had never met so adept an opponent, and to have each thrust of his sword turned away began to irk him just a little.

The King had expected no less than he was receiving from the Duke. He knew the man's skill and respected it, but he had no doubt of his own ability. What plagued him was the cut above his eye—a mere scratch, to be sure, but deep enough to bleed. Only a few drops, to be sure, but enough to form a mist before his eyes.

Enough it was so that those who had caught sight of the two on the balcony and had stopped their own battle to watch the deadly game between two consummate masters saw the sword of the Duke, fended off but poorly, flash through the King's guard.

The King fell. The Duke leaped upon him with sword and dagger.

Then a slight figure, a small piece of ragged fury, came from somewhere and threw itself upon the Duke, knocked him off balance and sent him sprawling beside the King.

Whatever had attacked the Duke was no match for the man. The Duke laid hands upon the worrisome creature— a boy it was—and hurled him half the length of the balcony. He then snatched up his sword to finish the interrupted task. But he found himself staring at the point of the King's sword.

He looked up in surprise at the man who held the weapon. For a moment disbelief showed on his face.

"You!" His jaw dropped and then he threw back his head in laughter. "Well, Kashka! I have you at last! You must consider it an honor to die by the hand of the future King!"

Kashka smiled cheerfully. "I should be more honored to die by the hand of the future late Duke of Xon!"

"Have done then!" cried the Duke and thrust his sword quickly at Kashka.

Somehow—he missed. He was chagrined. This fool! Again he rushed at him.

"Over here, my lord!" cried Kashka.

"I must get at the King while there is time," muttered the Duke. But he dared not turn his back upon the jester. Kashka was uncomfortably quick. He must kill the fool first. Indeed, it would be his pleasure.

The King had gotten to his knees. The boy was helping him rise to his feet.

"A touch!" cried Kashka. "You have torn my sleeve, my lord. What a shame! Perhaps your sister will mend it for me. I would not be ragged at my funeral—or yours!"

Down the balcony they moved step by step away from the King who leaned upon the boy.

"Kashka!" called the King. "You're no swordsman! What can you do against the Duke of Xon?"

"I shall teach him to dance, my King!" cried Kashka. "His steel sword jigs prettily but his feet are of lead!"

Again came a thrust of the sword.

"I cannot look!" The King turned his head aside.

But by now all other eyes in the great hall were fixed upon the two figures and the strange match between them. There was a commotion on the crowded floor beneath the balcony, but not a single glance sought its cause.

Now those that watched scarce breathed.

The Duke was close upon the fool. The jester's last step had been most awkward. His back was to the railing. There was no retreat. The next step was air and twenty feet of nothing to the floor of stone.

"Now," smiled the Duke. "I have no more time for games."

Sword poised, he lunged at the man before him. But it was his sword that found the empty air, and the body of the Duke of Xon smashed through the gilded dowels.

For a second the King's jester balanced precariously on his hands on the sagging rail. Then the splintered balustrade collapsed beneath his weight and he fell headlong.

The hush of death lay on the crowd.

Then a gasp rose in the air.

The tangled heap of arms and legs upon the floor began to disentangle themselves. Two jesters rose where one had fallen and dusted their sleeves and breeches. It was as if a bit of quicksilver had dropped and split into two identical parts.

"Cousin Kashka," one drop of quicksilver spoke in a voice of infinitely weary patience. "I wish you would stop tripping over fences, stumbling into wells, and leaping from ridiculously high places. I cannot *always* be there to stop your falls. Will you never learn?"

"Cousin Piff," replied the other drop of quicksilver in the meek voice of one thoroughly chastised, "I think I've learned."

25

The palace was ablaze with lights. The great council hall was filled with lords and ladies, servants, soldiers, knights, guests—all that lived or served or visited in the palace of King Aciam. Even the three ambassadors from countries far away were there with all their trains of attendants. Even the five ambassadors from countries near by were there with their personal servants. Even those whose doors had been barred and barricaded by the faithful servants because of their doubtful loyalty were there.

All were there except the Duke of Xon. His body had been removed.

At the end of the hall upon his throne sat King Aciam. He was pale and his shoulder was bandaged. Nonetheless, it was a true King who sat upon the throne. Beside him sat his radiant Queen Ekama. Beside her stood a dark-haired girl holding young Prince Bai asleep upon her shoulder. Everyone stared long at the Prince. There was no doubt that it was he, though he had lost his beautiful curls.

At the King's feet sat his jester, at the Queen's, hers. The two fools so resembled each other that they could scarcely be told apart. For many the only distinction was that one carried a flute, the other a lute.

One by one those who had risen against their King were brought before him, their heads bowed with shame. And one by one they were banished from their country.

Lord and Lady Vayn stood before their King. It is quite

possible that Lady Vayn was more upset by the thought of missing the mid-autumn ball than she was of never seeing her native land again.

"Vanity and greed!" The King shook his head. "For them you would commit murder and treason?"

"But your Majesty!" protested Lord Vayn. "The Duke said nothing of murder or treason. He merely said that you would die, may heaven preserve your Majesty, and that he would be the next king. We were deceived, it is true, but we wished only to serve our country. We had no thought of treason."

"They did bring Prince Bai safely to Nazor," put in the Queen who felt sorry for the foolish weeping Lady Vayn. The Queen could not help but feel kindly toward anyone who had the least bit to do with the safe return of her child.

"Your Highness," Piff spoke. "This man is not treasonous. He is too stupid."

Kashka snorted. "Stupidity is worse than treason!"

The King sighed. He was tired.

"What do you say then, Kashka?" he asked the jester. "I know you will be fair—in spite of your fondness for these two!"

"I say, confine them to their country estate," Kashka said with a grimace. "What could be worse punishment for anyone than to have to live with either of these two? For the love of heaven, make them live with each other. Besides," he added, "that way I shall always know where to avoid them."

"Fair enough!" said the King with a ghost of a smile. "You have heard your sentence. Go now."

Lord and Lady Vayn bowed and left the room. As they left Lady Vayn was heard to say.

"It's all your fault! I shall never be at court again! You're a stupid, ignorant idiot! You and your beard!"

And Lord Vayn, with surprising rudeness, was heard to tell the lady to close her mouth.

"Was that the last?" the King inquired.

He waited for some word, some sign that this was the end, that the victory was now complete and all the offenders had received their punishment. But there was no word, no sign, and the sound of his voice hung in the air like something that could be touched.

"Piff, there is one I have not seen," Kashka whispered to his cousin.

"Ay," Piff murmured, his eyes searching the faces in the vast hall. "What has become of her? My skin prickles when I think of what she might be doing!"

They waited, uneasy now. Who would break the stillness of the expectant air with an answer?

The Queen with a sudden movement took the sleeping Prince from the girl and held him close.

Then the tall doors at the end of the hall swung slowly open. A man-at-arms stepped in and his voice rang to the lofty ceiling with its announcement.

"The Lady Ysene!"

All turned and stared, and as if by magic a way was parted to give the lady passage through the crowd.

She swept through the door and toward the throne noticing neither the single movement of the crowd that made her path nor the isolated and surreptitious drawing back of skirts by those ladies past whom she stepped.

In a minute she stood before the King. Her face was pale. She bowed.

"Your Majesty, I have here a letter that informs me of a terrible thing. My brother has formed a plot to overthrow your reign. His treasonous behavior horrifies me. I have come to you at once for I have just read this letter." She held a parchment in her hand. "If I had had any inkling of this . . ."

Her eyes left the King's face for the first time, her glance sliding sideways almost against her will. She looked at Kashka as if daring him to deny her innocence.

It was then that she saw Piff.

The breath left her body. She stared at him with unbelieving shock upon her face.

At last her lips moved.

"You are dead," she whispered. "I know that you are dead. I sent my sisters to see to your final breath. They told me it was done."

She paused and sucked in her breath.

"I saw the place you died. I saw the stones that buried you. Yet you stand there. You have come back from the dead!"

As she continued to stare at him a gleam came into her eyes.

"Sweet Piff," she said suddenly. "You must tell me how you did it! Tell me how it is done! *Then* shall I rule the world! You and I together, we shall rule the world!"

"The powers of good protect us," a voice murmured.

"The lady is mad!" said another.

The Lady Ysene did not notice the hushed words. She leaned in excitement toward Piff and pointed to Kashka.

"Do you see him?" she asked. "I offered him a position of great honor under my rule but he refused it. I cannot bear such insolence. Besides he knows such secrets of mine that make him dangerous. You must kill him, Piff. The others—all but one—my sisters and I shall manage nicely. But there is that one who must be yours, Piff. He has some charm that defies my powers. But *yours*! Sweet Piff, who can resist the power of one come back from death! Ah, it will be so easy for you, Piff! Together we shall cast down all before us to their doom. Then we'll rule the stars themselves!"

"Stop! Oh, stop!" cried the Queen who had been looking

upon her stepsister with a mixture of horror and pity. "Piff, make her stop!"

"Lady Ysene," Piff spoke in a low and even tone. "I fear that I have given you a great shock. I assure you, though, that I never have been dead, nor if I had been, would I ever have been able to return from so final a resting place.

"It is known that you plotted with your brother. Cast that letter from your mind. It was I that wrote it. All my allegiance is to my King and there is no universe that could induce me to harm those I love.

"You would do well to find some quiet place where you might turn your mind away from those dark powers and look upon the world with different eyes."

Lady Ysene gazed fixedly at Piff.

"Fool!" she suddenly shrieked. "I shall lay a curse upon you as I did upon your cousin and as I shall upon all your kind!"

The company stood transfixed as the Witch Ysene threw back her head, closed her eyes, and stretched her arms upward.

"There shall be no curse from you this night, Lady Ysene!"

An old woman had pushed her way through the crowd to the witch and stood before her. Lady Ysene let her arms fall to her sides and stared at the withered creature.

"That power which you have used most wickedly has run its course. The time it takes you to renew your strength is given us to gain in strength against you."

"So it was you, Bargah, who kept my sisters from coming to the tower! All night I called and yet they did not come to me! You and your fools!" She glared at Bargah. "And so this night is yours! So shall it be! But there will be other nights. There are yet infinite nights to come!"

She turned and with a swift step passed once more

through the crowded hall. The gathering shrank back yet more lest they be touched by one so possessed.

The King rose to his feet.

"Stop her!" he commanded.

But no one moved. No one raised a hand. The assembly stood frozen in their terror.

She passed through the door into the hall and vanished from their sight.

For several moments no one stirred. Then the guards at the door leaped into the passageway and the soldiers of the King began their search for the Lady Ysene. But she was not to be found. There was no trace of her at all.

The King addressed the great assembly. His face was grave.

"My people! We have seen evil walk. How long it prowled and stalked unseen among us I do not know. But this night it came forth. It turned, showing us many faces like those of a gem cut by a malignant hand from a nocturnal world.

"Greed and hatred are the heart of this corrupting stone. And on this core are carved the facets of brutality, cruelty, and vengeance. There are a thousand others—malice, contempt, indifference—I cannot name them all.

"We are but humans. In all of us are faults. Discontented pride and envy, fear and ignorance—all such weaknesses lie open to the tempting jewel of evil whose surface glows with promise of fulfilled desires.

"Yet we are human! Our wish was to destroy this evil. But it is not yet our measure to live upon this earth free from its threat. Our battle with it must continue. We must ever be watchful. Tonight through courage and devotion and the love of brave and loyal friends we've come to victory. If we keep within us this strength we have we shall have victory again and yet again."

The King raised his head and his face cleared.

"Let us now forget the painful and unhappy side of this night's doings. I thank you all, my subjects and my friends, for your courage and your faith in me.

"Now there is one for whom I've looked but have not found whom I wish to see before me.

"Where is the boy who stopped the hand of the Duke of Xon else I should not be upon this throne?"

A rustle went through the crowd. Everyone craned his neck to catch sight of the boy. Everyone knew of the fight, blow for blow, between the King and the Duke of Xon. But who the boy was who had thrown himself upon the Duke they did not know.

When the assembly had gathered Taash had grown suddenly shy. He saw his two best friends sitting easily in the presence of the King and Queen. He saw Lia stand next to the Queen with Teyal in her arms. But Taash felt alone and out of it all. The great crowd of people, the royal couple and all the knights and lords and ladies of noble birth made him feel more and more like Taash, the woodcutter's boy.

He had looked for a corner where he might not be noticed. It was there that Bargah found him. She hugged him and patted him on the shoulder and whispered how glad she was to see him and how proud she was of him. He had felt better—at least more like Taash, Bargah's boy!

There had been time during the long trying and sentencing of those who had committed treason for them to tell one another of what had happened. Bargah related how the Queen and Lia and the Prince had hidden with her during the battle. She told him of the Queen's joy in having her child again in her arms. They laughed over the dismay the Queen had shown when she saw Prince Bai with his curls shorn, and then again over how she had kissed Lia for cutting them off!

But now the King was calling for him. Bargah pushed him forward.

As Taash walked toward the throne he was looked upon with curiosity. But there was one who watched his every step with mounting excitement.

"Ay, that's the lad!" whispered old Doro stretching his neck to see better. "And wait 'til the King sees his face!" He nudged his neighbor in the ribs with his elbow.

Kashka said I am the King's brother, Taash thought. I believed him. But what if the King doesn't believe me? What shall I say to him? I don't know! No matter then. Taash set his mouth firmly. I shall walk like a prince and I shall kneel before him the way Kashka taught me at the bottom of the well. I shall answer what the King asks me. Let Kashka tell him if he wants to!

The boy who approached the King's throne walked with a light step and a head held high. The eyes that were upon him grew more curious that a boy from the kitchen (for it was the new scullery boy) should have such a bearing.

Piff and Kashka rose to their feet and stood straight. The gesture startled King Aciam. They were accustomed to show such occasional respect for the royal family alone. They were notably disrespectful to everyone else! Ah, but he never knew what to expect from his fools! That was his greatest delight in them! After all, this boy had saved his life.

Now the boy bowed and knelt before him.

Piff and Kashka remained standing. The King stared at the head bent before him. He had prepared a little speech— words of gratitude—sincere and certainly sufficient. But what were those words? They had escaped his mind completely and all that he found there was a question. Who is this boy?

The assembly waited for the words of the King. But the King did not speak.

Aciam rose to his feet. He descended the steps of the dais and touching the lad on the shoulder bade him rise. He gazed into the boy's face, then raised his hand and brushed aside the shaggy hair that covered the lad's brow. A look of wonder came into his eyes and he turned first to Kashka and then to Piff. Then he returned his gaze to the boy.

"Who are you?" he asked simply.

"My name is Taash," said the boy.

The King smiled. "A name is nothing. I want to know who you are."

"I have been told," Taash began, and his voice faltered. Suppose it were not true after all! What an idiot they would think him! I don't know who I am, he thought desperately. I don't *know*!

"Yes?"

Taash turned his eyes toward Kashka. The jester, his eyes entreating, smiled faintly and nodded ever so slightly.

"I have been told," he spoke clearly now, "that I am your brother."

"And do you believe you are?" the king asked.

"Yes," Taash spoke firmly. "But I don't suppose you do."

Piff looked suddenly at the ceiling and half turned his back on the King and Taash. Kashka fell to one knee, his head bowed low. If the matter before them were not of so serious a nature one might swear they were struggling to keep from laughing aloud.

Indeed, the King's lips twitched. But he grew solemn at once.

"This is a serious claim," he said. "You have made it in public before a very great assembly. Do you have proof of your claim?"

"No," the boy answered. "I have nothing but the word of my friends."

The King gazed a moment longer at the boy, once again

glanced quizzically at his jesters, then addressed the girl who stood beside the Queen.

"Lia, the Queen tells me that Prince Bai wears two amulets around his neck. Give one of them to me."

"Yes, Sire," the startled girl replied and she bent over the child who still slept in the Queen's arms. In a moment she straightened her back.

"Sire," she curtsied and blushed. "I . . . I cannot lift either pendant. They are . . . too heavy!"

"Indeed! Then . . . Kashka, you will remove one of these pendants for me."

Kashka shook his head. "I cannot, Sire. You know that well!"

"Piff?"

"No, Sire, nor can I."

The King now looked at the boy.

"I would have you do it."

The assembly watched the boy approach the Queen. A few understood the matter. Many did not. But all watched with mute excitement.

Taash bowed to the Queen and looked down at the child in her arms.

"This one is mine," he said, and gently lifted the chain with its stone over the Prince's head and held it in his hand.

"Now put it around your own neck where it belongs," King Aciam told him. "And never take it off again."

He put his hand upon the boy's shoulder and looked into his eyes.

"You should never face such a one as the Witch Ysene without it."

Taash felt a chill at the mention of that name, but the hand on his shoulder was firm and the eyes looking into his own were steady and fearless. There was a strength that flowed through them to him.

Suddenly the King drew the boy to him and putting his arm around his shoulder held him close. With his head bent over the boy's he murmured in a voice so low that only those who stood next to them heard his words.

"Welcome home, my brother."

Then he turned Taash to face the people in the hall.

"Oh, my people," Aciam cried. "This is indeed a night of wonders! For not only has Prince Bai been safely returned to us but our brother, Prince Mittai, who has been lost to us these nine years, stands beside me!

"Let the bells be rung from all the towers. Let messengers be sent to all the cities and villages throughout the country to proclaim a fortnight of celebration! And let us here in the palace begin the celebration of this joyous occasion with singing and dancing and feasting!

"Let a banquet be prepared! Let food be served in the streets! Let everyone rejoice!"

It is too bad that Taash could not truly say to himself that he lived happily ever after. But he could not. The discovery of his identity seemed to promise a life of ease for him as Prince Mittai. But to seem is not to be, and Taash soon found himself with new and different cares.

The first of these he encountered almost at once. For when the excitement had worn thin at last and no one could any longer keep his eyes open, Taash was shown to a room such as he had never seen. He was given a voluminous nightshirt and a luxurious bed.

They both proved to be too much and tired though he was he could not sleep. Thoroughly miserable, he crept out of the monstrous mass of feather beds, searched the wardrobe for clothes that were less entangling and slipped out of his room. It might have been a shadow that glided through two corridors, four hallways, and three narrow passages. He

came to a stair. Down this he went and along another hall-
way until he reached a certain door. At this he knocked.

It opened at last.

"May I come in?" Taash asked forlornly.

Kashka yawned and nodded.

"Who is it?" Piff's half-awake voice came from a corner.

"It's only Taash," Kashka answered him. "I suppose he
can't sleep in all that finery. Here." He tossed the prince a
rough blanket. "You can sleep there on the floor if you like.
I have the bed tonight!"

Kashka blew out the light.

"I win!" Piff said in the dark.

"What do you win?" Taash asked as he curled down,
comfortable at last on a bit of straw.

"Oh," Kashka explained, "we had a little wager. I said
you would be down within an hour. Piff wagered two. What
took you so long to make up your mind?"

"They made me take a bath," was Taash's glum reply.

Piff chuckled, then yelped. Kashka had thrown something
and struck his target.

Taash heard none of the scuffle. He was already sound
asleep.

About the Author

ELLEN KINDT MCKENZIE lives in the San Francisco Bay Area of California and spends her summers in rural Wisconsin. She is the author of several books for young readers, including *A Bowl of Mischief, The King, the Princess, and the Tinker,* and *Stargone John,* a *Bulletin of the Center for Children's Books* Blue Ribbon Book and winner of the Bay Area Book Reviewers Award for 1991.